SAILIN̶̶̶̶̶̶ ̶̶̶̶̶̶̶̶

Praise for Elizabeth Adler's novels:

'The women in Elizabeth Adler's novels are courageous and creative . . . her books entertain and delight.'

*Cosmopolitan*

'The popular Adler gets the dynamics of a new relationship pitch-perfect . . . But it's the detailed, realistic description of the trip to France that makes her latest great vicarious vacation reading.'

*Publishers Weekly (The Last Time I Saw Paris)*

'Sensuously creamy suspense . . . a literal cliffhanger.'

*Kirkus Reviews (All or Nothing)*

'Like Tuscany's beauty, this book is helped with delicious words and literary creativity. It's thoroughly engrossing.'

*North Wales Chronicle (Summer in Tuscany)*

'A heartwarming, romantic adventure . . . a great one for Francophiles, features real places, restaurants and hotels in France.'

*Hello! (The Last Time I Saw Paris)*

*ABOUT THE AUTHOR*

Born in Yorkshire, Elizabeth Adler is married with one
daughter and lives in California.

*Elizabeth Adler*

# SAILING TO CAPRI

**HODDER**

Copyright © 2006 by Elizabeth Adler

First published in Great Britain in 2007 by Hodder and Stoughton
A division of Hodder Headline

The right of Elizabeth Adler to be identified as the Author
of the Work has been asserted by her in accordance
with the Copyright, Designs and Patents Act 1988.

A Hodder paperback

1

A CIP catalogue record for this title
is available from the British Library

ISBN 978 0 340 89662 4

Printed and bound by Mackays of Chatham Ltd, Chatham, Kent

Hodder Headline's policy is to use papers that are natural, renewable
and recyclable products and made from wood grown in sustainable
forests. The logging and manufacturing processes are expected to
conform to the environmental regulations of the country of origin.

Hodder and Stoughton Ltd
A division of Hodder Headline
338 Euston Road
London NW1 3BH

*To Ricardo—he knows why...*

# ACKNOWLEDGMENTS

Thanks, as always, to my editor, Jen Enderlin, who is simply the best; and to her assistant, Kim Cardascia, who is always there to help. And to my lovely agent, Anne Sibbald, and the wonderful team at Janklow & Nesbit Associates. Love you all.

# AUTHOR'S NOTE

Sadly, the beautiful *Blue Boat* is a figment of my imagination, a composite of every gorgeous, glamorous superyacht floating around the Mediterranean. I wish we could all sail on it!

# PART I

## The Mystery Begins at Sneadley Hall, Yorkshire, England

*No man is ever rich enough*
*to buy back his past.*

—Oscar Wilde

# 1

## Daisy Keane

It's snowing, great white starry flakes that cling to my red hair like a tiara on a princess for all of a minute, before melting and running in icy drops down the back of my neck. My mother, who was a stickler for proper behavior for young ladies, would have said it was my own fault, I should have worn a hat to the funeral out of respect for the dead. Of course she was right, but since I don't possess a hat, at least not one suitable for a funeral, I'd decided to do without.

So now here I am, standing with a small crowd of mourners at the graveside of Robert Waldo Hardwick, modern mogul, maker and loser of several fortunes and the proud winner of a knighthood, bestowed on him by Her Majesty the Queen, making him unto eternity, I suppose, *Sir* Robert Hardwick.

We are outside the Gothic, gray-stone church in the village of Lower Sneadley, Yorkshire, England. It's a freezing cold April afternoon, with the wind whipping across the Pennines, chilling the blood of those of us who are still amongst the living. At least we assume we are, because by now all feeling is numbed. Even Bob's dog, a small, stocky Jack Russell crouched next to me on his lead, looks frozen into stillness. He doesn't even blink, just stares at the hole in the ground.

Shivering, my heart goes out to him, and to the poor Brontë sisters who lived in an icy parsonage in just such a village as this, not too many miles away. When I think of them on cold, candlelit nights, of their poor, chapped little mittened hands desperately scribbling down the thoughts that became their famous novels, I can only wonder at their stamina.

Looking at my small crowd of fellow mourners I know most of them are asking themselves what am I, Daisy Keane, a thirty-nine-year-old American lass, doing at the funeral of a Yorkshire tycoon? I feel their curious sideways glances but I keep my eyes steadfastly on Sir Robert's velvet-draped coffin, pretending to listen to the vicar's final thoughts and prayers. Why, I ask myself, couldn't the vicar have gotten this over with inside his almost-as-icy church? Isn't he aware there's a spring blizzard blowing and that we are all slowly freezing?

I feel the tears sliding down my cheeks. Selfishly, I'm so cold that for a moment I've forgotten *why* I'm here. And no, it's not for Bob's money. I'm prepared to work for my living and I've no need for handouts from the rich. Which is exactly what I told Robert Hardwick the first time I met him, though then it wasn't *exactly* the truth.

It was at a cocktail party, one of those society events in London where everybody knew everybody else. Except for me. I didn't know a single soul. What's more, looking around I wasn't sure I even *wanted* to know them. The men were Savile Row suited, hair brushed smoothly back in that British old-schoolboy way, rich and talking business so they might get even richer. And the women were older trying to look younger, dressed too sexily by Cavalli and Versace, busy gossiping about women who were not there.

Bitches, I thought, snagging a second glass of dreadful white wine and a peculiar canapé consisting of a tiny pea pod filled with what looked like brown crabmeat. Starving though I was, I sniffed it suspiciously.

"It's curry," a voice said from behind my left shoulder. "And I don't recommend it."

I swung around too fast, slopping wine down the front of one of the biggest and ugliest men I had ever met. I mopped futilely at his dark pin-striped vest with my cocktail napkin. "I'm so sorry," I said.

"I startled you, it was my fault."

"How do you know it's no good?" I asked.

He gave me one of those aw-come-on-girl looks. "I've tried 'em before, of course," he said in a deep voice that expressed his exasperation at such an inane question.

"That was pretty stupid of me," I admitted. "Put it down to the company around here. Look at them, all talking about money and sex, who's got it, and who's getting it."

His pale blue eyes under grizzled brows had a flinty glint to them. I guessed he hadn't taken to my brash American gal comments, or maybe he didn't care for redheads.

"And so why aren't *you* talking money?" he asked.

I shrugged. "I have enough. Not a lot, but I don't feel the

need for more." I was lying, of course. I had exactly five hundred dollars to my name and no job. Which was the reason I was at this party, scouting prospects, though what a college-educated, divorced, former suburban American housewife would find here was hard even for me, ever the optimist, to imagine.

We stared silently at each other again. Then he said, "Okay, so then why aren't you talking sex?"

I gave him a cool upward glance. "Same answer."

He grinned, tight-lipped. "Are you hating this 'do' as much as I am, then?" He had an accent I couldn't place, vaguely Beatles but not the same, with flatter *a*'s and a harsher lilt.

"You mean you *noticed*?"

"So exactly *why are* you here?"

I shrugged. "A friend gave me the invitation. He couldn't make it. I'm a gossip page editor," I lied quickly. "For the American weekly mag *People Like Us*. Know it?"

"Thank God, no."

I smiled, guessing he'd been the butt of gossip columnists too often for his liking. I couldn't place him, though. I was on new turf here, didn't yet know the ins and outs of Brit society, but this was a rough-and-ready, take-no-prisoners kind of guy.

"You're in the wrong place," he told me firmly in his alien accent. "The people here don't give a damn about American magazines. They live in their own tight little world. For them, everything else is second-class."

That sounded to me very much like the boy locked out of the in-group at school. I stared curiously at him. He was maybe six-five, a massive bear of a man, hefty but not paunchy or soft, in a well-cut and very rumpled suit. He was in his early sixties, I guessed, clean shaven with a craggy brow, a wide nose, thin lips, a ruddy skin, and the worst haircut I'd ever seen. His hair was a thick gray tangled mop. I was sure no barber had been near it for years and was willing to bet he cut it himself. He brought to mind the ogre at the top of Jack's beanstalk. His massive hand clutched a glass of wine and his pale frosty eyes were taking me in from my long red hair and freckled face all the way down to my pointy-toe ankle-strap stilettos. Assessing my net worth, I thought, irritated.

"I'm Bob Hardwick." He paused as though waiting for me to react. I shook his hand but kept my cool. Of course, I knew who he was: the man who'd pulled himself up by his bootstraps from brash, poor, uneducated Yorkshire lad to famous global megatycoon, but I didn't let on.

"What say you and I get out of here? I'll buy you dinner," he said abruptly.

If he was after what I thought he was after he'd gotten me wrong. I threw him the under-the-lashes skeptical glance I'd had a lot of practice throwing at men over the past year. "I don't need anyone to buy me dinner," I said.

"Fine. Then you'll pay. Come on, let's go." And he had me by the elbow and was walking me out of there before I could even react.

# 2

## Daisy

A steel gray Bentley was parked right out in front. To my surprise, there was no chauffeur. Instead, a dog sat in the driver's seat, a plump Jack Russell, white with a brown patch over one eye and a whiskery chin.

"This is Rats," Sir Robert said, nudging the dog to one side.

Rats came and balanced on my lap, though he was obviously not looking for affection. He ignored me, staring intently out at the passing cars as though they were rabbits he was eager to chase.

Sir Robert drove too fast, though expertly. He did not address one word to me en route, though he had plenty to say—actually *snarl* would be a better word—to the tangled London traffic and its drivers, none of whom, according to him, should have been allowed on the road.

"At that rate you'd have the road to yourself," I said, tired of his complaining.

"And all the better for that," he retorted smartly.

Rats wobbled on my knee as Sir Robert made a fast turn into a quiet Mayfair street. He came to an abrupt stop in front of a flower-bedecked, red-brick town house, longtime home to the famous restaurant Le Gavroche. Moving quickly for such a big man, he had the door open and handed me out before I could even blink. I thought for an ogre he was in pretty good shape.

I knew the restaurant was in the grand-dressed-up category, the sort of expensive place you go to celebrate wedding anniversaries, lovers' trysts and big business deals. I checked my outfit. It was a cool autumn night and I had on a six-year-old black leather skirt and a button-up leopard-print sweater dusted with bronze sequins. I'd clamped the thick faux-fur collar shut with a whopping citrine starburst brooch and wore dangling amber glass earrings. My heavy dark red hair was swept up at the sides, kind of forties-style, flowing straight down over my shoulders. And on my feet were the sexiest pair of back suede stilettos ever dreamed up by man for the torture of woman, laced with wide satin straps just above the ankles. Very S and M, I'd thought when I spotted their pointy toes in Bergdorf's, marked down from the astronomical to almost nothing—obviously because nobody in her right mind would possibly want to wear them. Except crazy me, fresh out of suburbia and a bad marriage. And anyhow, the price was right.

All in all, I didn't look too bad for an expensive Michelin-starred restaurant, though perhaps the sweater was a bit "flash." But there again, I was just breaking out of the suburban mold and looking for love in all the wrong places. And besides, how would I ever get a job if I didn't draw attention to myself?

With Sir Robert's hand securely under my elbow, I walked up the front steps, past the banked flowers and into a small welcoming hall. Sir Bob waited for no one, not even the maître d', who hurried after us as we climbed down a tiny staircase and swept through the crowded dining room. Again before anyone could reach us, Bob ushered me into a corner table.

The room was small, intimate, clubby, lit by silk-shaded lamps. The dark red walls were dotted with charming paintings and there were flowers everywhere. The mood was gentle and I thought that for those diners rich enough to afford this elegant country-house kind of world it must feel a bit like coming home. It suited Sir Robert Hardwick perfectly. I could tell he was an old-fashioned man. Not for him the cool décor and fusion cuisine of the latest hot-spot restaurant. He'd brought me to a place where they obviously knew him well and treated him like a king. Or at least like a powerful man with money.

"Sir Robert, good evening, and welcome back." The maître d' had finally caught up to us.

"Thank you." Obviously Sir Robert was not one for small talk. "My usual, please." He raised a questioning eyebrow at me.

I wasn't a drinker but obviously something was expected of me. I remembered all those long, lonesome evenings in front of the TV with only *Sex and the City* and Sarah Jessica Parker for company. "A cosmopolitan," I said. I'd never tasted one but it was a pretty pink color and Sarah Jessica always drank them.

"Make that with Grey Goose vodka," Sir Robert instructed. He turned to me. "Of course the French make the best vodka."

"Of course," I agreed, as though I knew all about such things. Waiters hovered around us. Starched white napkins were swathed over our laps; menus were flourished; canapés—or *amuses bouches* as Sir Robert called them—appeared. A bottle of water arrived. I read the label. It was French. It seemed Sir Robert was a Francophile—French restaurant, French vodka, French water. All he needed was a French woman.

I watched, astonished, as he demolished his *amuse bouche* in one bite, then signaled for more.

"Wild mushroom tart," he told me, satisfied. "It beats those blasted pea pods with canned crabmeat in bottled curry sauce they were serving at that party. It's always the same at those dos—cheap white wine and somebody's sister who wants to get into catering rustling up a few dud eats. Christ, you could get food poisoning from that stuff. I'll bet there'll be a fair few being sick tonight! Serve 'em right," he added, unfolding his menu and studying its contents. "Never here, though," he added. "I've been coming to this place for twenty years. Can't fault 'em, lass, so choose whatever you want."

As if in answer my stomach growled loudly. I shot Sir Robert a wary glance from under my lashes, hoping he hadn't heard. I'd had a bowl of cereal for breakfast and that was twelve hours ago. Had I not met him I'd have been heading home—if my dingy bed-sitter in Bayswater could be called such—to a second bowl for dinner.

I was experiencing real poverty for the first time in my life and it was not fun. But when my husband ran out on me for another woman taking with him all the assets of our ten-year marriage, poverty suddenly stared me in the face. A lawyer, he had cleverly maneuvered our home and small investments into his own name, leaving me alone with the granite countertops and the fancy showerheads and a For Sale sign on a house that no longer belonged to me. Plus the memory of a cute blond twenty-year-old sitting next to him in "our" car as he drove away for the last time.

Which was why I'd come to London. Run away is more like the truth. I'd thought that distance would lessen the bad memories but so far my theory was not working. The pain of the past loomed as large as the poverty in my manless future.

The waiter was reciting the specials but Sir Robert waved him down. "This lass is hungry," he said throwing me a keen glance. "She'll have the lobster bisque to start and then your French chicken, roasted with veg. And bring plenty of bread and butter."

"The *poulet de Bresse*, of course, sir." The waiter wrote it down, seemingly unmoved by the fact that Sir Robert had arbitrarily ordered for me. Actually, so was I. Right then roast chicken sounded like some kind of heaven.

For himself, Sir Robert ordered the duck confit in pastry, then roast beef. Ah, so he was a meat and potatoes man, I thought, smiling.

"What yer smiling at, then?" he demanded.

"At the pleasure of being here," I lied quickly because I still wasn't sure about the pleasure factor.

"With *me*, huh?" He raised a skeptical bushy eyebrow.

I turned and looked him fully in his flinty blue eyes. I might have been putting my roast chicken in jeopardy by asking this question, but I needed to know. "Why did you pick me up at the party?" I said.

He leaned back, sipping his French vodka on the rocks,

thinking. Then he said, "You had red hair. You had good legs. You were alone." He took another sip and thought some more. *"And you were afraid."*

Shocked, I began to protest but he brushed me aside. "Don't bother to ask me how I know that. You know it's true."

I had no answer. We stared silently at each other for a moment. I took a sip of my cosmo. I liked it.

"Anyway, how old are you?" he asked.

"I'm thirty." I crossed my fingers at the lie, though I wasn't quite sure why I'd lied. It was becoming a reflex action, as though a couple of years here and there really made any difference in this youth-scape employment world. I was actually thirty-four then and fast coming up to thirty-five.

"You're lying."

I felt myself blush and snapped back at him. "What are you? Clairvoyant?"

He leaned his elbows on the table, hands folded together, a superior smile on his face. "Let's just say I'm a good judge of character."

I buttered a piece of bread busily, saying nothing. My lobster bisque and his duck confit arrived. Sir Robert ordered a bottle of white Bordeaux from the sommelier. We ate in silence for several long minutes. The soup was heaven.

"So what's your name?" he said finally, putting down his knife and fork.

I gaped at him, stunned. I was having dinner with a man who didn't even know my name!

"Daisy Keane," I said quickly.

"Daisy? What kind of name is that to inflict on a kid?"

"My mother had a sort of gardening mania. She named her three daughters Daisy, Lavender and Violet. It was a case of wishful thinking because our front door opened right onto a paved Chicago street. Not a meadow in sight."

The sommelier poured a little wine into Sir Robert's glass. He tasted it and approved. The glasses were filled.

"Try it," he said. So I did. It was delicious.

"Sort of like new mown grass on a summer day," I said.

"In keeping with your name, wouldn't you say?" He grinned at me, and his wide flat face lit with a spirit I hadn't seen earlier.

"I know you're supposed to drink red with beef," he said, "but this wine happens to be a favorite. And besides, you're eating chicken."

By now I was, and I was practically humming with pleasure. "This is the best chicken I ever tasted," I said, but Sir Robert was already attacking his roast beef. There is no other way to describe the way he ate. He was like a man with his last meal, intent on savoring every morsel. In his massive hands the silverware appeared smaller than life-size and his enjoyment had smoothed the scowl from his face. There was more than a faint resemblance to Shrek here, I thought.

"So what exactly are you doing here in London, anyway?" he asked suddenly.

"I told you, I work for an American magazine." Oh my God, the lies came so easily it was scary. Until now I'd been honest all my life. Yeah, and look where that got you, a cold little voice whispered in my head.

"Hah! You're no more a gossip columnist than I am. They're

a breed apart, recognizable at fifty paces at any party. And none of them ever looked like you."

My hackles rose. I put my knife and fork carefully onto my plate. "Oh? And exactly how do I look then?" I prepared mentally for his attack.

"Like a woman who got lost somewhere along the way."

He completely took the wind out of my sails. Was my past written so clearly on my face, like scars after a bad accident?

"Don't worry," he said, in a softer voice. "I've been there too, at the bottom of the emotional heap. Oh, I know, looking at me, reading about me in the papers, you'd never think this brash, common, ugly old bastard had feelings. But . . . I'm a man . . ."

I was silent. I didn't know what to say to this total stranger.

"Well?" He was looking at me, brows raised, awaiting an answer. I glanced down at my fingers, twisted together like high-tension wires. Here was my opportunity to tell my story, but I couldn't. It was too humiliating. I shook my head. I could not confess my plight to this man. I just could *not*.

He summoned the waiter and ordered coffee. The bottle of wine, only half-drunk, sat unwanted in its bath of ice in a silver bucket. The spark had gone from the evening. I suddenly remembered his dog. Worried, I asked if Rats might need to go for a walk.

"They'll have seen to that," he said. "But thank you for thinking about him."

I shrugged. At least I understood his love for his dog.

He signaled the waiter for the bill. When it came, he pushed it across the table at me. "A deal is a deal, right?"

Oh God, I'd forgotten that he'd said I should pay. I'd been living on cereal and cheese sandwiches for two weeks. If I paid, I doubted I'd be able to eat at all. I stared numbly at the breathtaking numbers. Pride up, I dug the last of my money out of my bag and counted out the correct amount.

"Mustn't forget the tip," he said, with a patronizing little smile. "Personally, I always give twenty-five percent here—it makes for good relations between me and the staff."

"And personally, I never give more than twenty," I snapped back. He was trying to control me, enjoying my discomfort at being stuck with the large bill.

He picked up the money, counting it. "You don't look like you're enjoying living up to your deal. Why not? You been lying again?"

"I never lie," I said stiffly.

He laughed, a loud, gruff bark that turned heads toward us. "There you go, doing it again," he said.

He put the money in his pocket, slid a credit card into the leather wallet containing the bill and handed it to the waiter.

"In fact, you look like a woman in need of a job to me." I glared at him. "What's up?" he said, still grinning. "Afraid to work your soft hands to the bone? Afraid of getting 'em dirty? Afraid of overtaxing your poor little brain? What's your real story, anyway?"

For a long moment, I stared numbly at him; then I suddenly crumbled beneath his onslaught. I apologized for lying. I told him my story. I told him about my mother, an Irish woman from minor aristocracy. "Believe it or not, I'm really a lady," I said. "Well, I mean I'm an Honorable. But my mom was. She married an Irish lord and became the Lady Keane and was poor with it. She was even poorer when he died and she moved to America and big-city Chicago, where she had relatives. The Irish are all over the place in America, you know. Anyway, we lived in a small apartment and she got a job in food services."

"She was a chef?"

"Actually, a waitress. She never told anyone about her title; she was such a modest woman she wouldn't have known how to use it to better herself. We got by somehow, got educated, grew up, got married."

"And divorced."

"Just me. Lavender is still married with three kids. Vi is single, works for the National Geographic Channel. She's always in places like Borneo or Mato Grosso." Our eyes met. "And you know all about me."

"Not quite all." His bushy brows rose in interest and suddenly memories I had deliberately kept hidden in the darkest recesses of my mind came flooding back, stinging with remembered pain.

I found myself telling Bob Hardwick everything. About how when my husband left me, taking with him everything we owned, driving away to start a new life with a gorgeous young woman on his arm, I cried bitter tears. I screamed and howled. I told myself endlessly that I must be to blame. I was not attractive enough, not sexy enough, not a fun companion. Not a good wife. In other words. I felt sure it must be my fault. Even now, I didn't know what I'd done wrong, and I was too wounded even to ask myself whether he was the one guilty of all those things.

I told Bob about how, when I finally got myself somewhat back together, I pushed those bad memories away. I hid from them and from my past, determined to find a new me, a woman who was no longer vulnerable to predatory men, and I wrapped my romantic heart in a shell never again to be broken.

"I'll take the man's role from now on," I told Bob Hardwick, who was sipping his wine, elbows on the table, pale blue eyes fastened intently on me. "And that's why I'm here in London," I said with a final shrug. "Now you know it all."

Bob was silent. Embarrassed, I grabbed my glass and took a gulp of wine, wishing I had not bared my soul to this complete stranger.

"It's over," he said at last. "The guy was a bastard. You should never have trusted him, but women are suckers for a pretty package. And good sex."

"Not even that," I blurted, then I blushed, once again wishing I hadn't said that. I'd always been this way; the words just came out before I could stop them. Besides, I'd never admitted this before, not even to myself, or my best friend, Bordelaise. And now Bob was laughing at me.

"Too much of the lady to enjoy it, huh?"

I knew Bob meant it as a joke to get us over the dark moment I'd inflicted on our evening, but when I thought about it perhaps he was right. Maybe I'd never let myself go enough, never really dissolved into the passion of the moment, never truly felt what the women's magazines told me I should be feeling.

"Perhaps you're right," I said, finally honest.

"So you're class then, despite appearances to the contrary."

I bristled again. "You have a way of getting at people don't you?"

"Works every time." He smiled triumphantly. "Anyhow, now you'll come and work for me. Right?"

"As exactly what?" I was suspicious. After all, this was still a man talking to a woman.

He shrugged. "My P.A. left to take care of her sick mum. I have a place in New York as well as a penthouse here, on Park Lane, and a house in Capri. Then there's Sneadley Hall, up in Yorkshire. They all take work to keep up. You'll be my major-domo, if you like. As well as my personal assistant, social secretary, public relations and all around gal Friday . . . whatever role I need you to play that day. You'll find me a hard taskmaster. I'm tough to work for, or so they tell me." He shrugged his big shoulders, exasperated. "It's just that I want things done *right,* and mostly they're not—unless I do 'em myself. But I'll pay you more than you ever thought you'd earn. So—think you can live up to that?"

He took my breath away. This man was a force of nature, larger than life, Shrek with brains. He was challenging me, and I was lured by his offer. Of course it was a lifesaver, but at the back of my mind I still wary.

He sat quietly watching me think. Then, "Listen, love," he said gently. "Once upon a time I was young like you. I was broke. And I was in love. Now I'm none of these things, but sometimes I ask myself, if I had the chance, which of the three would I like back? Would it be youth? So I could feel the exhilaration in the sheer strength of my own body again, the kind of feeling the young take for granted? Or maybe power? So I could have the opportunity of digging myself out of that deep hole of poverty, experience the pleasure of achieving my success all over again? Or what about love? Ah, *love*!" His eyes closed, and he groaned softly, thinking about it. "That quintessential emotion," he said. "No—never that. Love's too painful. That's all over with. There's nothing left for me but hard work. And then more hard work. That's the only thing that gives me satisfaction. That—and the love of a good dog."

I softened, listening to him unexpectedly baring his soul to *me*—a perfect stranger. Like me, he was alone, though not for the same reasons. He was alone by his own choice. Then he said, "Of course you'll have to come and live with me."

I might have known it was too good to be true. I gave him that skeptical sideways look, jumping when he slammed his glass down so hard the wine slopped over onto the tablecloth. A waiter hurried over but he brushed him aside.

"Listen to me, lass," Sir Robert said in a low, rough, angry voice. "And never forget this. *I am a rich man*. Women pursue me. Beautiful society women, young actresses, models; they pursue me with a lust for my money in their eyes. Women I've never met telephone to tell me how much they admire me and to ask me to dinner. Understand this, you dumb freckled redhead, *I can have any woman I want*." He poked a finger into my faux-furred chest. *"And I don't want you."*

My starburst brooch popped open under his onslaught, stabbing him. He inspected the blood oozing from his finger.

"Well," he said with a grin, "we're off to a good start, aren't we?"

And that was the beginning of my five years of employment, and of my friendship with Sir Robert Waldo Hardwick. Quite simply the most overbearing, most demanding, most exasperating man I've ever known. As well as the kindest, the most understanding and the most tender. How could he be all these things at once? That was the great mystery of Bob Hardwick.

It was also the foundation on which our relationship was built. Tempers, tantrums, tears—mine, of course. Icy dialogue, calm indifference—his. But what was ours too, ours to treasure, was love. We were alike. We were a team. We were friends. And in case you're wondering, no, he was never my lover.

That night at Le Gavroche, Bob Hardwick took my money because, he told me later, he wanted to see how honorable I was. Of course he'd guessed I was broke and faking it, yet I had lived up to my word. Or rather to his word. It didn't matter because he was equally honorable. *And* he gave me my money back in the car on the way home.

He also immediately gave me an advance on my very generous salary and told me to get a good haircut and some decent clothes. I moved into his life and into his world and he taught me all he could until I became indispensable, or at least he allowed me to believe that, but in my heart I knew it *was* true. Bob saved me. He gave me a second chance and I loved him for it. Which is why I'm standing here at his snowy funeral with the tears rolling down my frozen cheeks, saying good-bye to him because he was my best friend and I shall miss him to the end of my days.

At the same time I'm wondering why the other frozen-faced mourners—who include a beautiful French ex-wife and a gorgeous Italian ex-mistress, as well as various buttoned-up city types from Bob's business world—are here too, because not one of them could have been called his friend.

There was another man completely different from the businessmen mourners; tall and rangy, in a long black overcoat with the snow settling on his close-cropped dark head. He was standing alone at the back of the small crowd of mourners. His narrow dark eyes under stern black brows met mine over their heads and he nodded a greeting. I nodded back, acknowledging him, though in truth I had no idea who he was.

# 3

## Daisy

It was over. Done. The city people were turning away, hurrying out of the icy wind to the comfort of their cars, heading for the station in the town ten miles away and the fast train to London. A knot of villagers still clustered together under their umbrellas. Some worked at the Hall: the gardener, the housekeeper, the daily ladies. Then there was Ginny Bunn, the barmaid at the Ram's Head pub, dressed in black with the big-brimmed black hat she usually wore for the annual garden party at the Hall. And Reg Blunt, the pub's owner, square and stocky and Bob's good friend. Blunt had matched pints with Bob many a Saturday night, with Bob on his favorite hard wooden settle near the fireplace. These local people knew him as one of themselves and they came over now, offering their hands and sympathy, some wiping away a tear.

"He was a real good man and a good friend," Ginny said, choking up, "despite what other folk might say."

I nodded, wishing desperately I could smile or find the right words, but there were none.

"The Lord said 'Blessed are the meek,'" Blunt said. "But if you ask me, it's strong men like Sir Robert that are our blessing. He'll be missed around here. Aye, that man will be truly missed." And to my surprise he took my hand and pressed it to his cold lips. "Take care, Daisy," he said. "And remember, everyone here in Sneadley will be looking out for you."

Touched, I watched him walk away. In just five years I had become part of this village, a member of a small community where people still "looked out" for each other. Reg Blunt was telling me that if I needed help they would be there for me, and I was grateful for that. I was alone again in a cold, snowy world, unprotected by Bob Hardwick. And also, I realized, unemployed again, though at least this time I had a savings account amounting to a great deal more than the five hundred dollars I'd had in my purse when I first met Bob.

Rats was still staring into the dark hole where somehow he knew his master lay. "Come on, boy," I said, tugging on his lead. He did not move. "Rats, come here, baby," I said, but he lay down on the snow. I bent to pick him up but he clamped himself to the frozen earth. The villagers were gone and I could see the other mourners getting into their cars. They didn't even look back. No one cared. He was just Hardwick's old dog.

Bitter tears fell down my cheeks as I tried to get my hands under Rats's middle but he clung like a limpet to a rock.

"Here, let me help."

I glanced up through my tears. It was the stranger.

"Animals have a way of knowing," he said quietly. "He doesn't want to leave his master."

"Nor do I," I said, before I could stop myself.

The stranger's dark eyes held mine in a long deep sympathetic glance. Then he turned to the dog, running his hand along the coarse white fur on his back. "Come on boy," he said gently. "It's time to leave. Everything will be all right now."

The dog lifted his head to look at him for a second; then he put his snout firmly back between his paws and heaved a sigh that shook his stocky body.

"Now listen, old fella," the stranger said firmly, "you have to look after Miss Keane, so let's get on with it. Come on, it's time to go."

Whether it was the stranger's no-nonsense tone or the mention of my name, or simply his charm with dogs, something got Rats to his feet. He sneezed loudly then gave himself a thorough shake, spattering the two of us with mud, and suddenly we were laughing.

"That's better," the stranger said, still smiling. "Now let me get both of you out of the cold."

With his hand under my elbow, and with Rats dragging behind on his lead, we left Bob Hardwick in his last resting place.

We walked back down the slippery church path where the city folks' footprints had already been obliterated by the heavily falling snow, and out through the lych-gate that in summer would be covered in heavy-blossomed purple wisteria. The village street was empty now except for my red Mini Cooper and a sleek black Jaguar convertible, both with a covering of snow.

I looked properly at the stranger for the first time. He was in his early forties and very tall, about six-two, broad-shouldered, in a long loose black overcoat buttoned to the neck and black boots. His lean face was the kind that spoke of experience, and not all of it good, all planes and angles with a bluish hint of stubble already growing in. His nose was slightly hooked and his narrow gray eyes looked at me from under straight black brows. He was kind of offbeat attractive, a little sinister even, with furrows in his forehead and crinkles radiating from his eyes, and his hair was cropped almost to the skull, leaving just a dark haze over his well-shaped head.

"I don't know who you are but thank you anyway," I said.

"But I know who you are. Bob told me all about you."

I was astonished. I thought I knew all of Bob's business associates and social acquaintants.

"You're Daisy Keane, helpmeet, social director, confidante, and good friend." He gave me a slight bow. "And I am Harry Montana."

I shook his hand. It wasn't until later that I realized that while he had told me his name he had not told me who he was. "Look," I said, brushing the snowflakes from my hair, "you must be as cold as I am. There's to be no reception, Bob once said he'd never want that, but why don't you come back to the Hall? At least let me give you some hot coffee before you drive back to . . ." I didn't know where he was driving back to and he didn't enlighten me.

"Thanks, I'd like that" was all he said.

"Well, it's not far. Sneadley Hall is right off the main street in the village, through the big iron gates on the right. You can't miss it." I climbed into the Mini, which had always been too small for my long length. "Just follow me."

I suddenly realized that, like me, Harry Montana was American. He had some kind of southern accent, Texan perhaps? Whatever, he was a long way from home. As I drove carefully down the snow-covered village street I wondered again what he was doing at a small funeral in a Yorkshire village in a snowstorm.

# 4

## Daisy

Sneadley Hall had been in the Oldcastle family for five generations before Bob Hardwick bought it. It was a large square Georgian-style building in the dark gray stone that was typical of Yorkshire, with a long straight driveway leading up to a columned portico. The casement windows were tall and the front door had two long windows with an arched fanlight over. It was not a pretty house but its square solidity had suited Bob's personality.

"Everybody who owned this place was in wool," he'd told me when he first brought me to see it. "There were sheep on these hills, as far as the eye could see and then beyond. Wool was what made Yorkshire rich and the day we turned from sheep to acrylic was the undoing of many of the fine wool merchants and mill owners in these parts. It was rags to riches and then back to rags again faster than you'd ever have thought possible. And now it's men like me, the cowboys of the financial world, the opportunists, the hardheaded what's-the-bottom-line fellas, that own homes like Sneadley Hall."

I heard the Jag's tires crunching on the gravel behind me as I drove through the arched wrought-iron gates still embellished with the monogrammed *O* of the Oldcastle family. Mrs. Wainwright, the housekeeper and cook, had the front door open before I'd even parked.

"Eh, come on in, Miss Keane," she said. "We were getting worried, leaving you there all alone in the churchyard. I was about to send Mr. Stanley back to fetch you."

Stanley was the gardener. He lived in the gatehouse with his wife, while Mrs. Wainwright had her own cozy apartment in the annex. "No need to worry, Mrs. Wainwright, here I am," I said, walking up the steps onto the portico. Behind me, I heard Montana parking. "And I brought a friend of Sir Robert's back with me. Mr. Montana helped me with Rats. The poor dog didn't want to leave."

Mrs. Wainwright heaved a sigh. She was a big pear-shaped woman with a generous bosom, curling iron gray hair, a square jaw and piercing blue eyes that missed nothing. Including the man now coming up the front steps right behind me, carrying a laptop case.

"No doubt y'll both be wanting coffee then," she said briskly. "Though in my view, a nice cup of tea goes down a lot better, especially when you're feeling under the weather. And I've made my jam sponge, I know it's your favorite."

She turned to walk away but I called out her name. Puzzled,

she looked back at me. I ran to her and threw my arms around her in a great big hug. "Thank you. Thank you for everything. Thank you for caring," I muttered into her wiry hair.

"Well then, it's nothing, nothing at all." She smiled, embarrassed, as I let go of her. Hugging was not in her Yorkshire vocabulary, though love was. "You're dripping water all over my fresh-polished hall floor," she admonished. "I'll send our Brenda out with a cloth." "Our" Brenda was her married daughter who lived in the village and who also worked at the Hall.

"Sorry, Mrs. Wainwright," I said with a rueful smile. Then I remembered the man I'd invited back for coffee.

Harry Montana was glancing approvingly at the paneled walls and the polished chestnut floors, at the tall windows with the heavy gold curtains half-shutting out the snow, at the fire blazing in the massive stone hearth. "I half-expect to see foxhounds lounging in front of the fire and hear the hunt going by," he said. "All those men in red coats on big black horses."

"You'd never find hounds indoors; they'd be out in the kennels near the stables," I said. "Anyhow, dogs are not allowed out with the hunt anymore."

"Still, you get the picture. Isn't it what we Americans always think about the English country life?"

"I guess so." I smiled. "I've learned a lot in the past five years, about that English country life. But please, let me take your coat."

He put down the leather laptop case and shrugged out of his almost ankle-length black overcoat. It was as light as a feather, cashmere I guessed, with an expensive Italian label, but underneath that coat was a different man. Narrow frayed worn-in jeans, black boots, a black turtleneck sweater. His shoulders under the sweater were broad, his hips in the jeans, narrow, and on his right wrist he wore a silver and leather bracelet studded with turquoise stones. I felt a flutter in the pit of my stomach. With his cropped head and lean looks he should have been auditioning for the role of the bad guy in a Hollywood western, not attending the funeral of a Yorkshire tycoon.

I hung his coat in the hall closet alongside my own, then took out the old towel kept there for that purpose and went to dry off Rats who had already parked himself in front of the fire. "Good boy," I murmured. "Good boy, Rats. It'll be okay now, I promise. And I promise I won't leave you."

"You inherit the dog, then?" Harry Montana said from behind me.

"I've inherited nothing." I scrambled to my feet. "I'm just an employee. But of course I'll take care of Rats, because Bob would have wanted that. Anyhow, now I feel as though he's my dog, even though I know that for him there'll only ever be one master."

I felt Montana's eyes on me as I put the cloth away. I remembered I still didn't know who he was or why he was here. I suggested we move into the drawing room and he held open the heavy door to let me pass.

This was my favorite room in the house. Even in a snowstorm it seemed sunny. Light ocher walls, golden brocade sofas with cushions squashed from much lounging around over the years, soft pale rugs a little frayed from wear, lamps that shed a warm golden glow and a fire sparking in the grate. In fact when

I thought about it, this wasn't so far removed from the country-house comforts I'd first noticed in Le Gavroche, when I'd thought how nice it must be to come home to a place like this. Soon, though, I would be gone.

Mrs. Wainwright bustled in pushing a two-tier Victorian mahogany tea trolley piled with plates of tea sandwiches and biscuits and the famous jam sponge, plus the silver coffee things. She said good afternoon to Harry Montana and left me to do the honors. I poured steaming hot coffee into fragile blue-and-white Wedgwood china cups and handed one to my cowboy. He was completely relaxed, knees apart, long legs crossed at the ankles, sleeves pulled up, revealing a glimpse of a tattoo in what looked like Chinese script running around his forearm.

I ate a piece of the jam sponge. Usually, it tasted of summer strawberries. Today it tasted like dust.

"So how d'you know you didn't inherit?" He stirred two sugars into his black coffee. "The lawyers read the will yet?"

I frowned, suddenly on the alert. I'd asked a perfect stranger into Bob's home. He could be anyone! A business rival trying to find information. A reporter on the scent of a good story. A long-lost relative on the make. I stared at him again. He looked like a fashionable version of a Marine, with his haircut, his frayed old jeans, his bracelet, his tattoo. I pushed my heavy, still damp hair from my forehead, hot with anxiety. Had I inadvertently let the enemy within Bob's gates? "Who the hell are you, anyway," I snapped, "asking me all these personal questions?"

"I'm kind of a friend of Bob's."

"There's no such thing as 'kind of a friend,'" I replied tartly. "A friend is a friend and that's it. How did you know him?"

"I met Bob ten years ago. He was having some personal problems. He'd heard about me from someone he knew. He called me in Dallas, and I flew to New York to meet him. He thought I might be able to help."

I wondered what Montana meant by "personal problems" but decided it was better not to ask. There were some things Bob had not wanted me to know and I respected that. Still, I needed to know who the man sitting opposite me in Bob's house really was. I was about to ask him again when he beat me to it. He got to his feet, took a wallet from the back pocket of his jeans, removed a business card and handed it to me.

"Harry Montana," I read. "Risk Management. Security. Private Investigator." There was a New York address and one in Dallas, and phone numbers, plus the usual e-mail info.

I wasn't surprised by his profession, just puzzled. Bob had used private investigators when he'd needed to dig up information on his business rivals, but from what Montana had said that did not appear to be the case this time.

"Did you ever wonder about the way Bob died?" he asked.

"Of course I did. I still do . . . endlessly. He was driving alone at night on a mountain road he didn't know well and went over the edge. I should have been there, with him, I should have been the one driving . . ."

"And if you had, you would have been dead too."

I felt my face go slack with shock. I stared blankly at the stranger. "No, you don't understand," I said quickly. "Bob al-

ways drove too fast. He expected other cars to get out of his
way. I wouldn't have let him drive that mountain road, but I
had the flu. I was in bed at the apartment in Manhattan. I
should have been with him. *I should have been there . . .* "

"And now you're drowning under a sea of guilt."

The place in my heart that had been numb came suddenly
to life and the power of grief swept over me. My shoulders
sank and my head drooped as wave after wave of sobs swept
through me. The stranger did not move. He sat watching me
until it was over; then he said quietly, "Guilt won't bring him
back, Daisy Keane, and you know it. And know this too. We
are all ultimately responsible for our own actions. Bob Hardwick did not die because you were not there; he died simply because *he was.* It was the wrong moment, the wrong place, the
wrong time."

I heard the clock ticking. A log shifted in the grate and
fresh flames flickered and were reflected, pink, in the silver cof-
feepot. Adrift in my misery, I was peripherally aware of the old
landscape paintings, the faded coral and greens of the rugs, the
brass and leather fender encircling the fireplace, of Rats's
sleepy snort as he turned in front of the fire . . . all the familiar
things and sounds. But it was just me and the stranger now in
the sudden deadly silence.

I jumped at the tap on the door. Mrs. Wainwright came in.
Shifting her gaze hastily from my tear-ravaged face, she said,
"You'll not get out of here tonight, Miss Keane. Mr. Stanley
tells me all the roads are blocked and the plows won't be out till
tomorrow, providing this blizzard stops, of course."

The Hall was set back from the village street in tree-studded grounds. Down the long straight driveway and through the driving snow I could just make out the hazy yellow glow of the lamps by the gate. In the parking circle in front of the portico, both cars were already under a lavish white blanket.

I got up and closed the heavy silk curtains. My heart sank at the thought as I said, "Looks like you're here for the night, Mr. Montana."

He was already on his feet, looking at his watch. "I hate to put you to the trouble . . ."

"You have no choice. I'm afraid you're stuck with me."

"It's no trouble, sir," Mrs. Wainwright said, taking charge. "I'll put Mr. Montana in the Red Room, Miss, if that's all right with you?"

I nodded of course, then said to Montana, "We'd better get our cars into the garage before they're completely buried."

He thanked Mrs. Wainwright, thanked me again, looked at his watch. I got the feeling he was anxious to leave but knew he had no choice.

I led the way to the boot room at the rear of the house, where I found a pair of wellies that fit him, and gave him Bob's old green quilted Barbour jacket. I put on the same outfit, tucked my pants into my wellies and dragged a black woolen ski cap all the way down to my eyebrows. I handed Montana a flat checked cap.

We were quite a sight. "You look like the English country gent," I said.

"And you look like a refugee from Siberia." Despite myself, I grinned.

The falling snow was hard, tipped with ice, driven sideways

at us by the wind. Telling Montana to follow me I stepped bravely into the blizzard. Mr. Stanley had salted the front steps but the snow was already drifting into the portico, and I slipped.

Montana grabbed my arm. "Take it easy," he said, holding me firmly under the elbow.

I liked him close to me, protecting me; it made me feel small, feminine again. It had been a long time since a man had held me and I had to remind myself that this one was only making sure I didn't break my neck.

Montana swept the Mini's windshield clean. The snow came halfway up its tires, and he looked doubtfully at me. "Why don't you let me drive it?" he said.

"I'll be fine. Besides, I have to lead the way; the garages are around the back of the house in the old stable block."

I waited while he cleaned off his windshield and heard his car start up. Another hour in this cold and neither of these cars would have started. It seemed like some kind of miracle they did now.

I put my foot on the gas. The tires whirred but nothing happened. I put my foot down harder and the car jolted forward. It was like driving through a sand dune. I saw Montana's low lights behind me and signaled right, taking the corner carefully. Even so, my back end swung out. I took my foot off the gas and righted the car quickly. I didn't want to end up in the shrubbery. Down the side of the house, then a right into the big cobbled courtyard, pristine under its snowy cover. I pressed the garage-door opener, breathing a sigh of relief as the door swung up. I'd been afraid they wouldn't work in the icy conditions.

The garage somehow still smelled like the stables it used to be, though now it held Bob's collection of cars, including a 1929 Bugatti, a 1964 E-Type Jaguar, an early sixties Corvette, a fifties turquoise blue Chevy convertible with fins, and a '64 Ford Mustang convertible, plus a new Mercedes and the latest beautiful bright red Ferrari. Bob loved cars. It was ironic that he'd had to die in one.

I drove the Mini in then signaled to Montana to bring in the Jag. He parked next to me. As he got out I handed him a soft broom.

"Better brush off the snow if you don't want your beautiful convertible spoiled." I watched as he wielded the broom, first on his Jag, then on my Mini.

"Didn't think you'd be a red car girl," he said over his shoulder, still busy sweeping snow.

"I don't think I am really. Bob bought it for me, said it was time I brightened up my life a bit."

Montana turned to look at me. "And was he right?"

"Bob was always right."

Montana propped the broom back up against the wall and we walked outside. The electronic doors closed behind us and we were alone in the dark. The big black sycamores laden with snow groaned in the wind and the cobbled courtyard was a cold white rectangle, untouched even by bird tracks.

The snow had temporarily stopped and we stood silently, breathing in the clean icy air. I glanced sideways at Montana.

Steam blew from his nostrils the way it does with horses after a long ride, and snowflakes settled on his dark head.

"This reminds me of my childhood on my dad's ranch in Texas," he said quietly. "Snowy nights like this I'd go out to the bunkhouse and sit with the cowboys around their stove, listening to them talk horse talk and cattle. Afterward, I'd walk back to the ranch house alone. Sometimes the snow came up to my knees and I'd be frozen by the time I got home. I envied those guys in their warm bunkhouse, the jolly smoky camaraderie, their shared interests, their easy chat. Home for me was just my dad and me and the housekeeper—some old guy recruited from the cowboys because he was too old to ride out anymore."

It had begun to snow again and I shivered. "You must miss it," I said.

"Not a bit. I'm a city dude now. Want to make snow angels?" he asked with a grin.

"Absolutely not, I'm already frozen." With him holding my arm we set off across the courtyard. The deep snow forced us to lift each foot then place it carefully down again, making for slow progress. When we finally reached the back door my face was layered with snow and I was panting with the effort and the cold.

Warm yellow light spilled from the windows and we stumbled thankfully inside, casting off our soggy jackets, both of us hopping on one foot as we pulled off each of our wellies, laughing at how silly we looked. Mrs. Wainwright met us as we emerged into the hall, telling us that dinner would be ready in an hour.

"Just time for a hot bath and some dry clothes," I said.

Then, remembering my guest had no luggage, I told him Bob's things would certainly be too big for him so he was stuck with what he had on.

Montana picked up the laptop case, and we walked together up the wide shallow stairs to the galleried hallway. Rooms led off on either side. Bob's was the main one, over the portico with the view across the village to the Yorkshire dales, rolling gently into infinity and still, in summer, dotted with sheep. I turned left and showed Montana to the Red Room and he said it lived up to its name, all red brocade with a big carved Jacobean four-poster swathed in red silk. Bob had chosen the furnishings himself and I'd told him in my opinion it looked like an Indian restaurant. He said no it didn't, it looked like a Bombay whorehouse, which was exactly what he'd wanted. I said I hoped Montana wouldn't feel too out of place sleeping in the red whorehouse and he laughed.

Then I showed him the attached dark-paneled bathroom with the white cast-iron claw-foot tub, left him to it and went to my own sanctuary at the opposite corner of the house.

# 5

## Harry Montana

Montana stood under the hard hot shower for a long time until he felt his bones begin to thaw out. He hadn't been this cold since he was a kid. He dried himself, wrapped the towel around his haunches, and stood in front of the mirror, running his hand over his stubbled chin. He wasn't thinking about the way he looked; he was thinking about the woman he'd just met and her relationship with Sir Robert Hardwick.

Daisy Keane was attractive, chic with that severe modern look many women adopted as the easy way out when they were not too sure of their own personal style. It didn't marry too well with her appealing country-girl freckles and mane of glossy red hair and her full, sweet mouth. Nor with her husky, low, sweet voice. He'd expected a hard-faced money hunter out to take Bob for all she could get; instead there was a hesitancy about her, an uncertainness, an air of vulnerability. Either she was a good actress or she really cared about Hardwick. He shrugged. Who knew? With Hardwick's kind of money at stake, anything could happen. He'd liked the way she behaved with the dog, though. There was hope for her yet. And he'd bet she hadn't expected to meet anyone like himself at the funeral either. They were poles apart, together tonight only because of Bob Hardwick and a snowstorm, and because he had a letter for her. He'd intended to drop it off at the Hall after the funeral but she had invited him anyway.

He put on his clothes, checking the bracelet that never left his wrist, zipping up his jeans, buckling the silver-studded belt, sliding his feet into the black boots. Still chilled, he would have killed for a bourbon. Listening to the snow on the windows, he remembered his stormy youth.

Montana had been just twelve years old when his father had died penniless and he'd been evicted from the ranch. The authorities had quickly dumped him on a foster family living on the fringes of an urban ghetto. It was light-years away from the silent plains of the ranch where he'd roamed on his horse, and the worn-out broken scenery of despairing urban life indelibly seared his young soul. Because he'd had no choice, he stuck it out for a couple of years; then he took off with nothing more than a few bucks in the pocket of his Levi's and a black denim jacket that had belonged to at least three other kids before it was handed down to him. He was fourteen looking sixteen when he began his solitary yearlong journey on the back roads of Texas that made him wiser and tougher than your average teen. When he ran out of money, which was often, he always managed to get a job, but he never stayed anywhere very long. He'd be back on the road, on his endless way to nowhere, no future shining hopefully before him. That is, until he met the man who changed his life. The man who took him in and opened him up to a world of books and learning, and a spirituality he'd never before experienced.

His name was Phineas Cloudwalker and he was a full-blooded Native American of the Comanche tribe, though he always described himself as "Indian." Phineas Cloudwalker made sure Montana got a good education, and eventually he'd graduated summa cum laude from Duke University.

After that Montana abruptly changed course and joined the Marines where his loner, nonconformist attitude soon landed him in trouble, but then, in recognition of his intelligence and his leadership qualities, he was co-opted as a lieutenant into the special division called Delta Force. And it was there, amongst the other nonconformists, the fearless young men who were up for any challenge, ready to take any risk, ready to die for each other and their country, that Montana excelled.

Ten years and several grueling campaigns later, he left the Corps to take care of the dying old Comanche who had saved his life, and his soul. It was this man's bracelet he wore, this man's values that were now his standards, this man's strength from which he had learned. This Native American was the man he considered his true father.

From his mentor Montana had also learned the art of living each day as it came. Here in the quiet comfort of Sneadley Hall, where tradition still ruled, he realized he had almost lost that art. Mostly, now, he worked. There was no space and no time in his life for a dog like Rats, or for a real home, though that was not something he'd ever wanted. His nomadic ways were too deeply ingrained.

He walked to the window and held back the curtain, staring out at the snowy landscape. He hadn't expected a storm so late in April and nor apparently had the weather forecasters. You'd have thought with all their Doppler radars and global weather patterns they'd have managed to predict this one. He should have been back in London by now; he had a date waiting. Taking out his cell phone, he dialed her number.

"Sorry, babe," he said when she answered, "I'm stuck up north in a snowstorm." He listened to her grumble for a bit, apologized again, said it was unfortunate but there was nothing he could do about it. She bitched some more, and, impatient now, he said abruptly, "Honey, that's showbiz. I'll call you later." She was cute, sexy and way too demanding. He didn't need a demanding woman in his life. In fact he didn't need any woman in his life. He was quite happy the way he was. Owned by no one.

The Red Room was beginning to get to him. Red was not his favorite color. Taking a large manila envelope from his case, he left the red silk behind and walked back downstairs. Rats was still hunched in front of the hall fire. The dog rolled an eye at him, snuffled wearily then glanced away. "Poor old boy," Montana said gently.

He put the envelope on the hall table then picked up the long iron poker, shifted the logs around a bit and stood with his back to the fire, hands thrust into the pockets of his jeans, thinking about the reason he was here. With his death, Hardwick had presented him with a mystery, one Montana was determined to resolve. Plus he'd been entrusted with a mission he would take care of tonight. It was part of his job and the reason he had been at the funeral and not back at his London apartment with the cute girl who drove him crazy. Analyzing things, he wondered if he wasn't better off after all, in the Yorkshire snowstorm, facing the emotional storm that he knew was about to get even worse.

# 6

## Daisy

Of all Bob's homes, Sneadley was my favorite, though I had not yet seen his villa in Capri. Somehow we had never gotten around to that. Bob said he was too busy to take a true vacation, though that was the reason he bought the Villa Belkiss in the first place. I sat on my bed and pulled off my damp socks, looking around at the familiar room that soon would no longer be mine.

Sneadley was the house Bob had brought me to the day after he offered me a job. After the dingy bed-sitter in Bayswater, this room looked like paradise, and when he told me I could decorate it any way I wanted, I drove into the nearest small town where I bought cans of paint and brushes, then came back and painted the place myself.

"You're a competent lass," Bob had said, standing in the doorway watching me perched on a ladder running a roller over the ceiling. "I could have had the lads in to do it, y'know, you'd no need to go to all this trouble."

"Trouble?" I cried, elated. "This is the best thing that's happened to me in years. I'm loving it. Besides, I used to do it when I was married. I decorated our home myself, every room."

"And what was your house like?" He expressed curiosity about my past life for the first time.

"Suburban. Boring. Lonely. I'd hoped for children but it didn't happen."

"Probably because you weren't getting enough," he said drily, making me laugh. And anyway, he was right.

I sponge-painted the walls of that beautiful room a pale terra-cotta, until it looked the way I imagined an old Tuscan villa might, sort of faded by the years and the weather. Maybe sponge painting is now a designer cliché, a bit passé, but every time I step into that room, it welcomes me. I simply love it.

The frames of the three tall casement windows are set deep inside paneled embrasures, with interior shutters that actually shut. I painted them a dull white and had curtains made in a heavy taffeta striped in bronze and muted gold, then put in a creamy soft carpet. The furniture was thirties, pale burled walnut. There was a sleigh bed with a plump cream silk quilt and a dressing table with little shaded silver sconces on either side of an ornate Venetian mirror. By the window was a chaise lounge in pale chenille, piled with velvety pillows, where I liked to sit and read on summer evenings with the scent of new mown grass wafting in and the faint bleats of the sheep coming from the hills.

I put on a Diana Krall CD, went into the bathroom, went to the tub, turned on the faucets, threw in some jasmine bath oil and lit a couple of candles. Thankfully, I stripped off my funeral clothes. I left them where they lay and stepped into the bath's soothing warmth, closing my eyes, soaking away the memory of the awful day, of the bitter cold and of my despair.

The sound of Krall's soft voice singing old standards drifted toward me. What lay in store for me now, I wondered, now there was no Bob Hardwick to save me? There were a lot of decisions to be made. Would I stay here in England? Go back to Chicago? Maybe try my luck in L.A. the way everybody else seemed to? My sister Lavender was married with three kids and lived in San Francisco. She was older by seven years, and the age gap was too big for us ever to be really close. My other sister, Vi, also had a busy life, and though we all cared about each other, I knew it wasn't fair to my sisters to impose myself suddenly on them. And that, as no doubt Bob would have said, left me free to do whatever I wanted.

"Always look on the positive side," I could hear him saying now. "You're not at a dead end, you're simply at a crossroads. It's up to you to choose your route."

I needed a hug. I picked up my cell phone and dialed the Chicago number of my best friend, Bordelaise Maguire. I know Bordelaise is an odd name but her pregnant mother happened to be taking a French cooking course when she unexpectedly went into labor. *Bordelaise* was the first word she'd uttered after the baby was born. Which is how my friend came to be named after a French sauce.

Of course, I had called to weep long distance on her shoulder when Bob died and of course she'd said she would get a flight and be with me the next day, but I wouldn't allow it. I told myself this time I had to stand on my own two feet, I had to take care of things the way Bob would have expected me to. He had helped me become this new strong woman and this was my time to prove it. Foolish, I know it now, when I could have benefited from the company of my dearest friend, but when we're under stress we do foolish things.

Bordelaise had e-mailed me every day since and I told her that I was okay and that I'd soon be leaving Sneadley Hall for good and perhaps I'd be coming back to Chicago after all.

Now Bordelaise answered on the first ring, and without even asking who it was, as though she'd been expecting me to call, she said, "You okay?"

"Sort of."

"The funeral's over then."

"It's over," I agreed mournfully.

"So what you do now is go to bed with a large glass of hot whiskey and lemon. Just snuggle under those blankets and get some sleep. I'll bet you haven't done that in a while."

Sleep belonged to the nights before Bob died. "You sound like my mom," I said.

"Somebody's got to look after you, even if it is long distance."

"I'm okay, really I am. I'm taking a long hot bath. There's a storm here, we're snowed in."

"And here too," she said. "Are you really okay, though?" She sounded doubtful and I assured her I was all right and said I was going downstairs to have dinner with a friend of Bob's.

"The roads are closed and he's stuck here for the night," I explained. "So you needn't worry, I'm not alone. I just wanted a hug from you, that's all."

"You've got it, girl," Bordelaise said softly as we rang off with promises to call tomorrow.

Bordelaise and I had known each other since grade school. Her mom and dad owned the restaurant where my mom worked, and we'd both done teenage stints there as mini-waitresses, washers-up, table clearers, and gossipmongers, speculating about which of the customers we fancied and who was dating whom and which wife was cheating on which husband.

Bordelaise was a bright-eyed pixie of a girl, petite with rough blond hair hanging over her dazzling blue eyes in a too-long shaggy fringe that drove her mother crazy. She swore her daughter couldn't see through it. Bordelaise attracted men like bees to the proverbial honeypot; all she had to do was run her hands through that blond hair and give them that flirty upward glance and her impish smile and they were goners. She had a track record to prove it. Two husbands down and one about to go. Not that that fazed her; unlike me she was always game for the next adventure.

The bathwater was already cooling. I climbed out and wrapped myself in the luxury of a big soft warm towel, and I stood looking at my reflection in the mirrored walls.

So here I am, I thought, staring at myself, a tall cool drink of water on the outside and still trembling on the inside. I've never been a beauty, I was just a freckled, lanky kid who grew up into a freckled lanky woman. My boobs are too small for the current bosomy fashion; my long dead-straight dark red hair has a mind of its own which is why I usually wear it pinned up at the sides or pulled back out of my eyes, which are the color of green olives. My legs are my best feature, long and slender and I've progressed from the S and M stilettos to smarter, more flattering and horribly expensive shoes that are my greatest indulgence. I have a good clear skin under its dusting of freckles, a straight nose and full lips, and I am one of the few women I know who can wear red lipstick—namely Armani No. 9. Actually, I'm not too bad for a woman who doesn't even try, always hiding my vulnerability behind my black suits.

In fact, I'm a successful fraud. The superefficient, clever P.A., fair but harsh when I need to be; always cool, always in charge. Only Bob knew the true me; he'd seen through me right from the beginning. And Rats knows who I am too; he jumps on my bed at night, ignoring my bed socks (I always have cold feet, which Bob said was "significant") and my cozy but dowdy nightie. The dog snuggles up to me, a warm living being to whom I pour out my heart just as though he understands. And who's to say he does not? Anyhow, *I* believe he does, and only Rats and Bob—and my friend, Bordelaise, about whom more later—know the real me.

Now, naked in my pretty bathroom, I felt the same way I had when the For Sale sign had gone up on my house that was no longer mine. Out in the cold. Alone again.

I dressed quickly in a black sweater and loose black velvet pants; then, sitting at my pretty dressing table, I powdered my nose, put on some lipstick and brushed my hair. I dabbed on Guerlain's L'Heure Bleue—a gift from Bob and a far more exotic scent than I would ever have chosen myself—pushed my bare feet into a pair of flat black ballerina shoes, and walked downstairs to have dinner with Harry Montana.

# 7

## Daisy

Montana was standing before the hall fireplace, hands shoved in the pockets of his jeans. He looked up when he heard my footsteps, holding my eyes with his as I walked toward him.

He gave me a smile. "Less of the Siberian refugee, more the lady of the house," he said.

"Think it's an improvement?" Was I *flirting* with him? How could I? At a time like this.

"Definitely."

"Anyhow, as you know, I'm not the lady of the house. I'm merely an employee."

"More than that. You were a friend."

I smiled. "That's better than 'kind of a friend.'"

"I didn't know Bob well enough to be more than an employee," he explained. "But—simply because Bob was the kind of man he was—I had the privilege of becoming a 'kind of a friend.'"

Of course I wanted to know why Bob had employed him in the first place, but I didn't ask. Discretion was part of my job. Instead I offered Montana a drink. The dog followed me as I led the way into the drawing room where an array of bottles and glasses arranged on large silver trays on the massive seventeenth-century oak sideboard constituted the bar. I glanced inquiringly over my shoulder at him.

"I guess you don't have bourbon?" he said.

"I certainly do. On the rocks?"

"Please."

I poured the drink and handed it to him then busied myself fixing my usual evening tipple, the cosmo I'd developed a liking for after my first at Le Gavroche. I shook the silver flask vigorously, poured the drink into a martini glass, added a spiral of lemon.

Montana watched me with a bemused expression. "A girly cosmo," he said. "I'd have expected more from you."

I bristled at the implied criticism. "Such as?"

"Oh, maybe a malt whiskey, a rare Russian vodka . . ."

"What makes you think I look like a drinker? Am I that tough?" I offered him Mrs. Wainwright's homemade cheese straws, still warm from the oven.

"Not tough. Just, maybe . . . a façade of toughness. These are good."

"Mrs. Wainwright's an excellent cook." Things were suddenly a little awkward between the stranger and myself. A definite coolness had set in. I thought wearily this might be a long night.

I went over to look at Rats who was lying on his belly in front of the fire. I put my drink and the bowl of cheese straws on the coffee table and plopped down into the squishy old sofa. "Come here, boy," I said. He gave me a long mournful look, then got to his feet, walked slowly over and climbed onto my knee.

He gave my chin a lavish lick and I wiped my face with the back of my hand. "Jack Russells think they're little lapdogs," I informed Montana who had taken a seat opposite.

"At least it's a sign of life," he said.

He sipped his drink silently, and I sipped mine. "So you live in Dallas, Mr. Montana?" I asked finally.

"Among other places."

He certainly wasn't giving anything away. "But not on your dad's ranch?" I prodded.

"The ranch went into bankruptcy just before Dad died. I was twelve then. I've not been back since."

"I'm sorry." I was flustered by his sudden frankness. "I didn't mean to pry."

"I have no secrets," he said calmly. "After Dad died I was placed in a foster home. They were decent enough people, there was just no love to go around." He grinned at me. "Maybe that's why I've been looking for love ever since."

"And have you found it yet?"

"Several times." His narrow dark eyes held mine again, and I felt myself get hot in the place where my heavy hair fell onto the nape of my neck. I noticed his eyes were the deep gray of Yorkshire stone.

"Did any of them stick?" I would have killed him had he asked me such a personal question but he didn't seem fazed.

"Not a one. You're probably looking at the only straight, unmarried forty-four-year-old man left in Texas."

I laughed. "At least we got that out of the way," I said.

I was flirting again. What was wrong with me? I didn't think I even liked him. Not really, anyhow, though he was kind of tough-attractive. I sighed. He was certainly different from the other men I'd had designs on over the past few years. As always, I'd been looking for love in all the wrong places. Kind of my pattern, Bob had said. "Another bourbon, Mr. Montana?" I was doing my best imitation of an English lady.

"Don't you think it could be Harry now? After all, we're stuck here for the night in a snowstorm."

"Another drink, Harry?"

"No thank you, Miss Keane."

"Okay, okay, so it's Daisy."

We stared silently at each other. Then he said, "What's your story, anyway, Daisy Keane? Where do you come from and how did you end up here?"

"You're the investigator, I thought you'd already know." He gave me a level look that said I was being ridiculous. I shrugged. "Chicago originally. I ended up in a suburb in Illinois with an unfaithful husband who sold the house out from under me and took off with a twenty-year-old blonde. A familiar story in your line of business, I'm sure."

"I don't do that kind of investigating."

"Then exactly what kind do you do?" There was frost in my voice, and I didn't know why. I just knew that all of a sudden I was weary. Weary from the long dreadful mournful day, weary from trying to keep my emotions in check, weary from weeping in front of this stranger. I just wanted to be in my bed with the lights out, the blankets up to my neck and Rats fast asleep on my feet. Alone with my memories.

"I'm a crime investigator."

I glanced at him, astonished. What was a crime investigator doing with Bob?

"I investigate theft, fraud, extortion." He paused. "And murder."

I jolted upright and Rats slid protesting from my lap onto the sofa. Montana's dark eyes stared meaningfully into mine. "Wait a minute, are you saying you think Bob was *murdered*?"

"Maybe." I felt my heart flutter and jump and then settle like a lead weight somewhere in my stomach.

"So, Daisy," he said, "what exactly do *you* stand to gain from Bob's estate?"

I stared blankly at him. "I told you, I'm an employee. I have no expectations. And anyhow I didn't expect him to die!"

"You were also the closest person to him, you know everything about him, all his secrets. Surely you must have thought about it sometimes? After all, he's listed in Forbes one hundred as one of the world's richest men."

It sank in what he was getting at. I glared angrily at him. "Surely you can't be suggesting that *I* killed Bob?"

He gave me that cool grin. "Well? Did you?"

# 8

*Daisy*

There was a tap at the door and Mrs. Wainwright poked her head in. "Dinner's ready, Miss Keane. I've got the Yorkshire puddings just coming out of the oven, so if you'd like to sit down . . ."

"Right. Yes, of course, Mrs. Wainwright." I pulled myself together, got up from the sofa and walked with the man who thought I might be a murderer into the dining room.

Mrs. Wainwright had set places opposite each other at one end of the long refectory table. Montana pulled out the heavy chair for me and I sank into it before my knees gave way. A bottle of Bordeaux waited in its silver coaster. He poured me a glass and said, "I'm sorry I shocked you, but you were Bob's friend. I had to tell you. And it's only a hunch. I have no proof."

I nodded. "I understand now. It's the reason you're here."

He took a seat opposite just as Mrs. Wainwright bustled in carrying a sputtering hot Yorkshire pudding tin.

"This is the way we like to serve 'em in these parts, sir, piping hot and crisp," she said to Montana, spearing a fluffy pudding onto his plate. "It's traditional to serve them as a starter, you see, with a good gravy. Why not have two, sir. I'm sure you're going to like them. I'm known for my Yorkshires."

"Mrs. Wainwright makes the best," I assured Montana, passing him the gravy boat. Bob had liked his table set simply, just plain white plates and plain silverware. The glasses were beautiful, fine crystal, but also plain. Bob hated drinking good wine out of a thick glass. But why was I thinking about table settings? I must be losing my mind.

Under the table I felt Rats come and slump on my feet. I bent to pat him, watching Montana devour the puddings.

"These are fantastic," he said, glancing up at me. "The only ones I've had before were in steak houses back home and they were like tough old pancakes."

"This is where they originated, you're getting the real thing now. Would you like another?"

He shook his head. "You should eat something. You can't get through the night on one piece of jam sponge."

I took a sip of the good wine. I checked the label. It was the one Bob had always served with roast beef. Mrs. Wainwright had remembered and opened it earlier. She came in now, along with her daughter, Brenda, who was about my age, with streaked blond hair, the clear pink skin of a countrywoman, and her mother's blue eyes. She had two teenage children and

her husband worked in the supermarket in the local town. I
asked Brenda if he'd managed to get home and she said no, he
was having to stop with his cousin that night, nothing could
get through. Brenda lived a couple of houses down from the
Hall gates but despite the drifts she said she'd make it back all
right.

They set the dishes on the table, cleared our empty plates,
gave us fresh ones and left us to it. On automatic pilot, I offered Montana the roast beef; passed the new potatoes tossed
in butter and parsley, the roasted parsnips, the Brussels sprouts.
I served myself some just for the look of it but I couldn't touch
a thing. Instead I gulped down the wine. Harry Montana
poured me some more.

"They're good people," he commented.

"They're all good people around here," I said. "And there
was no one better than Bob. These people have reason to know
it; he looked after them the way the village squires used to in
the old days."

Montana did not look impressed.

"Let me tell you this, Montana," I said, fueled by wine and
fear. "It may sound odd to you, but Bob Hardwick was a man
of infinite goodness. Ask anyone around here. He was always
giving, and without any fuss, without asking for acknowledg-
ment or praise. If someone was in need and he knew about it,
he quietly helped out. What he always said was that he'd been
there too, at the bottom of the emotional and financial heap.
Which is why he understood me. He knew where I was coming
from at that low point in my life when I met him, and he
helped me without any questions. He just . . . understood.

*That's* who the real Bob Hardwick was." I stared hard at Montana. "Nobody would want to kill Bob," I added. "Nobody!"

"I hope you're right."

The door opened and Brenda came in to clear our dishes. She brought a platter of cheeses, crackers and grapes, then got the port decanter from the sideboard.

"Mum'll bring the coffee in a minute, Miss. I'll have to be off now, back to my girls."

"Thanks, Brenda." I glanced at the snow still swirling against the windowpanes. "And take care. It's not getting any better out there."

I heard the door close after her. The French enameled clock with the little bronze nymphs holding up the crystal dial ticked loudly and Rats shifted his position on my feet. The room was cozy, quiet, with the lingering smell of roast beef and the aroma of good wine. Warm and dimly lit, it was a good place to be on a stormy winter night, or at least it would have been if Bob had been pouring the port and not Montana. A wave of resentment overcame me. Why did this stranger have to come here, casting these terrible doubts over Bob's death? Why did it have to snow, leaving me stuck here with him? Any other time I could have told him to get out, but tonight that was impossible.

I refused the port and instead, with a shaky hand, poured myself another glass of wine. My third. I was counting. Plus a cosmo. *And* on an empty stomach. I told myself I'd better eat something and took a cracker and some of the crumbly local Wensleydale cheese. I said nothing, waiting for Montana's next move. I had no doubt now I had let the enemy in Bob's gates.

Mrs. Wainwright came in with the tray of coffee things. She said good night and left us alone again.

I felt Montana's eyes on me. I crumbled the cheese in my fingers. If I put it in my mouth I knew I would choke. Rats slid from under the table. He headed for the door, looking back at me. "I have to let Rats out," I said, getting up.

Montana followed me. "He's just a little guy and the snow's deep," he said. "I'd better shovel a place for him."

I nodded my thanks, wondering how he could be impervious to the waves of animosity emanating from me, as tangible as the cartoon cloud around Charles Schulz's Pigpen. He was used to it, I supposed, the big-time P.I. called upon to save billionaires and no doubt making a fortune off them. God knows how much Bob had paid him. And for what? As far as I knew, Bob kept no secrets from me, business or otherwise. Bob was as open about his faults and failures as he was about his triumphs.

Rats hovered, shivering on the kitchen steps watching as Montana, coatless, shoveled a clearing in the snow. He propped the shovel against the wall, picked up the dog and deposited him in his own icy space.

Rats sniffed miserably, did the quickest pee on doggie record, and stumpy tail down, skidded back up the steps and into the warm kitchen. Despite my misery, I was forced to laugh.

We stopped to watch as the dog dragged the old sweater Bob had given him to his usual spot in front of the Aga, turning round and round before finally plumping down on it. The Aga was a wonderful creation: a massive cobalt blue cast-iron stove that emanated a gentle heat and was one of the best things I'd discovered about English country life. Its ovens never went out; somehow they kept a permanently even temperature suitable for the baking of soufflés or the slow braising of casseroles or roasting of meats, and its hot plates with the shiny steel covers never needed lighting. The Aga also partly fueled the Hall's hot-water system and kept the kitchen the coziest room in the entire house.

Bob and I and his guests had often ended our evenings here, clustered around the big scrubbed-pine kitchen table that had been in the house since it was built, sipping wine and nibbling on Mrs. Wainwright's excellent gingersnap cookies. Some of the best nights of my life had been spent with convivial company around this table. Now, though, the kitchen was immaculate. The dishwasher whirred gently, and the hardwood floors had a dark gleam from much polishing. The housekeeper was proud of her domain.

"Mrs. Wainwright's finished for the night," I told Montana, who was still standing by the door watching me. It was unnerving, as though he was looking out for any false move I might make. Well, darn it, the only move I was going to make was to clear the last of the dishes from the dining room table and then I was off to bed.

When I told him this, Montana immediately said he would help. He stacked plates efficiently, holding the silverware down with his thumb so it wouldn't fall.

"You're pretty good at table clearing," I said.

"When I was a kid I was a busboy at a diner in Galveston."

"Maybe you should have stuck to it," I said nastily.

He made no comment, simply followed me into the kitchen

with the dishes. I ran water into the sink, squeezed in some Palmolive, swished the dishes around, rinsed them off, set them on the wooden drainer. He didn't offer to dry them, which for some reason irked me. I took paper towels and ostentatiously dried the glasses, polishing them slowly to a gleam. I put them in the glass-fronted cupboard next to the dozens of others. I turned to face my silent, watchful guest.

"Time for bed," I said, walking past him into the corridor that led from the kitchen to the front hall.

"Wait!"

It wasn't a request, it was a command. I spun around. "Wait for what? So you can expound on your stupid theory that Bob was murdered? Well, I'm sorry but I don't want to hear it." He was standing next to me by now, but I turned angrily away.

He grabbed my shoulder this time. "Please, Daisy Keane, wait a minute. It's not for me, it's for Bob. He gave me something for you. Please, sit here while I go get it."

He pulled out a chair, sat me in it, then walked down the corridor to the front hall. I waited, sullenly. He was soon back, holding a bulky manila envelope which he handed to me.

"Do you know what's in here?" I asked.

He shook his head. "Bob simply asked me to hold on to it. I was to give it to you 'should the need arise.' And I'm quoting his exact words."

He pulled out the chair opposite and sat, elbows on the table, hands clasped in front of him, looking at me. I caught sight of the strange turquoise-studded bracelet again and wondered in passing why such an obviously tough honcho would wear such a thing.

I turned the manila envelope over and over. For some reason I didn't want to open it. I didn't want to know whatever it was Bob had to tell me from beyond the grave, I just wanted things to be the way they had always been. Why, oh *why*, couldn't I simply turn back the clock and start all over again? By not getting the flu, not staying home in bed, not allowing Bob to drive alone? Then I remembered what Montana had said: that if I had, I would be dead too.

# 9

*Daisy*

I clutched the envelope to my chest. Whatever it contained was personal, from Bob to me. It had nothing to do with this man; he was only the messenger. The weariness I had felt earlier returned, draining me. "I can't deal with this now," I said, getting to my feet. "I'm off to bed."

"I think that's sensible. It's been a long emotional day."

Remembering that after all Montana was my guest, I told him to help himself to anything he wanted. I said there was bourbon and bottled water in his room and leftovers in the refrigerator if he got hungry. He'd find cookies in the biscuit tin on the shelf over there, tea—

"Thank you," he stopped me. "I'll be fine."

I paused awkwardly at the door. "Well then, I hope you'll be comfortable in the Red Room."

"I will," he promised.

The flight of stairs had never seemed longer as I hurried

back to the sanctuary of my room. I heard Rats's claws pattering on the wooden floor behind me. I also heard Montana's footsteps on the stairs, then muffled by the old Chinese silk runner as he walked to his room at the opposite side of the house. I waited till I heard his door close then quickly closed my own. For the first time ever, I locked it.

I breathed a deep sigh of relief. I felt safer away from sinister Harry Montana's dark all-seeing gaze, forever looking for secrets or for answers to questions I hadn't known existed and anyhow didn't want to know about.

The lamps were lit and their gilded shades cast a pleasing glow. The bed was turned down, the pillows plumped, the extra blanket folded across the bottom because Brenda, who took care of these things, knew about my notoriously cold feet. I put the large manila envelope on the bed then went into the bathroom and washed my face. I went and sat at my pretty little dressing table and rubbed cream into my skin then slowly brushed my long hair, staring at my miserable reflection, at my swollen eyelids and my tight mouth, putting off the moment when I would have to open that envelope. I knew that if Bob could see me now, he would tell me straight out I looked like hell. "Get yourself together," I could hear him barking at me. "Tomorrow, go to the beauty parlor, the spa, wherever it is you lasses go to get yerselves fixed up. Just don't walk around looking long-faced at me."

Baring my teeth, I practiced a smile in the mirror. I looked like a plain, tired woman. I snapped off the little silver-sconce lamps, slipped off my shoes, got out of my clothes and hung them carefully in the closet. I put on a nightie: white cotton lawn down to the ankles and buttoned to the neck with long sleeves. I put on my comfy old pink bathrobe and girly over-sized fluffy pink slippers, then I went and lay on the bed.

Rats, who'd been waiting patiently, jumped up and came to sit on my feet. He was heavy and I was desperately uncomfortable but I wasn't about to move him. I needed him as much as he needed me.

I lay propped against the pillows, eyes closed, reviewing the day. It seemed ages since we had stood in the biting wind as Bob was finally laid to rest. I could hear the little jeweled clock Bob had given me on my birthday ticking softly. This was a house of many clocks; Bob loved them. The dog made snuffly sleepy noises and the wind pushed the snow softly against the curtained windows.

I could put it off no longer. I sat up, took the envelope and ripped it open. Inside I found three more envelopes. The largest one said, "Do Not Open." The other two were letter size. One said, "To be opened at the appropriate moment. You will know when." The other, "Open now."

I opened it carefully and unfolded the sheets of lined yellow paper torn from a legal pad.

*"Daisy, love,"* Bob's letter began,

*I hope you may never need to read this because it will mean that I am dead. But if you do, then I know I am in good hands. In the years since I picked you up at that party you have come to mean more to me than almost any other woman. I say* almost, *because though I never discussed it, there was a woman I cared deeply about many years ago, long before I knew you.*

*Remember I told you that night we met, that I'd been there too, at the bottom of the emotional heap? Well it was Rosalia Alonzo Ybarra I was referring to. Remember I said I'd asked myself if I would like to be young again, ambitious again, in love again? Well it was Rosalia I was thinking about.*

*When I was with Rosalia I was all those things: young, broke and in love. I was twenty, she was eighteen. She put up with the poverty and there was no doubt she loved me and I loved her, but she couldn't take the other part of me: my burning ambition, the need to win at all cost. She left me because of it. All she wanted was a normal family life with a husband who came home nights and a lot of children. I'm telling you the truth now—and this is the first time I have ever really talked about her. I never saw her again and I've never gotten over her. I sacrificed her to a part of my life that seemed more important at the time. It was only as the years passed that I realized how selfish I'd been.*

*So you see, lass, when I saw you alone and afraid that night at the party, something in me from the past reached out to you. It was as though by saving you I could make amends, maybe even find a kind of happiness through you. And I did, my sweet Daisy girl (your mother, God rest her soul, should have been shot for giving you that name. You're much more of an Eleanor or an Isabel, a Juliet even, because you are a true romantic, even though you try to hide it from yourself). But that's beside the point and anyhow, lass suits you just fine. And by the way, even without even seeing you I know you need to get your hair done, it'll be straggling all over the place like always. Go get a hairdo, a massage, a facial, and bloody well cheer up! No use moping around now it's all over.*

*I suppose I was never a good man in the best sense of the word and anyone who called me a son of a bitch probably had good reason. But I*

*tried and I cared, and in time the money meant less to me. It became*
*merely a reflex action, making more and more. But when it gets down*
*to it, "enough" is all a man needs.*

*If the worst happens to me—other than dying in my own bed of*
*natural causes with a glass of good Bordeaux and you by my side—you*
*can be sure I was murdered.*

My heart skipped a beat. It was here in Bob's own handwriting. Swallowing back the shocked tears I read on.

*I'm imagining you reading this and realize it will come as a shock,*
*but a man like me doesn't get to my age—sixty-four, in case you've*
*forgotten—without making an enemy or two. And no doubt some of*
*them would like to see me under the earth instead of basking on top of*
*it in the sunny South of France with my latest—and most lovable—*
*redhead. Namely—you. But for some time I've had the uneasy feeling*
*that someone from the past was out to get me. At first I thought it was*
*just a joke, some crazy with a bee in his bonnet about a wealthy public*
*figure. Now, though, I'm not so sure. But who? you might ask. I have no*
*idea, and anyhow, I hope it's all a figment of my overactive imagina-*
*tion, though Lord knows I've probably offended enough people (and*
*that's putting it mildly) and I've beaten enough of them out of a busi-*
*ness deal or in a game of high-stakes finance to fill a good-size down-*
*town Manhattan bar, where at six p.m. no doubt they will all*
*cheerfully drink to my demise.*

*I have given Harry Montana a list of possible suspects I've "of-*
*fended," though I can't be certain it's actually any one of them. After all*
*there are plenty of other loose cannons out there in the world of high fi-*

nance, both male and female. Anyhow, Montana knows the score and how all of this came about, and no doubt he'll fill you in.

On this list are six people I tried to help in my lifetime, though I daresay none of them would admit it, or even believe that was my motive. Could one of them be my killer? (I say "killer" because if you're reading this then obviously I am already dead.) Again, who knows, though I'm personally of the opinion that there's more to each of them than their current lives show.

Here's something else to think about, Daisy: It's my belief that if you take folks out of their normal habitat and put them in a strange place with other strangers, they become different people, or rather they show themselves for the people they really are. And now I've come up with the perfect idea to test out that theory.

My feeling is if I have been killed for my money then at least let's have some fun out of it. So now I'm going to play a game, and I'm setting it up for you.

Remember those old movies where all the suspects are gathered together in the big country house? Somehow there's always a thunderstorm with the lights flickering on and off and a sinister old butler; there's creaking floorboards and poisoned wine and knives gleaming, and faces at the window and shadowy figures glimpsed in darkened hallways. Well, it's going to be a bit like that, only instead of a gloomy country house, Daisy lass, it's going to take place on a high-class yacht, namely the famous Blue Boat, and at the Villa Belkiss.

I'm sending you and all six of the suspects on a Mediterranean cruise. Tell them it'll be a kind of wake, a "celebration of my life" as the pompous funeral people insist on calling it, though personally I rather enjoyed celebrating my life when I was alive to enjoy it. This is not the

*real reason I'm inviting them though. I involved myself in these peo-*
*ple's lives. Now I want them to acknowledge the truth about them-*
*selves, to reveal their deepest emotions to each other, and also to you,*
*Daisy. I want you to find out their reason for living and how what I*
*did affected their lives. Maybe then they will come to terms finally with*
*who they are. And if they do, maybe they would have surprised me, and*
*maybe they'll get a second chance.*

*It's an interesting thought, and a perfect way to find out the truth*
*before they finally get to hear my will read and discover if there's any-*
*thing in it for them.*

*How can I get my suspects on board? you might ask. Money, of*
*course. It's always the bait rats are eager to snap up. Again, Montana*
*will have all the details.*

*So you see, I'm looking to you and to Montana to solve my murder.*
*Montana will also guarantee you will never be in any danger. And*
*trust me, Daisy, that wherever you are . . . and wherever I am . . . I*
*will be always there, keeping an eye on you.*

*The large sealed envelope marked "Do Not Open" contains a copy of*
*my Last Will and Testament, fully executed by me in the presence of my*
*lawyers, who have the original in their safe. It's to be read by Montana*
*on Capri on the last day of the cruise, and I can guarantee it's full of*
*surprises.*

*Do not read the will now, no matter how tempted you are. It's to be*
*a surprise for everybody. And by the way, everyone will be your guests*
*on this cruise, so don't let any of those toffee-nosed snobs try to patron-*
*ize you. Remember, I could buy and sell all of them and they know it.*
*After all, isn't that the reason they'll be there?*

*The third envelope is to be opened by you after the "game" is all over*
*and the mystery solved. This one is personal, lass, just between you and*

me. I never said this to you in life but I must say it to you now. I love you, Daisy Keane. You have integrity, even though you do tend to lie a bit. You had no designs on my money. And you certainly never had any designs on this big, common, ugly old Yorkshire lad. I can't blame you for that, though I must admit that, with your red hair and freckled nose, it crossed my mind a couple of times. Only joking, only joking. Pure love is pure love and that's all there is to it, dead or alive.

I know you'll take care of Rats for me. And please, lass, take good care of yourself. Find yourself some happiness, I know it's out there waiting for you. In fact, I guarantee it.

Bob had signed his missive the way he signed all his notes to me, simply with the gigantic "BH."

I sat for a few minutes stunned, then, shoving Rats out of the way, I got up and began to pace the room nervously. *Why* hadn't he confided in me? *Why* hadn't he told me who he suspected and the reason they wanted to kill him? And now I had to take these murder "suspects" on some crazy cruise.

I pulled back the curtains and stared out into the night. The snow had stopped and the windowpanes had those curved white snow corners. They looked the way they used to at Christmastime when I was a kid and we'd fake them with that spray-on stuff from the drugstore. Outside was a winter wonderland, a smooth thick blanket of snow that muffled the normal country noises. The silence was so absolute it throbbed against my ears.

The letter clutched in my hand fluttered in a sudden breeze. Surprised, I stared at it. I glanced at the window but it was tight shut and there was no draft. The back of my neck prickled. Was it Bob, coming back to keep an eye on me as he'd promised in his letter? I swung around, half-expecting to see him. I thought I heard the curtain rustle and turned quickly back, but it hung perfectly still.

Heart thudding, I ran and switched on every light in the room, then I sank onto the chaise. "*Jesus!* Don't you do this to me, Bob Hardwick," I said in a quavering voice. *"Just don't you do this."* Eyes closed, I pictured him standing there, a trace of a smile on his big ogre face. Laughing at me.

"Okay. It's okay," I told myself loudly. "I'm just imagining things. I'll be all right now. Everything's okay."

But Rats jumped from the bed and ran to the door. He stood there, whining. *He knew someone was there.* I willed myself to walk across and open it.

*"Jesus Christ!"* I jumped about three feet into the air. A man was standing in the shadows, looking at me.

# 10

*Daisy*

Mouth agape, hand clutched to my heaving chest, I stared blankly at Montana. He was wearing a white terry robe and carrying a tray with a blue kitchen teapot, two blue-striped mugs and a plate of gingersnaps.

"I'm sorry I startled you," he said politely. "I was just about to knock. I knew you wouldn't be able to sleep once you'd read the letter so I made you a cup of tea. I saw the light under your door . . ."

"You scared the hell out of me." My voice sounded brittle, snappy.

"I'm sorry."

He looked so repentant I almost forgave him. He was bare-foot and I thought dazedly how cute he looked, the tanned cropped-headed, tattooed hard-man P.I.

Exhaustion swept over me and suddenly a nice English cup of tea seemed exactly what I needed and Montana's company seemed better than none. I stood aside for him to pass then showed him where to put the tray, on the small glass table next to the chaise.

Rats put his paws on the table, sniffing the gingersnaps. I gave him one, then poured the tea. The chaise was the only chair in the room apart from my little vanity stool and since I didn't want Montana sitting that close to me I showed him to the cushioned window seat. He took the mug I offered him and still standing, he stared out of the window with its Christmasy decoration of snow.

"It's odd," he said, "the kind of peace that comes with a blizzard. I don't know whether it's because we're temporarily cut off from the reality of day-to-day living, or whether it's the complete silence." He closed his eyes, listening. "There's not even the sound of the wind blowing anymore."

"It must remind you of your childhood," I said.

"Nothing in my childhood was ever peaceful."

I thought I'd better not get into that, but then it occurred to me that I was so used to being discreet I missed out on a lot of things. For instance, if I'd asked Bob more about his past he might have told me about the woman he'd loved and why he'd never gone back to her.

"So what happened in your childhood?"

Montana took a seat in the window. He leaned forward, elbows on his knees, the mug clasped in both hands. I felt that little flutter again in regions I didn't even want to think about. He looked so incredibly masculine in my very feminine silk-curtained boudoir.

"My father was a harsh man," he said. "He rarely spoke, except to give orders. He rode out with the cowboys and was gone sometimes for weeks on end, leaving me alone with the old man who was supposed to keep house. But when Pop was away, the old man drank and I was left to fend for myself. All I had was my horse. I loved that mare. Believe it or not I rode her twenty miles to school every morning, and twenty miles back again, that's how remote we were. I'd hitch her to the post, give her a feed bag and go inside that little country schoolhouse. Just one room and seven reluctant kids, all of different ages, all showing up to get some learning. But learn we did—I could conjugate verbs in Latin before I ever learned how to do it properly in English."

I took a sip of my tea, temporarily forgetting about Bob.

Montana's charcoal eyes searched my face. "You're looking a bit better," he said. "There's color in your cheeks now."

Embarrassed, I tucked my feet under me. In my old pink robe and giant fluffy slippers, I felt like an overgrown junior high school kid at a sleepover. The dog sneaked a second cookie and crunched it loudly, dropping crumbs all over the carpet. I didn't care.

"I think you should read this." I handed him Bob's letter.

I was very aware of our fingers touching as he took it. I also noticed he was still wearing the American Indian–style turquoise bracelet. I guessed he never removed it.

He read the letter carefully, studying every word as though he could find double meanings or hidden references I had missed. I doubted there were any, because Bob always said exactly what he meant. He glanced up.

"Do you believe him?" he asked.

"Bob never lied."

"So, do you have any idea who might have wanted to kill him?"

"No one I can think of."

Montana folded the letter and handed it back to me. "Remember your Bible? The Ten Commandments handed down by Moses?"

I did remember. "Thou shalt not commit adultery," I said. "Thou shalt not steal. Thou shalt not bear false witness against thy neighbor. Thou shalt not covet thy neighbor's wife, nor his male servant, nor his female servant, nor his ox, nor his donkey, nor anything that is thy neighbor's."

"Put it in context," Montana said, "and what have you got? Sex, money, jealousy, envy. Enough to kill for."

"But Bob was a good man. He would never knowingly hurt anyone. I told you earlier, he always helped people."

"Hardwick was a hardheaded businessman in a tough dog-eat-dog world. How do you think he got this successful? This rich? He did what he had to and he was as ruthless as anybody else when he had to be."

I said nothing but I knew in my gut Montana was right.

Montana got to his feet and began to pace. "Money, power. That's motive number one." He turned to look out of the window again. His back to me, he said, "Then there's motive number two. Passion. Sex."

"I know nothing about that part of Bob's life," I said stiffly, because I knew Montana was wondering if Bob and I were lovers.

He swung around and looked me in the eyes. "Why not?"

"Bob told me he didn't want me," I said, regretting the words almost before they were out of my mouth.

Montana's brows rose. "Well now," he said, half-smiling. "You *have* surprised me."

"He didn't mean it like that," I said defensively. "We'd just met, he offered me a job and I thought he was propositioning me. He told me in no uncertain terms that he could have any woman he wanted, and that he certainly didn't want me. He didn't mean it as an insult," I added, "it was just that he wanted me to get it straight in my head that all he was offering me was a job."

"And quite a job for a woman with few or no qualifications."

Anger simmered as I found I was defending myself again. "Bob wasn't after qualifications. He wanted to help me. You read his letter. Anyhow, as you might have noticed, I was a quick learner. He said I was indispensable to him, he said he couldn't run his life without me."

"Then you're saying there's no way you could be suspected of murdering him?"

Furious now, I leapt to my feet. "Stop it," I snarled. "Just stop! And no, I did *not* sleep with Bob Hardwick. No, I was *not* after his money. No, I did *not* 'covet' anything he owned, except the time he had to spend with me. He was my best friend as well as my employer and . . . and . . ." I ran out of words and steam.

"Just wondered," Montana said mildly.

I glared at him. "You know what? If I was ever going to kill anybody, right now it would be you."

"That's exactly the way it happens. Passion of the moment."

Furious, I flung myself backward onto the bed, arms over my head, slippered feet kicking the air. "Ohhhh," I yelled. "Why did I ever have to meet you anyway?"

"Because Bob arranged it. He's given both of us a job. Now it's up to us to carry it through, regardless of our personal feelings."

I sat up and stared icily at him. "I don't know that I can do that," I said, stiff as Her Majesty the Queen.

"Tough," he replied coolly. "We have our orders. And anyhow, you're not doing it for me, you're doing it for the man you really cared about." He walked to the table and picked up the teapot. "More tea?"

"No thank you."

He refilled his mug, looking quite at home in his bathrobe in my bedroom. Rats trotted over to Montana, then settled down at his feet. *Traitor*, I thought.

I got up, kicked off my slippers, slipped out of my robe. "I'm going to bed," I said, remembering too late the granny nightie, buttoned to the neck and down to the ankles. I climbed hurriedly into bed and pulled the covers up to my chin.

"Okay, we'll talk some more in the morning, around ten, make some plans," Montana said. He walked around my room, checking the windows, closing the curtains, turning off the lamps. He gave Rats a final pat as he walked to the door.

"By the way . . . cute nightie," he said as the door closed behind him.

I could swear I heard him laughing.

I turned my head in to the pillow and was asleep within seconds.

# 11

## *Montana*

Montana did not sleep. He lay on the bed for a long time, hands clasped behind his head, staring up at the pleated red-silk canopy, lost in his thoughts.

He'd met Bob Hardwick ten years ago, when the mogul called him in to investigate the backgrounds of certain applicants for a high-powered executive position within his company. Montana had taken care of the job rapidly and efficiently, then he'd gone to see Bob.

Hardwick had leaned back in his oversized leather chair behind his impressive rosewood desk in his lofty Manhattan offices, looking expectantly at him. Secretaries bustled in and out with papers for him to sign, which he did with barely a glance. Various assistants came to warn of his imminent lunch meeting at Four Seasons and to say that his tailor was on his way up with the new suits to be fitted, and that a woman with an impressive society name wished to talk to him. He wafted them away with his big hand like so many annoying flies. "I'll be there when I get there" was all he said, and the assistants rolled their eyes as they went to try to placate those kept waiting. He looked like a wild man in his rumpled suit, his thick gray hair standing on end, his flinty blue eyes under his grizzly, scowling brows, his pink complexion hinting of high blood pressure. He was impressive in his stature and his ugliness.

Montana's raised eyebrows must have expressed his disbelief that Hardwick was actually listening to what he had to say, what with all the interruptions.

"Don't worry, lad, I'm listening." Hardwick leaned across his desk, taking him in fully for the first time.

Montana presented him with the truth about the job applicants, and his misgivings about the one who on paper sounded the best.

"I'm going on my gut instinct but I'm advising you not to take him on."

"I like a chap with gut instinct. I've made my way to the top on exactly the same thing. You like it then, what you do? Detecting and snooping, all that stuff?"

"There's more to my job than just investigating backgrounds of potential employees, or finding what rival international companies are up to and what their problems are. We're also a security company. We ensure the safety of our clients."

"Men like me, you mean?" Hardwick looked interested.

"Men like you, sir. Billionaires, royalty, celebrities."

"You mean Hollywood stars?"

"Among others, yes."

Hardwick twiddled a pen between his fingers, looking down

at his desk, thinking. "And how would a man know he's in danger—from a stalker, let's say?"

"It's best to employ someone like me before you get to that stage."

Still twiddling the pen, Hardwick sighed. "I couldn't stand that, though, being guarded, my every move tracked. What kind of life is that anyhow? No, I'm a man who values his freedom. And, oddly enough, a man who values his solitude." He gave Montana a long searching look. "A man like you, I'd guess."

Montana had to admit he was right.

Hardwick picked up the application he'd been considering. He scanned it, thinking about what Montana had just told him about his gut instinct. "Tell you what, why don't I offer you the job instead? I'll pay you twice what you're earning now." He was using the same bribe tactic he always used when he wanted something badly enough. "You've no experience but you'll get the hang of things quick, I can tell that. And what you don't know about takeovers and leverage and finance I'll teach you myself. What do you say to that, Montana?"

"Why me?"

"I like you. Gut reaction. Right?"

"Right. And it's a great offer but I'm sorry I can't accept."

Hardwick studied Montana carefully; then he said, "Of course I see now, a man like you couldn't take to normal office hours, being tied to a schedule, repeating the same task day after day. You're a free ranger, Montana. Besides, if you worked for me you'd have to get a different haircut and get rid of that damn bracelet."

An assistant poked his head around the door. "Four Seasons, sir . . . lunch . . . ," he mouthed.

"Get out," Hardwick said to the assistant. Montana was on his feet, ready to be dismissed. "And you sit down, Montana. You're too interesting to let go just yet. How old are you anyhow? Thirty-four? Young and still malleable, right? I need young men like you around, men who don't always say yes to me, men with integrity. Are you sure I can't offer you a job? I'm upping the ante. I'll offer three times what you earn now."

Head thrust forward, Montana looked Hardwick straight in the eye. "Mr. Hardwick, I'm available any time you want in my capacity as investigator or for security purposes. I like my job and there's no way I will ever change it."

"Not even if you find a good woman, fall in love?"

"Not even then. She'll have to take me as I am."

"I tried that once, when I was young and poor and struggling. Didn't work for me," Hardwick added with a wry grin. "She loved me but she took off and left me. It wasn't the money, or rather the lack of it then; it was my own bloody self-centered ambition. 'Take me as I am,' I said to her, and she turned me down. So there you have it, Montana. It's risky with women. But I respect your feelings and I think you're very good at your job."

He got to his feet and so did Montana. They shook hands and Hardwick walked him to the door. "Any time you change your mind let me know," he said.

Over the next ten years Hardwick had often called on Montana. They lunched many times at a diner on East Forty-ninth Street where Bob was partial to the burgers and shoestring fries. They'd talk about Montana's growing business; about the new offices he was thinking of opening in London; about Bob's French wife who soon became his ex; about the temperamental Italian mistress who also became an ex; about how he never had time even to visit his villa in Capri and that he'd always dreamed of sailing around the island because in his opinion it would be even more beautiful seen from the water.

"It's a dream of mine," he confessed to Montana, "which is why I bought the place sight unseen. It belonged to Vassily Belkiss, a famous ballet dancer, and when he passed on it just sort of sat there for years. It's the one thing I can thank the Italian for; she found it, persuaded me to buy it, told me it was a good investment. I'm not sure she was right about that but I fell in love with the photographs and the romance of it all. I guess one day I'll find the time to visit; meantime, it's a nice dream. Perhaps you'll come and visit me there? What would you say to that, Montana?"

"Any time you say," he'd replied, but it had gone no further than that because in the next breath Bob was telling him he had a small problem that was beginning to irritate him.

"It's the damn e-mail," he said. "The instant communicator that invades a man's privacy any time day or night. I keep getting these threatening little notes, simple stuff, juvenile really, like 'I know where you are right now. Remember I'm watching you.' And 'I know who you were with last night. My eyes are always on you.'" He shrugged. "Of course it's too daft even to think anyone is really able to keep tabs on my every movement without my noticing."

"I could," Montana said.

Bob looked up at him, surprised. "As easy as that, is it?"

"No, but my men are good at their job."

"And this nutcase—could he be that good?"

"Never assume anything. It might be a woman."

"A jealous female, huh?"

Montana grinned. "Know any like that?" he asked, and Bob grinned back and said he knew a few.

Montana told him that he would have the e-mails monitored and that he would assign round-the-clock security immediately, but Bob refused point-blank.

"I told you earlier I couldn't handle that," he said. "It's not in my nature—nor yours either, Harry Montana—to live like a trapped animal." Then he handed Montana a list of six names and asked him to investigate them.

"They are all people who at some time or other were involved in my life, either personal or business. Each one of 'em has a flaw. And each one resents me, even though I did what I thought best for them. I want to know exactly where their lives are at now, what they are doing, and with whom. I want to know if they deserve my help."

When Montana asked him why, Bob shrugged again and said, "Gut instinct. Any one of 'em might want to kill me." But he laughed as he said it. "Just kidding," he added.

Two days later he was dead.


Sir Robert Hardwick's death had not been judged a murder; in fact, quite the opposite. It was an accident: he'd misjudged the turn, and the car had gone off the road and burst into flames. By some miracle, Hardwick had been thrown clear.

A verdict of accidental death was given and Sir Robert Hardwick made his last flight home to Yorkshire. The local rescue services hauled the remains of the vehicle up the mountain and Montana was granted permission to have the scorched mass of metal towed to a garage he used in New Jersey. It remained there, crated up, awaiting his next move. But first he had to decide if Bob's hunch that someone wanted to murder him was right. He was in for a sleepless night in the Red Room.

# 12

## Daisy

The next morning, pulling myself together, I wrote responses to some of the notes of sympathy from Bob's contemporaries in the world of high finance, as well as to a couple of heads of state, and even one to a young Royal whom Bob had befriended at a polo match and with whom he'd kept up a correspondence, along with the occasional lunch.

An hour later when I emerged from the library Montana was waiting in the hall. He lounged against the fireplace, hands in the pockets of Bob's old Barbour jacket. With the Jack Russell dog sprawled at his feet he looked almost like a country gentleman, though I doubted *gentleman* was a word that could properly be used to describe this hardheaded American P.I.

"Glad to see you're on time," he said with that little smile that narrowed his gray eyes and that I felt uncomfortably sure lent a double meaning to his words.

I hurried to the boot room to put on snow gear. Scruffy but

warmly dressed, I returned to the hall. Montana unfurled his long length from the fireplace where he'd been toasting his bones. "Come on, boy," he said to Rats, who got to his feet and stood looking expectantly up at him. As though Montana was his new master, I thought bitterly.

Outside, I sniffed the icy air, thinking of spring and crocuses and snowdrops, to say nothing of the drifts of daffodils that should already have swathed the gentle slopes of the Hall's grounds in optimistic yellow.

I felt Montana's hand under my elbow, steadying me as we walked down the steps, but I moved quickly away from him on the narrow path carved through the snow in the driveway. The dog had perked up at the thought of a second walk so soon, and now he bounded ahead, making a right when he got to the gates as though he knew we were going to the Ram's Head. Rats had spent a lot of time in the pub with Bob and everyone there always made a fuss of him. Bob would buy him an English banger, which he'd devour in two fast gulps then looked pleadingly up for more.

"We need to talk about Bob's list," Montana began before we were even out of the driveway. "I want you to tell me about the people on it, who they are, what you know about them."

"Aren't you supposed to know all that? After all, you're the detective."

"Detectives find things out by asking questions," he said patiently, as though talking to a spoiled child.

"Okay, so what d'you want to know?" I said sullenly.

He threw me a wary glance that I caught out of the corner of my eye but I kept my focus determinedly on the snow-cleared path down the middle of the village street. I did not want to know about murder. I did not want to know about "suspects," and I certainly didn't want to go on a cruise with them. I wanted everything to be the way it had always been. How *could* Bob do this to me?

"Remember, this is for Bob," Montana said, as though reading my mind. "Look upon it as your final job for him."

"Of course," I said, ashamed. "I'll do anything to help."

When we got to the pub Rats was already sitting by the door. He dived in ahead of us, tail wagging and I heard Ginny, behind the bar, say, "Eh, Rats luv, it's grand to see you again. I'll have your sausage ready in two shakes of a lamb's tail."

We followed the dog into the seventeenth-century inn and were immediately engulfed in the pleasant fug of heat blasting from the radiators, as well as from the huge wood fire in the walk-in-size stone grate. The scent of apple logs mingled with the cigarette smoke and the fruity aroma of draft beer, overlaid with a strong hint of gravy. I waved at Ginny, shrugging out of my coat as I walked through the low-ceilinged room with its battered wooden counter, blackened old beams and nicotine-colored plaster. There were wooden sconces with red shades on the walls and small red-shaded lamps on the broad wooden window ledges, and the diamond-paned windows were fogged with condensation from the heat inside and the bitter cold out. A few older men sat over their beers at little tables dotted with coasters advertising Tetley's ale. The wooden settles they sat on were high-backed and hard, but they'd spent a lifetime on them and looked at home.

I stopped to say hello, introducing Montana as a friend of Sir Robert's. Then Reg Blunt came out from behind the bar to shake hands. I told him we'd take a table in the snug, the small room to the side where it was quiet and we could discuss business.

"The shepherd's pie's good today," Reg said. "Unless you fancy steak and chips, Mr. Montana?"

"He's from Texas," I warned.

"Better forget about that steak then. You're better off with the shepherd's pie, or bangers and mash. And o' course there's always a plowman's or a pork pie."

I remembered I hadn't eaten the day before, and now I was starving. I ordered a pork pie as well the plowman's, which consisted here of Cheddar and the local Wensleydale cheese with a hunk of bread and the spicy dark brown relish I'd become fond of called Branston pickle. Montana decided on the shepherd's pie and we both ordered pints of Tetley's draft bitter.

Ginny came in with the sausage for Rats, already cut in pieces. "If I don't cut it up he'll just gulp it down," she explained, giving Montana the eye and a smile. "I remember you from the church yesterday," she said. "Good to see you again, sir. This is the best place in town, y'know."

Montana told her it was the *only* place in town and she laughed as she strode away on her spiky-heeled black leather boots, her ample red butt twitching.

Montana looked me straight in the eyes and raised his glass in a toast. "To us, Daisy Keane," he said. "Because we are going to get to know each other really well."

I took a sip of the bitter I drank only when I came to the Ram's Head, staring down at Rats, who had polished off his sausage and stared back at me, hoping for more. I slid my eyes back to Montana. He was still looking at me, waiting for some kind of reaction to his toast I supposed.

I put down the glass. "And why is that, Montana?"

"We're going on a cruise together, you and I," he said, with that little half smile playing around his lips.

"What makes you think *you're* going? I didn't invite you."

"No. But Bob did."

Mutual antipathy flickered between us. I picked up my glass and took a good slug of the beer, wiping the foam off my lips with the back of my hand. I saw him grin but it was too late to be ladylike. Lord knows why Bob had employed him and even worse, why he'd asked him to go with me on this ridiculous cruise. But if anyone knew anything deeply personal about Bob and his life, it was I. I'd bet Montana knew only the business stuff.

Reg came over carrying a steaming mini-casserole of shepherd's pie. It smelled so good I almost wished I'd ordered it myself, but then Ginny set my pork pie and cheese and bread before me and told me to enjoy it, adding that I looked as though I could use a bit of fattening up. I ate it silently, contemplating my future on a cruise with Montana.

"How do I know Bob invited you?" I asked at last.

Montana put down his fork and took a folded piece of yellow paper from his jeans pocket. He handed it to me then went back to excavating his shepherd's pie.

It was a letter from Bob.

"*Montana,*" it began.

*We've worked together for almost ten years now and I know I can trust you. I've already given you a list of people I was once close with and who I think in some way believe they would benefit from my death. Nothing is written in stone, you understand, but if it proves true and one of them wanted me dead, then only one of the six is guilty. I hope you never have to use this list, but should the occasion arise, I know I'm in your good hands and you will not let me down.*

*Here's what I want you to do. You will have Daisy invite each one of them on a Mediterranean cruise to "celebrate my life." A sort of floating wake, you might say. You'll need to give them a sweetener—and I'll bet this will get them where it counts. You will offer each of them one hundred thousand dollars to go on a luxury cruise, all expenses paid. You will also tell them that my will is to be read at the Villa Belkiss in Capri the day the yacht puts in there, and that some of them can expect to benefit. Make no mistake, Montana, each one of these people will think they are mentioned in my will.*

*Tell them that I personally wanted to invite them and that, had I been alive, I would have joined them as their host. They'll be dying to know what's in it for them—if you'll excuse the pun. Anyhow, I always wanted to go on a cruise and never had the time, so I'm thinking why not also invite a few more friends? Fill out the ranks of suspects, so to speak. These sorts of mystery stories always had a few red herrings and we'll use these other guests as ours. I'll give you a separate list of names for this, or you can choose some.*

*Call me an eccentric old bugger if you will, but I always liked those* movies where "the butler did it," and I thought this would be a good way to find out who my "butler" was.

Blue Boat is the yacht I've chosen. It's owned by a friend and I suggest you contact her as soon as possible. It's the Ritz-Carlton of luxury yachts—big, elegant, classy, and with an excellent crew, so my friend tells me. I wish I could come with you but maybe I'll be watching the proceedings anyway. You never know. Anyhow, I want them all to have a damned good time—except my killer, of course.

You're a good man at your job, Montana, the best, I'd say, and I know you'll carry out my last commission in your usual excellent fashion. Your fee, as always, is already taken care of, as will be all expenses. My lawyers, Grady, Marshal, Levin and Frost, whose offices are in Moorgate, London, have been fully apprised of the situation and will carry out your orders.

One more thing. I'm handing my most precious possession over to you for safekeeping. I use the word possession in its loosest sense because I never owned Daisy Keane. Still, she is my only family. I love her, though I'm sure you know by now she can be as exasperating as any woman you've even known and then some. It will be your job, Montana, to keep her safe. With you at her side, I know I'm not putting her at risk, and who knows, you might even enjoy each other's company.

Good luck on your quest. Then, when it's all over and done with and the murderer has been apprehended, I will surely be able to rest in peace. Until then, don't bet on it!

Having written all this, I'm not currently planning on going anywhere and these events may never have to be played out. But if they are, then good luck. Enjoy the cruise.

He signed it *"Sincerely, Bob Hardwick."*

My heart began to thaw. Bob had called me his "family," he'd also said he loved me. But he'd also said I might be in danger and I'd need Montana's protection. For the first time I felt a pang of fear.

I glanced at Montana, enjoying his lunch, oblivious to my possible danger. My fate was in his hands. Thanks to Bob, I was to cruise the Mediterranean on a luxury yacht with a man I scarcely knew and certainly didn't want to know, as well as half a dozen murder suspects, whom I would be expected to entertain under the ploy that it was Bob's idea of a farewell memorial.

"Okay." I sighed, resigning myself to my fate. "So where's the list?"

# 13

*Daisy*

Montana took another sheet of yellow paper from his pocket. Without looking he handed it over and continued eating. *"Thanks,"* I said, but sarcasm seemed wasted on him.

It was Bob's handwriting all right and with one exception I knew all of the people on it. The ex-wife, Lady Diane Hardwick, headed up the list.

"I know what Diane's motive for murder would be," I said. "Greed. Bob told me that when he married her he was marrying 'class.' That's exactly the way he put it. She's some kind of French aristocracy, though Bob never met her family. I remember her maiden name though, it was de Valentinois . . . Diane de Valentinois. Very romantic, I thought.

"Bob met her at the Cannes Film Festival. She was handing out information pamphlets, and he told me she was wearing a sexy red evening dress that showed off her gorgeous body to perfection. 'One look and I was a goner,' he told me. 'I'd have done anything to make her mine.'

"That was ten years ago. Diane must be about my age now, maybe a little older. I met her once or twice. She would simply descend on us, in Paris or the Riviera, always ready to cause trouble. She's beautiful though. Red hair, lighter than mine, and emerald green eyes. And she does have fabulous legs. Bob told me he fell for the legs first, then the hair. I sometimes wondered if it was because of nostalgia for Diane and the red hair that he picked me up at that awful London party, though he always swore it wasn't. Anyhow, their marriage was turbulent; it lasted only a year, but Diane insisted on keeping her title. She made it a condition of the divorce, and now she's still Lady Hardwick. Bob was generous too; ever the gentleman, he gave her an enormous settlement. 'After all, she was my wife,' was what he said."

"So when Diane 'descended' on Bob in Paris or the South of France, she was after more money."

I nodded. "God knows why she needed it, he'd already given her a fortune, but she's the kind who always wants more. Anyhow, now she lives in Nice."

I went to the next name on the list.

"Filomena Algardi was Bob's ex-mistress. A modern-day Italian Brigitte Bardot: the pout, the blond ponytail, the bikini—sexy as all get-out. Bob had an on-and-off relationship with her for years, but she was greedy, and in the end he couldn't take her demands, or the tantrums when she didn't get what she wanted. It's easy to find motives for her. How about jealousy *and* greed?

"I never told Bob this," I added softly, "but I felt sorry for him. He wanted so badly to believe Filomena loved him, *really loved* him, for the man he was and not just his money. So many times I wanted to say, 'She doesn't, don't do it, Bob, get rid of her, you're worth a million times more than she is'—and I wasn't just talking money. I wanted to tell him he was looking for love in all the wrong places and with the wrong sorts of women. There were nice women right here in the Yorkshire countryside, attractive women, women he'd understand because basically they were the same kind of people. I invited one or two to dinner parties but Bob was always a sucker for the glitz and the glamour girls. 'I wanted to flaunt Filomena on my arm,' he told me one night after too much after-dinner port. 'I wanted 'em all to know that ugly old Bob Hardwick was good as they were.'" I sighed, remembering. "So you see, despite Bob's success and his wealth, at heart he was still the poor homely lad from the wrong side of the tracks.

"I only met Filomena once," I added. "She came charging into Bob's London offices screaming he was a cheap bastard and that she'd get back at him, just you wait. Security took care of her but it was an ugly scene. She'd wanted to embarrass Bob and bring him to heel. I always felt that with Filomena anything might happen, and too often it did."

I took a long draft of my Tetley's bitter before I read out the next name.

"Davis Farrell. American. I never met him, he was before my time, but he and Bob were partners in a project for several years. I don't know what it was but I know it wasn't successful. I guess Farrell just moved on."

The next on the list was Charles Clement. I said, "In his fifties, flashy in a smooth British kind of way. I remember he spent a couple of weekends at Sneadley. They'd play golf and tennis and he was there for the August grouse shoot on the moors. They were very much 'guy' weekends—no women, lots of booze and food and man-talk over port after dinner. They certainly didn't want me there; I'd make sure everything was organized then head back down to London, out of their way."

"You have friends in London?"

"Sure, one or two; career women like myself, tied to their bosses' whims and lives and travels. It doesn't leave much time for a private life, but we get together occasionally—lunch, shopping, that sort of thing."

"No special friend then?"

"Bob was my special friend. And Bordelaise, of course."

Montana raised his brows at her ridiculous name so I told him the story of how she got it.

He laughed. "And is Bordelaise *saucy* then?"

"As all get-out. She'll charm you in half a minute. You'll fall in love with her. Everyone does."

"She's alone and fancy-free?"

"Two husbands down and one on his way out. She gets bored easily."

Montana leaned closer, elbows on his knees, hands held loosely in front of him. His eyes had an intensity that I found disturbing and I went quickly on to the next name.

"Marius Dopplemann." I glanced up again. Obviously Montana knew the name, everyone did. Dopplemann was a genius, a German national who'd taken American citizenship and become famous and influential, first in the space program, then in other top-secret projects. "The German scientist?" I said. "I never met him and Bob never talked about him except once to say he admired his work. I've no idea of a possible motive."

"And the last name?"

"Rosalia Alonzo Ybarra. The first I heard of her was in his letter to me. She's his long-lost first love."

Montana said, "There's no address for her, or for Dopplemann. Nor for Clement and Farrell."

I shrugged. "They might be on Bob's personal Rolodexes."

It was time to go. Montana helped me on with my jacket; he lifted my hair off my neck and settled the collar snugly. I felt myself go warm all over and turned my face away so he wouldn't see that I was blushing. It was silly to react this way simply at the touch of a man's hands. I decided I really must get out in the world more.

Montana walked over to the bar to pay, stopping to chat with Ginny and Reg while I collected Rats from his chosen spot in front of the fire.

I waved my good-byes and stepped outside to wait for Montana. The cold bit my nose and sneaked down my throat, and I almost turned around and went right back inside, but then Montana swung through the door, buttoning Bob's jacket. I figured he might as well keep it now, but maybe the expensive black cashmere coat was more his true urban style. Hadn't he said he was a city guy? I realized I had no idea even in which country he lived. Perhaps he was simply "a man of the world."

We walked back to the Hall, each lost in our own thoughts. I was wondering how I was going to cope with the scary cruise, and I assumed Montana was wondering how he was going to find all these people and persuade them to come on that cruise.

"If necessary, you'll have to do the persuading," he said.

He'd read my thoughts again. "Me?" I asked in a voice squeaky with nerves.

"You're the person closest to Bob. You're also the hostess, the person inviting them on this memorial cruise."

"The wake," I said gloomily, sniffing up my runny nose and pulling my woolen ski cap farther over my ears against the icy wind.

"Exactly. They'll call you, of course, wanting to know more. Tell them it'll all be very jolly; say that Bob wanted to make them happy after he'd gone. It was his dying wish and he left you a letter asking you to do this for him. Your one final task."

"Okay." With the toe of my hot pink Moon Boot I kicked moodily at the snow piled by the Hall's iron gates. Stanley, the gardener, was outside the gatehouse where he lived with his wife and three black cats, two of whom hurtled at Rats, spitting and snarling. Tail down, Rats made a run for it back to the Hall while the cats, shouted at by Stanley to behave themselves, settled on a patch of ice and preened their whiskers, having won the day's battle.

"Afternoon, Miss Keane, Mr. Montana." Stanley touched a hand to his deer hunter's cap. "Might be a bit more snow later but I heard the plows will be out our way tonight, so there's a chance you might get out of here, sir."

"Glad to hear it, Mr. Stanley. And no doubt so is Miss Keane."

"I'll keep you posted then, sir," Stanley said as we walked on.

Rats was already waiting by the back door. We went into the boot room and silently stripped off our coats and tugged off our boots. Montana followed me as I walked in my stocking feet, down the corridor past the kitchen and into the front hall. Rats immediately took up his position in front of the fire, and we went into the library that Bob always used as his office. I showed Montana the three big Rolodexes and left him to search for the suspects' addresses.

Telling Montana I'd see him at dinner, I left him to it. Rats lifted his head as I went by but he didn't follow me, and slightly put out, I realized he wanted to stay with Montana.

Back in the safety of my room, I undressed and put on a robe. I rubbed Vaseline into the frost-bitten bits around my red nose then lay on my velvety chaise lounge and covered myself with a soft blanket. Eyes closed, I thought about the events of the last twenty-four hours. My life was suddenly set on a different course, one I had no wish to take. I was afraid, but I could not let Bob Hardwick down.

# 14

## Daisy

When I came downstairs that evening, Montana was gone and Rats was sitting next to the hall table with his nose pointing at an envelope with my name on it. I don't know how the dog knew it was from Montana and whether it said he'd gone out for a while and would soon be back, but personally I was kind of relieved it was a message of good-bye.

"Daisy," he'd written,

*(remember we agreed I could call you that instead of Miss Keane? Just reminding you so you don't think I'm being presumptuous!) I heard the roads are clear and if I hurry I can make it back to London before the next storm. Didn't want to wake you so I'll say good-bye now. I'll keep you posted as events unfold, which I expect will be pretty quickly, plus I'll take care of the invitation with Bob's lawyers and have them get it off right away by messenger.*

*It was good meeting you, Daisy Keane, even though, as Bob said, you can be "exasperating and difficult." Give a guy a break, can't you? I'm only doing my job. Can't we be friends?*

*Meanwhile, better stock up on some cruise wear! I'll be in touch— soon.*

He'd signed it "Harry C. Montana."

I wondered what the *C* stood for. And what did he mean I was "difficult"? Hadn't I rescued him from the storm, given him shelter? What more did the man want?

It was dark out but not yet snowing. I went into the kitchen. Mrs. Wainwright had the night off but there was a plate of leftover roast beef and vegetables keeping warm for me. I emptied the last of yesterday's good Bordeaux into a glass and swallowed a smooth mouthful. I gave Rats his dinner, took my plate, and went and sat at the kitchen table. I sipped my wine, listening to the clock in the shape of the old cartoon character Felix the Cat ticking on the wall. Every room here ticked away the time. It only emphasized the silence and my loneliness.

The warmed-over roast beef was still good. I finished the wine, found another bottle, opened it, filled my glass again and slumped back into my chair. I was desperately lonely. I stared at Montana's note lying on the table.

"Can't we be friends?" he'd written. Did he really want to be my friend, or was it simply until the "case" was solved and he was no longer on Bob's payroll? I remembered his lean, hard face, the well-shaped dark head, the narrow gray eyes and that half smile that made me think uncomfortably he was laughing at me, and despite my better judgment I suddenly wished he was still here, sharing the bottle of wine with me.

"Better stock up on some cruise wear," he'd written, mockingly. I got up and began to pace the kitchen floor, mulling over my strange situation.

Rats levered himself from the sweater in front of the Aga and began to follow me around, hoping for a walk, but it was too cold. Instead I just let him out the back door and waited, shivering, glass in hand, until he'd finished and we both hurried back inside.

I eyed Montana's note again. "I'll be in touch—soon," he'd said. I put it in my pocket, then rinsed off my plate and glass, put them in the dishwasher and wiped off the table. Rats trotted after me as I walked back upstairs, but instead of going to my own room, I turned left at the top of the stairs and headed to the Red Room. I opened the door and peeked inside. If I was expecting to find any trace of Montana, any lingering vitality, any hint of his hard masculine persona still hanging in the air, I was disappointed.

Are you nuts? I asked myself as I hurried down the hallway to my own room. You meet a guy who's definitely going to drive you crazy and you act like you miss him? Forget it, baby, he's being civilized only because it's his job.

I slammed my door behind me just as the phone rang. I pounced on it. "Hello?" I said.

"Just thought you'd like to know I made it back safely."

I sucked in my breath, happy to hear Montana's voice. "I was worried," I admitted softly, realizing I meant it. "The roads are so icy."

"You missing me then?"

"Not a bit." I made my voice crisp as iceberg lettuce. "It's simply a natural concern for my fellow men."

He laughed then, a good, deep sound that made me smile. "Okay, then this fellow man may have some news for you late tomorrow. I'll call back then."

"I'm going back to London," I said, unable to bear the silence at Sneadley any longer. "You have that number?"

"I do. And it'll be my turn to worry about you on the icy roads."

I didn't know what to say to that, so I said nothing.

"I mean it," he said gently.

"Thank you."

"Speak to you tomorrow then."

He rang off, and I sat holding the phone. Suddenly London seemed like a great idea.

I hurried to my closet and picked out a black dress I particularly liked, one suitable for a dinner date, just in case. Then I turned on the TV, flopped onto the chaise lounge, and with Rats on my knee, numbly watched a reality show until I fell asleep. Tomorrow would be another day. And soon those invitations would be arriving at the suspects' doors.

# PART II

# THE SUSPECTS

*The truth is rarely pure,*
*and never simple.*

—OSCAR WILDE,
*THE IMPORTANCE OF BEING EARNEST*

# 15

## Lady Diane Hardwick

Ex-wife, Suspect No. 1

When she was married to Sir Robert, Diane Hardwick lived in a palatial apartment in one of Monte Carlo's best buildings, complete with a white-jacketed houseboy, personal maid, chef, and housekeeper, plus an ever-changing staff of day workers who kept the place polished, dusted and germ-free. Diane had a phobia about germs. Even though every door handle, every faucet and every bathroom was cleaned twice a day she still wore gloves in the house, but because she didn't want people to know of her eccentricity she never wore them when she went out. Instead she surreptitiously dusted things with Handi Wipes before touching them. Except, of course, for the gaming chips at the Casino.

She wouldn't have been permitted to play the tables in gloves anyway, though how they could suspect a woman of her stature of cheating was unthinkable. And of course she did *not* cheat. She simply lost. That's why she was now living alone in a small apartment on the Place Charles-Félix in the old part of Nice, close by the house where Matisse once lived. It was also close to one of Nice's oldest squares, the Cours Saleya, site of the famous outdoor market.

Since Diane did not enjoy food she was not thrilled to be living close to the market and its lavish displays of fruits, vegetables, and flowers. The smells of cooking wafting into her apartment from the booths selling *socca,* the local chickpea pancakes, and the aromas from the many restaurants lining the square made her feel ill. Only the market's magnificent displays of flowers pleased her. No matter how tight money was, and it was *always* tight, Diane filled her four-room second-floor apartment with the scent of tuberoses and lilac, jasmine and freesia, anything to dispel the odors coming in from the streets.

It wasn't a bad apartment. In fact, anyone but Diane would have found it charming. Granted, the ceilings were a little low but the narrow French windows reached all the way to the top and were fronted with small iron balconies, onto which she crammed ferny plants to prevent her neighbors across the way from peeking in. The plants also succeeded in cutting out whatever sunlight might have come into the apartment but Diane liked the subaqueous greenish glow filtering through the ferns. It was rather like living in an aquarium.

One room had been allocated to her clothes, a wall-to-wall, floor-to-ceiling display of couture through the past fifteen years, plus hundreds of pairs of designer shoes and as many handbags. As Sir Robert had scathingly told her, she would never need to go naked in this world. In fact she could still adorn any party and look like a million dollars, though now the eighteen-carat square-cut emerald surrounded by diamonds was a copy of the original Cartier that Bob had given her, as was most of her other jewelry.

A couple of items she'd hung on to, though, by hook or by crook, even when disaster befell her at the tables. These were what she called her everyday jewels, for the good enough reason that she wore them every day. They consisted of a pair of four-carat diamond earrings and the thin rope of diamonds she wore twined around her neck. They were her first real jewels and had been given to her long before Bob Hardwick appeared on her horizon. She was just seventeen when she donated her youth and beauty as well as her virginity to an older man in exchange for a couple of months of luxury at a Caribbean resort. In return he gave her the diamonds and a good time. It was, she thought, a fair exchange.

Her living room—or *salon*, as she called it in the French manner—was hung with a padded silvery scrolled brocade. Unable to bear the dull unevenly plastered walls that reminded her of a peasant hovel, she had hocked a bracelet and bought the expensive fabric. She had personally nailed up some four-by-twos, covered them in batting for padding, then stapled on the fabric. It looked sensational.

When it came down to it Diane could still fend for herself, still put on a show the way she'd had to in the beginning. Diane

was all about making a great impression. With the good Art
Deco furniture salvaged from the sale of her old place in
Monte Carlo, all mirrored surfaces and crystal lamps and white
rugs on dark polished floorboards, the room was really quite
beautiful. As was her bedroom, tiny though it was and almost
filled with a giant bed covered in a white crochet spread, which,
unlikely though it seemed, was made by Diane herself in her
futile idle moments, every stitch hooked with anger.

The anger was directed at Bob Hardwick, the ex-husband
who had left her in this sad state, down on her luck. "What?
Again?" had been his withering comment when she'd descended on him at the Hôtel du Cap, where he'd been week-
ending with a redhead he said worked for him. She'd heard
that one before. Only by then Diane was already divorced and
could do nothing about the other woman, except plead poverty,
which had gotten her exactly nowhere.

She had learned to crochet from her grandmother, though
that was something she would never admit to. She would not
even admit to *having* a grandmother except to claim aristocratic lineage. She never talked about her family or her past, because there was a lot about it she preferred to forget. She only
ever talked about the time when she was the wife of the
megatycoon Hardwick. And of course, still being Lady Hardwick meant she was invited places even though she could no
longer reciprocate those invitations.

She could never invite people back to the poky apartment
on Place Charles-Félix and admit to her reduced lifestyle. She
was aware that people were beginning to comment on this, to

talk about her, speculating on her finances. She didn't like it
and she didn't like Bob Hardwick, but now he was dead and as
his ex—and only—wife she knew she stood to inherit his estate. After all, he had no other "family."

She had been calling Bob's lawyers from the minute she'd
gotten the news of his death, wanting to know when she could
receive an advance on the estate. And she'd shown up for the
funeral, frozen and furious because the Italian mistress was
also there, along with the few stuffed-shirt businessmen who,
after shaking her hand and muttering a few words of condo-
lence, ignored her. As did the "mistress." And also Arnie Levin,
the lawyer, who only when she'd confronted him had told her
the will was to be read at a later date. What had he meant by
that? How long was she supposed to wait anyway? The lawyers
were keeping mum about it, and Diane suspected uneasily
something had gone wrong and by now she was desperate for
money.

It was ten-fifteen in the morning. The windows were open
and she could hear the racket coming from the market. The
smell of cooking drifted in. She was forced to leave the windows open though because the day was already hot and there
was no air-conditioning. Frowning, she squirted her tuberose
scent in the air to mask it.

Still in her lace-trimmed pale blue satin pajamas, she
walked into the kitchen to prepare coffee. She had not changed
a thing in the kitchen; it was the way it had been for decades: a
drab, narrow brown-tiled room with tired gingham curtains
stretched on wires across the cupboards under the sink and

next to the stove. A few plates and cups were stacked on open shelves and a small refrigerator gurgled in one corner. Kitchens were not Diane's domain.

The coffee can was empty. Frustrated, she walked to the living room window, staring out through her leafy plants into the busy street. Children clattered past, yelling at the tops of their voices, dragging their schoolbags behind them. Diane had never wanted children. Didn't understand them. Her own childhood was something she would rather forget and she'd never wanted to be any part of that world again.

Two doors down across the street the ballet school was in progress. The hunched old woman who played the piano was mercilessly grinding out a chunk of Tchaikovsky the composer would surely never have recognized, while little girls in pink tutus flitted across Diane's line of vision, imagining themselves, she supposed, to be great ballerinas on a world-famous stage. Diane was not an optimist. She did not share their vision of themselves.

A large brown dog sauntered down the street. It stopped in the doorway opposite, sniffed, then nonchalantly lifted its leg. Pleased at having left its mark, it trotted on. Diane heaved a bitter sigh. Who would have thought she would ever live in a place where dogs peed in the doorways?

She went to her bedroom and sat at the vanity table with its beautiful Venetian mirror, a gift from Bob. "To reflect your beauty forever," he'd said when he presented it to her at the beginning of their relationship. But what Diane was seeing reflected now was not beauty. It was not that first flush of youth, when she would wake up to face herself and her skin was rosy and perfect and her eyes shone with the luster of the emerald on her finger, and she had a body she knew would never let her down. She could wear anything, strip naked without needing candlelight, do anything, be anyone. Until she discovered gambling, that is.

She glanced wearily at the tiny gold travel clock on the glass vanity. It said 10:30. Damn, she was late.

Hurriedly throwing a raincoat over her satin pajamas, she thrust her feet into a pair of canvas wedge espadrilles, lacing them around her narrow ankles. She pushed back her long red hair, dragged a straw hat low over her brow, and donned a pair of large Jackie O sunglasses. Then she ran down the narrow flight of stairs and out onto the cobbled street. The heavy wooden door slammed behind her as she hurried in the direction of the Cours Saleya and the market.

When she'd made the appointment, the man had said 10:30 prompt. He would not wait and because of what had happened she simply could not afford to be late or the past would catch up with her. Painful as it was going to be to let go, she needed the money.

Diane turned heads with her eccentric appearance but she shrugged off the glances and astonished smiles. She didn't care how she looked. There was nobody there who knew her, nobody who mattered. Her sort of people did not go to markets. Nor did she, except like this morning, when driven equally by a desperate need for hot, strong coffee and by the appointment for which she was now late, she had to go for it.

She did not notice the tail, the nondescript man in T-shirt, shorts and sneakers following her. Her mind was on other things.

She took a seat at a terrace café on the shady side of the square, wiped off the table, ordered an espresso and glanced carefully around. The man she was supposed to meet was not there. Her heart gave a lurch of apprehension. Where was he? She was relying on him. He couldn't do this to her. After all the long months of planning, she couldn't lose now.

A thousand thoughts spun through her head, all of them bad. Nervous, she took off her hat, pushed her sunglasses up into her hair, downed the strong sugary espresso then ordered another. He would come, she was sure of it; he wouldn't let her down now; he wouldn't give away her secret. She shook her head. After all, how could he? He was part of it.

The tail sent by Montana to follow her was sitting a few tables away. He saw her shaking hand, the perpetual nervous swing of her crossed leg, the way her eyes tracked the passersby. He wondered if she was doing drugs.

A few minutes later he saw her rise from her seat, a look, half apprehension, half relief on her face as a man wound his way around the tables to where she was sitting. He was younger than Diane, not good-looking, not bad-looking: an ordinary young man in white shorts, a T-shirt, and dark glasses. He carried a small bag, the kind European men use to hold their essentials: wallet, keys, that sort of thing.

Taking his cell phone from his pocket, the watcher got them in his sights and took a quick series of photographs. The ordinary young man waved away the waiter. Obviously he was here on business, and he meant it to be quick. A few minutes later, the tail saw Diane, her face tight with anger, take the diamonds from her ears and slide them across the table into the young man's waiting hand. The young man looked carefully at them then said something that caused her to exclaim angrily, though she kept her voice too low for the watcher to hear.

The ordinary young man pushed back his chair and stood up. Diane scrambled to her feet too. She put back the sunglasses, hiding her eyes so the watcher could no longer read her expression. The young man said something, then turned and threaded his way back around the tables, into the throng coursing through the marketplace.

He had left his small handbag on the table. The watcher saw Diane pick it up, open it, take out the bundle of money and count it. Her body language expressing defeat, she flung some coins on the saucer for the waiter; then she too hurried away.

The watcher did not follow her. Instead he followed the young man.


There was a sound like a rifle shot as Diane hurried tearfully down Place Charles-Félix. Nerves frayed, she screamed and ducked quickly into a doorway. Peering out, she saw that it was only a motorbike messenger and that he had stopped outside her building and was pressing her bell. She ran the rest of the way.

"Are you looking for Lady Hardwick?" she asked, out of breath from the unaccustomed exercise.

"Is that you, madame?"

She nodded, taking out her key and opening the door to prove that indeed she lived there. "I am Lady Hardwick," she said, just in case there was any doubt left. Besides, she always liked the way it sounded.

"Sign here, please."

She signed his receipt book and he handed over the envelope. From its size and shape and the beautiful calligraphy, Diane guessed it was an invitation. She hurried upstairs, tearing open the envelope as she went and pulling out the engraved white card.

*Miss Daisy Keane requests the pleasure of your company on a Mediterranean cruise to celebrate the life of Sir Robert Hardwick.*

Diane clutched a hand to her throat. A *cruise*? Were they *mad*? Why was Daisy Keane asking *her*?

*It was Sir Robert's last wish that his friends join together, at his expense, on the yacht Blue Boat, sailing from Monte Carlo on the 25th of May, for a five-day cruise, stopping at Saint-Tropez, Sorrento, and Capri, disembarking at Naples on the 30th of May. All expenses will be taken care of by Sir Robert's estate.*

*Upon hearing that you accept, a check for one hundred thousand dollars will be waiting for you onboard.*

*On the last evening, Sir Robert's will is to be read at the Villa Belkiss in Capri.*

The RSVP line gave a phone number and Sir Robert's business address in London.

One hundred thousand dollars. The zeros danced in front of Diane's eyes like balloons at a kid's birthday party. *A hundred thousand dollars!* Oh my God, she thought, I'm saved. And she wanted her earrings back!

She read it again and again. Then she read the last line: "Sir Robert's will is to be read at the Villa Belkiss in Capri." The first smile of the day lit up her lovely face. It had all worked out. She was to inherit after all. *That* was why they had invited her. At last she would get what was coming to her.

Of course, she would go. She was already planning her wardrobe. She picked up the phone and called Daisy Keane.

It was over. And fortunately, who and what she truly was and what she had done, would be her secret forever.

# 16

*Filomena Algardi*

Ex-mistress, Suspect No. 2

It was raining in Venice. The hard, drenching, torrential kind
of rain that, combined with an exceptionally high tide, had already flooded the Piazza San Marco to a depth of over a foot
and was still rising. The domes of the basilica were lost in the
mist, and the famous rival caffès, Florian and Quadri, where
Filomena spent too much money on expensive cups of coffee,
were shuttered, their awnings closed, chairs and tables stacked
inside, the string quartet gone. There were no tourists to delight with sweet music today.

Narrow wooden planks had been placed across the flood as a
temporary walkway. Accustomed to them from birth the Vene-
tians strode confidently across while the inexperienced and
foolhardy tottered then stumbled up to their knees in the oily
water.

Unfortunately for Filomena, she could get to her apartment only over those planks or else via a long, circuitous route involving many back alleys and at least half an hour more in the pouring rain. She chose to walk the planks. High heels were not the ideal footwear for such a journey and she stepped slowly, placing one foot carefully in front of the other, the way high-fashion models did when "pony-walking" the runway. Swathed in a fashionable white trench coat that did little to keep out the rain, she had tucked her expensive Fendi alligator bag inside to protect it and pulled a plastic bag over the blond hair she'd inherited, along with her blue eyes, from her northern Italian mother. The woman Montana had assigned to follow her was not so expert. She slipped off the plank and stood scowling angrily, almost knee-deep in the water as Filomena disappeared in the gloom and the rain.

Filomena made it safely across and into a side street, sloshing through the puddles, giving up any hope of saving her expensive shoes. Her apartment was in an old palazzo fronting onto a wide canal where in weather like this the first floor inevitably flooded, making her second-floor apartment surely the dampest in all Venice. Anyhow, *apartment* was too grand a word for the single large room with a tiny bathroom carved from one corner. She'd taken it only because the address—the Palazzo Breva—was a good one, even though in the heat of summer the place stank of the canals, and when winter came it was freezing. And whatever the season, it was eternally damp. The saving grace was that the old building had a certain elegance and charm and the corner view across the canal of the gold-domed churches and secret leafy patios was magical.

Filomena waded through the narrow alleys until she came
to the street entrance of the Palazzo Breva. A grumbling
woman concierge greeted her sourly as she stepped inside, in-
forming her that she'd mopped up the worst of the floodwater
in the foyer but that the canal side was inundated. Shivering,
Filomena walked up the flight of marble stairs, worn to a
groove in the middle from centuries of use, as was the ornately
carved balustrade. The ceiling frescoes were still lovely, though
dulled by decades of smoke and grime, and a chill emanated
from the paneled walls that had once been a pretty celadon
green but from long neglect were now somewhere between a
sad beige and a dull gray.

Filomena was a woman who loved sunshine; she loved heat
and tropical climates, the beaches of Rio and Saint-Tropez.
With her shiny golden hair, her sexy pout and her lithe body,
she could still adorn any beach with her own particular style.
The trouble was, she was getting older. Filomena was twenty-
eight, and in her kind of world eighteen was the only age to be.
Even twenty-five was considered over the hill. How could it
not be when there was an endless supply of nubile young beau-
ties, eager for the gold and glitter of a life they couldn't afford?
Just the way she had once been.

Opening the door, she stepped into her one-room world.
What a comedown, she thought, hurling her soaking trench
coat, uncaring, onto the floor. She kicked off her ruined stilettos and dragged the dripping plastic bag from her hair. She
looked like an old bag lady. No man in his right mind would
give her even a first look, never mind a second. Her skirt was
wet too. She unzipped it, stepped out of it and left it where it

fell. Her shirt followed. Wrapped in a blanket and still shivering, she walked to the window, staring out at the lashing rain and the angry waves sweeping from the storm-tossed lagoon, sending the overflowing canals into a whirling frenzy.

It was the end of April and the weather should not have been misbehaving like this. For Filomena, May, with its pale sunshine, was the most beautiful month in Venice, though she loved November best, when the alleys and bridges were mysteriously aswirl in a dense woolly fog that rolled quickly through, muffling footsteps and shrouding people in mystery. In Venice in November you could be anonymous and sometimes Filomena preferred that.

She was brought up in the Veneto, the region of hills and vineyards behind Venice, in a small village where her father was the baker. It was far from the social glitter of the city but though poor, Filomena had had a happy enough childhood, attending school in the nearest small town, where she was a good student. Her disgruntled father used to tell her that she had brains but she was just too lazy to use them.

It wasn't just laziness. Filomena had discovered she was beautiful. At the time she believed the two assets, brains and beauty, to be an unbeatable combination. Now she wasn't so sure. After all, look where she'd ended up: alone in a second-rate studio apartment, selling clothes she could no longer afford to buy, waiting to see if everything would work out as she'd hoped and planned, and that with Bob Hardwick, finally dead and buried, he had left her some of his damn millions.

She'd gone to the funeral, of course, wanting to stake her claim over his very grave, make the lawyers and everybody else aware that she was someone who counted. Including his bitchy ex-wife, with her crocodile tears sending black mascara rivulets down her cheeks. Filomena had been careful not to wear eye makeup, and certainly no blusher. She had planned to look pale and interesting and had succeeded in drawing more than a few appreciative glances from the mourners, two of whom pressed their business cards into her hand as they said good-bye, but she knew they would all be married and she wasn't about to go that route again. When she got what was coming to her from Bob—he'd always promised he would take care of her in his will, otherwise she wouldn't have done what she had done— she would be her own woman, able to pick and choose her man from the world's available best. And this time she would stick out for marriage.

So far, though, it hadn't worked out that way. After the funeral, the will had not been read as she'd expected, and there had been no word on when it might be. Now her grandiose plans had disappeared into the rain swirling around Venice.

Staring out the window, she wondered gloomily if her father had been right after all. Perhaps she should have stayed home and become a schoolmistress instead of a tycoon's mistress, taught class instead of teaching older men how to enjoy life. Maybe she should have married the local builder or someone like him, and had a nice warm villa and three sons to look after her in her old age.

There she was, back to age again. She was too old to model, though she'd done some of that when she was in her teens. She was not a natural in front of the camera, nor could she act, though she'd tried that too. And it was too late now to consider becoming a schoolmarm. She shivered, wrapping the blanket closer. The truth was, no man, not even the village builder, had ever asked her to marry him. All Filomena was good for was to be a mistress.

Tears stung her eyes, running over the delicate planes of her cheekbones, down her lovely face until she tasted their salt on her lips. "What happened to me? What did I do wrong?" she asked the bare four walls. "What's to become of me?"

There was a rap at her door. Hastily brushing away the tears, she went to answer it. It was the concierge, old and brown and withered, wrapped in knitted woolen shawls with clumpy granny shoes and wrinkled stockings. Sunk in her misery, Filomena thought one day she would look like that: she'd become a concierge, ignored by everyone, spying on other people, living vicariously.

"A letter for you. Delivered by messenger," the woman said, holding out a large square envelope. "Though how he got through in weather like this I don't know."

Filomena took the envelope, thanked her and shut the door quickly in her face. She could tell the nosy old woman was dying to know what news needed to be delivered so urgently but it was none of her business.

Sinking onto the narrow bed that pretended in the daytime to be a sofa, Filomena studied the envelope. It was fine-quality stationery and looked the right size for an invitation. She ripped it open and took out the engraved card. Her eyes flew wide. It *was* an invitation, though not one she'd ever expected to receive. It came from Bob's personal assistant, bidding her to join them to "celebrate" Bob's life on a Mediterranean cruise. If she accepted, she would receive one hundred thousand dollars. *If she accepted.* Were they *crazy*? Did Daisy Keane seriously think she would *refuse*? Plus, it said Bob's will was to be read on the final night.

Filomena's quick brain sifted through the infinite number of possibilities implied by this invitation. It was obvious to her that all her plotting, all her campaigning had not been in vain after all.

She was smiling for the first time in days as she wrote her RSVP. Of course she accepted, but just to make sure, she also telephoned Miss Daisy Keane at the London number. It was answered on the first ring.

"Hello, Miss Keane?" she said. "Filomena Algardi here." She positively purred into the phone. "About the invitation to poor dear Bob's wake. Yes, of course I'm planning to be there. I wouldn't miss it for the world. See you there, Miss Keane."

Snuggled on her bed in her blanket, Filomena began planning out the rest of her life.

# 17

## Charles Clement

### Ex-friend, Suspect No. 3

Charlie Clement laughed when he read the invitation and immediately tossed it into the wastebasket. He had to hand it to that bastard Bob Hardwick, he'd even come back from the grave to get you. He was a man who always got what he wanted. Still, Charlie was nervous; he was sure there was more to this invitation and its bribe than met the eye.

Sitting behind the dull slab of steel that was his modernist version of a desk, he leaned back in the leather chair, fingers steepled, still smiling, though it was not a smile of pleasure. He was a tall, fleshily handsome man in his early fifties, with long slicked-back dark hair that curled just a little at the nape. His restless dark eyes missed nothing, and his mouth was a thin sensual line. As always, he was impeccably dressed in a dark pin-striped suit with a handmade shirt of the kind he ordered by the dozen from Ascot Chang, monogrammed, of course, on the cuffs. His shoes were made by Lobb, and his large gold watch was a Rolex. He looked like what he was—a smooth operator.

Charlie Clement played the role of upper-class Brit to the hilt. After all, hadn't he been to the best schools and grown up with some of the top names in society? He was certainly not aristocracy, though, or even landed gentry. Charlie's father had made a bundle in paper goods, then lost it all in bad long-shot investments, which had left Charlie, aged eighteen, at a loose end because he'd counted on that cushion of money to provide him with the playboy lifestyle he preferred.

They say everyone gravitates to what they know best and Charlie knew what was best for him. He'd opened up what he advertised as the first "high class" escort service, providing traveling businessmen and tourists with a "companion" for the evening. Because of Charlie's connections it had been a big success from the word go, and High-Class was never short of customers, nor of willing "escorts," both male and female. Despite the rumors, there was never any mention of sex. What Charlie always told people who inquired with a smirk about the nature of his business was that loneliness was "a commodity." Take care of that, he said, and you have a business. Not everyone believed an antidote to loneliness was the truth about what Charlie sold, but he was clever enough to ward off any implications of sexual favors. His girls, he said, were gorgeous; they were well-dressed, good conversationalists, fun companions. They made good money and got to dine at the top restaurants and dance at the best clubs. No more than that was expected of them.

He'd met Bob Hardwick at a dinner party, and spotting

what he thought was a prospective client, he'd talked to him about loneliness. Hardwick had invited him a couple of times to Sneadley Hall and later for the grouse shoot that took place every August. He'd gone, of course, but he'd been forced to leave early after a little misunderstanding. At least Charlie considered it little; in fact, Hardwick had punched him. Then Hardwick had had his escort business closed down and threatened further retribution.

Bob Hardwick was a man with clout in the corridors of power and his threat sat uneasily on Charlie's mind. For months he'd felt like Damocles with the sword hanging over him by a hair, ready to drop any second. He hadn't really felt safe until he'd made sure Bob Hardwick was dead and safely in his grave. Now the man was coming back to haunt him. And this woman, Daisy Keane, had the balls to ask him to celebrate Bob's life on some crazy Mediterranean cruise.

He fished the invitation out of the wastebasket and read it again. *One hundred thousand dollars.* Bob surely knew how to bait the trap, he thought with a thin smile. And "Sir Robert's will is to be read at the Villa Belkiss in Capri." Well now, wasn't that interesting?

He thought for a moment, then still nervous, picked up the phone and dialed the RSVP number. "Charles Clement for Daisy Keane," he said when the operator answered. He was asked to hold; moments later she came on the line.

"Mr. Clement? I assume you're calling in response to my invitation?"

"I am. And I'm asking myself why Bob Hardwick would like my presence at his wake."

She laughed, a pleasant sound, and he remembered that he'd met her, a tall redhead with a sexy mouth and no clothes sense.

She said, "Sir Robert's last wish was to have a group of his friends get together in a sort of celebration. Actually, it's just that he wanted everyone to have a good time at his expense. It's for the last time, you see. And believe me, if Bob could be there with us, he would."

"I believe it," Charlie said, suddenly making up his mind. "I'll be there, Miss Keane."

He put down the phone and glanced at his watch. Time for lunch. It was still cold out and he shrugged into his overcoat and walked down the stairs to street level. London's Soho was its usual crush of too many cars and too many people in too-narrow streets.

He'd noticed the fellow earlier, lounging opposite his office, reading a newspaper. Aware that the man had fallen in behind him as he walked away, Charlie felt little prickles of goose bumps rise on his skin. Was it the police? A plainclothes detective? He shot a quick glance behind him. The man was still there. Charlie quickened his pace. He stopped and lit a cigarette, glancing over his shoulder again. The man had gone. He heaved a sigh of relief. With Bob Hardwick's invitation from the grave where he'd thought he had him safely dead and buried, he'd become nervous. Smiling, he strode on. He didn't notice the new man who fell inconspicuously into line behind him.

Charlie walked fast, pushing his way arrogantly through the crowd until he came to a small club with photos of scantily clad girls outside. The sign over the closed dark blue door said MARILYN'S. The seedy doorman in a pale blue suit with a gold-braided cap unfolded himself hastily from against the wall where he'd been smoking a cigarette and contemplating the racing form, and Clement gave him a sharp lecture, then pushed past him into the club.

They always drew a good crowd at lunchtime. The men came to watch the girls strip, do their pole dances, lap dance if you had the price. Though of course, the real pricey "show" took place elsewhere, in an upmarket mansion in Paris, which was where Charlie was headed next. It was, after all, his favorite place in the world. In his view there was nothing to beat the École de Nuit.

He caught the Paris train out of Waterloo, thanking God for the Chunnel—the tunnel that linked London and Paris via rail. In a couple of hours he'd be there.

And so would Montana's man who was trailing him.

# 18

## Davis Farrell

Ex–business Partner, Suspect No. 4

It was a pleasant day in Queens, New York, but the sun filtering through the cloud cover only emphasized the littered gray streets and shuttered storefronts of the poorer part of town, populated by immigrant families, often illegal and living on the fringes of society. The blackened brick tenements zigzagged with iron fire escapes looked out onto treeless streets that blended into slightly more prosperous areas of fourplexes. Farther out were the small single-family homes that were all the immigrants, most of them Hispanic from Central America, could hope to strive for. That is if they could get jobs that paid enough to live more than hand-to-mouth, because without that elusive green card that pro-claimed them residents of the United States of America, they had no bargaining power in the employment market.

The women worked as domestics in the suburbs or even

Manhattan, bringing back tales of the kind of lifestyle none of them had ever dreamed of, while the men were picked up for employment on street corners where they grouped, waiting to be selected for a day's work moving furniture or hauling equipment or gardening, and any other backbreaking job no one else wanted for under the minimum wage.

They sent their children, of whom there were many, to school using false identities, and when school let out, the older children went to work in the small local stores: the bakery, the butcher, the hardware shop. In fact life wasn't much different from that in the country they'd left, the country they still referred to as "home," even though it was a country to which they never wanted to return. America was the promised land, and they wanted to catch hold of that promise, to make something of themselves. Their only alternative was to lie and cheat and grab at whatever opportunity presented itself: drug dealing, protection rackets, armed robbery, gangs. After all, nobody was perfect and everybody had to survive.

Walking down the treeless avenue, Davis Farrell didn't look much different from any of them. A little more eccentric perhaps: his long dark brown hair straggled across his shoulders, his skin was olive color and his eyes brown. A beard hid the lower half of his face and he wore a gray T-shirt, jeans and worn sneakers. He stopped at a storefront, its windows crisscrossed with metal security gates, as was the door, which he now unlocked.

Stuck on the storefront window was a banner on which was written in Spanish, "Farrelisto. Assurance. Specialista en Immigracion." But Davis was more than just an insurance agent; he helped the immigrants with their visas and their housing.

He was not surprised to find people waiting outside his door. Worry drove people to him, searching for answers to insurmountable problems. Davis Farrell knew these people. He lived where they lived, in the same tenements. He dressed like they did. He spoke Spanish like they did. Here, he felt more Hispanic than in Connecticut, which was where he came from.

He opened his door and ushered his customers in. Telling them to wait, he'd be right with them, he pulled up his window shades, took a seat behind the wooden desk that had seen better days, leaned back in the Windsor chair, the seat of which was polished to a sheen by many years of bottoms, then pushed the button on the answering machine, listening to the distraught rattle of Spanish from his clients while he ripped open his mail.

He glanced up as the doorbell pinged. The door was kept permanently locked. Around here you never knew who might be outside. This time, though, it was a bike messenger. Farrell pressed the button to allow him to come in, signed for the envelope he handed him and made sure the door lock clicked as he left. He turned the envelope over, surprised. A thick white envelope with his name and address in calligraphy. He hadn't seen quality like this in many years. He grinned. Maybe he was being invited to dinner at the White House.

He put it to one side while he dealt with the waiting clients, conversing with them in their own language. One of the men he knew well; he'd helped him get a visa two years ago. Now he'd progressed; he worked steadily, had just bought an old car and needed insurance. Farrell got him a good deal. The second was a youth, no more than seventeen, Farrell guessed. He was illegal, just off the boat, scared as hell and with nowhere to go. Farrell made a couple of calls, then told him to wait, he would personally take him to a house that would give him shelter, and the people there would try to straighten out his situation. It was better than leaving him on the streets, easy prey for drugs and gangs and guns.

The third was a woman desperate to obtain a loan. Farrell knew it was impossible; he couldn't help her, but he took out his money clip and peeled off a couple of twenties; at least she and her kids would eat today. He promised to speak to the immigrants' association and see what they could do for her. It was only one of the many requests he would receive that day, and no day was any different from any other.

Alone but for the silent waiting youth, he picked up the envelope and studied the writing. Puzzled, he slit it open and removed the white card.

He laughed uproariously when he read it. Obviously he'd thought about Bob Hardwick a lot these past years. Hardwick had always been a joker, but this time the joke had been on him.

One day, out of the blue, Hardwick had cut Davis Farrell's life in two. One minute he had been the young hotshot Wall Street guy; the next he was out on the streets, and nobody—not one single person he knew—would employ him. He hated Hardwick for that, hated him with a passion that he'd known would never die—until Bob Hardwick did.

After he'd taken care of the scared young illegal immigrant, Davis locked up his office. He took the subway to midtown

Manhattan, then walked to the parking lot where his BMW waited. He changed his shirt and slipped on a dark well-cut cashmere jacket and a pair of good loafers, changed his shabby bag for a leather case containing a laptop, then walked over to Lexington. In just a few minutes he was in another world; a modern minimalist office, all leather and steel. A well-dressed shiny-haired young woman sat at the reception desk. She smiled in a greeting, saying she hadn't expected him back today.

In his own large office, he took out his laptop and called the receptionist to get him some coffee—hot and strong—from the deli downstairs. He hadn't been able to work like this out in the open again until Bob was dead and unable to talk. But now Davis Farrell was back in biz.

Picking up the phone, he called Daisy Keane in London. Suddenly worried, he figured he'd better accept the invitation and find out what was going on.

# 19

## Daisy

When I'd gotten back to London, a messenger had arrived with a copy of the invitation to the cruise and a note from Montana saying they had already been sent out and I should expect replies very soon. He was on his way to New York and would be in touch later. The note was brisk and businesslike. He said nothing about our night together at Sneadley, only thanked me for taking him in out of the storm.

Restless as a cat, I prowled Bob's huge Park Lane penthouse, stopping to stare out the windows at the gray sky hanging over Hyde Park. The trees were just showing their first early skin of green, like moss on a damp stone, and here and there daffodils poked their way through the stale clumps of gray snow, spring bursting through what was left of last week's blizzard.

While I waited to hear from the suspects and Montana, I filled in my time by going methodically through Bob's papers, putting aside those I considered needed his lawyer's attention.

I'd never had access to Bob's personal safe before, but now I had
the key and I knew it was my job to check what was in there. It
was only a small wall safe, half-hidden behind a rail of jackets
in the closet off his bedroom, and when I opened it I found
there wasn't much in it, just another of those manila envelopes
he always used like a quirky personal filing system.

There was no name written on the envelope, nothing to in-
dicate what might be inside. Not wishing to pry into Bob's personal affairs I hesitated to open it, but then I decided better me
than anyone else. If the contents proved too intimate and definitely not for other eyes, I would destroy them.

Bob had sealed the envelope with strips of Scotch tape. I
peeled them back and removed a packet of letters in old-
fashioned, flimsy airmail envelopes clasped with a rubber band.
All of them were to Señorita Rosalia Alonzo Ybarra at an address near Málaga, Spain. And every one of them was unopened and marked "Return to Sender."

I knew at once these were Bob's love letters to Rosalia begging her to come back to him. And she had not even opened
them. Sadly, I imagined how desperate he must have felt as he
wrote her yet again. The postmarks on the envelopes dated
from forty years ago and spanned a period of three years. Three
years of hoping, waiting.

I put the letters back in the safe and locked it. I wasn't about
to read Bob's outpourings of grief and love. They had been
meant for only Rosalia's eyes.

But at least now I had an address for Montana to follow up
on, though after all these years, who knew if Rosalia would still
be there? I put her out of my mind, cleared out my desk and

packed up the office, then went to tackle my own suite of rooms.

Bob had installed me at the opposite end of the apartment from his own. "For propriety's sake," he'd said with that mischievous grin that lit his big face and sparkled his eyes like a candle on a dark night. "Wouldn't want anybody to get the wrong impression now, would we?"

As I had at Sneadley Hall, I'd made my rooms at the apartment my home, and it wasn't easy preparing to leave, packing the mementos and the gifts.

Rats lumbered slowly around after me as I worked. I could tell he was upset by the changes and I took him for frequent walks in the park, trying to make life feel normal for him. I didn't know yet where I was going, but wherever it was, he was coming with me.

Three days crawled by. I wondered what had happened to Montana, but I didn't call him with the news about Rosalia. After all, there was no way she would be suspected of killing Bob; in fact, she might not even be alive. I couldn't stand waiting for the phone to ring and since I was doomed to go on this cruise, I decided I might as well take his advice and do some shopping, so I walked through Hyde Park to Knightsbridge and Harvey Nichols.

Two hours later I slumped in a chair at the store's upstairs restaurant surrounded by bags containing the kind of clothes I'd never worn before: gauzy things in pretty colors, chiffon dresses, jeweled sandals, soft fringed shawls, and an armload of clanking gold bracelets with huge hoop earrings to match.

I told myself that, of course, I wasn't thinking at all of the way the new me might look to Montana. I just wanted to look good when I came face-to-face with the glamorous Diane and Filomena. Famished, I devoured my lunch and about a gallon of coffee, then took a taxi back to the apartment. Perked by all that caffeine, I took Rats out for another walk in the park. It surely beat sitting around waiting for Montana to call.

# 20

*Daisy*

The shrill of the phone met me as I walked back into the apartment. Somehow I knew it was Montana. My legs turned to jelly at the sound of his voice, but I told myself it was only because I was so relieved finally to hear from him.

"Daisy," he said.

"Montana," I replied and heard him sigh. "I thought you'd forgotten about me," I added.

I knew he had a grin on his face as he said, "Missed me, did you?"

"And what do you expect me to answer to that?"

"*Yes* would be nice."

"Then I'm not nice."

"Of course you are, I knew that the minute I met you. Too nice, I thought, to be involved in murder and mayhem."

"Murder and mayhem?" I was a worried, half-afraid echo, wondering what he was going to tell me now.

"I'm in New York," he said. "I'll be in London tomorrow. Can we meet?"

"Yes, oh yes." I was unable to keep the relief from my voice this time. "And I hope you're going to tell me this is all a joke and I don't need to go on a cruise with you."

His laughter came over the phone. "Then why did you buy all that glamorous cruise wear today?"

Dumbfounded, I said, "You're spying on me."

"Just keeping an eye on you, long distance, you might say. After all, Bob left you in my safekeeping."

I thought about that for second, then, my voice small and grateful, I said "Thank you," though I still didn't believe there was someone out there looking to kill me.

"All part of my job," Montana said briskly. "So, what d'you say we have dinner tomorrow night? I'll pick you up about eight. Okay?"

"Where shall we go?" Why did I say these things? A man asked me out to dinner and all I thought about was where we were going.

"McDonald's," he said. "See you at eight." He was laughing as he hung up.

The phone shrilled again almost immediately. Of course he'd called me back, how could he leave on a note like that? "I'd like a Big Mac with large fries," I said.

A strange voice said, "Really?"

"Oh, oh . . . I'm sorry . . . I was expecting someone else . . ."

"Nothing wrong with a Big Mac," the stranger said. "Am I speaking to Daisy Keane?"

"You are."

"Well, hello there, Daisy. My name is Davis Farrell."

"Oh! Yes. Of course . . ." I was caught off guard, not knowing what to say.

"I want to thank you for your kind invitation. I read Bob's obituary in *The New York Times*. Tragic, absolutely tragic. Bob and I go back a lot of years, you know . . . a lot of water under both our bridges, you might say. Bob was always there with a helping hand when a guy needed it—if he thought it justified, of course. And Lord knows, Miss Keane, his generous offer of a hundred thousand to go on this cruise is not the only reason I'll be going, but it certainly helps. I'm admitting that to you now so you won't think I'm coming under false pretenses."

My heart warmed to Davis Farrell; he was speaking so glowingly of Bob. At least he was coming on the cruise for the right reasons. The money was just a sweetener. "I'll look forward to meeting you then, Mr. Farrell," I said.

"Davis, please. And I'll look forward to meeting you too, Daisy. I may call you that, may I not?"

I could just imagine him, preppy personified: dark blue blazer, khakis, loafers, blue shirt, striped tie, good manners. The perfect gentleman. It made a change, I told myself as I agreed that he might call me Daisy, and that I too was looking forward to meeting him. We said good-bye, or "*hasta la vista*" as he put it.

I sat gazing out of the floor-to-ceiling windows overlooking the traffic zooming down Park Lane and at the park beyond, misty in the gathering dusk, thinking about Bob and the times we'd had here. The parties, the intimate dinners, the discussions over my future—always a matter of concern for Bob.

"Somebody's got to marry you and take you off my hands," he'd grumbled after a particularly stormy fight. I forget the reason for it now, something to do with him not getting to an appointment on time then blaming me, and me telling him he was a lazy bastard and he should bloody well look after himself. "You're becoming too English," he'd complained. "I thought I'd got myself one of those nice compliant women, the kind that'll do anything for a man with money, not a feisty lass who doesn't know how to treat a rich man and expects equal rights or something."

I believe I told him that my rights were more than equal and I could find any number of men to take me off his hands, if I so wanted. Which, of course, I did not, because by then I was independent, and my occasional on-off relationships were more about sex than about love and marriage.

"Sex? Are you sure you know what that is?" Bob had laughed at me, making me even madder. "In the end, it'll be up to me to fix you up with somebody, I suppose," he added, ignoring my angry tears and gazing thoughtfully into midair. "And dammit, I do believe I've got just the man."

I told him I did not want or need any man, I was fine just the way I was, thank you very much. I smiled, remembering his answer.

"Daisy, my love, you're the kind of woman who'll never be complete without a man. Right now, you've got me. After that, what yer gonna do? As usual, I expect I'll have to be the one who looks out for you."

The daily housekeeper had gone and I was alone in the big apartment. It was dark now. Headlights glittered down Park

Lane and the lamp globes gleamed golden amongst the trees in Hyde Park. A sudden, strong breeze rustled through the unlit room, and from his perch on the bench under the window, Rats lifted his head, bright eyes looking hopefully past me.

Heart in my throat, I swung around, staring into the dark room, but of course no one was there. "Just you and me, Rats," I said loudly, hurrying to switch on the lamps. But I glanced nervously around because I wouldn't have put it past Bob to come back, just so he could have the last laugh. But of course, even he couldn't do that.

# 21

## Daisy

With Rats slumped in my lap snoring heavily, my mind drifted to Bordelaise. I'd still not told her about Montana or the cruise. I speed-dialed her number. She answered immediately, though rather sleepily.

"Hi," I said.

"Hi to you," she replied, yawning. "What's up?"

"Did I wake you?"

"No . . . Well, not exactly . . ."

I could just see her, sitting up in bed, pushing back her short blond hair with her fingers and reaching for her glasses. She was blind as a bat, and she always put on the glasses when she was on the phone as though doing so also helped her hear better. "Am I interrupting anything?" I asked, smiling, wondering who the man in her bed was.

"Nothing important," she assured me with a sigh. "I wish it

was," she added mournfully, making me laugh because, despite three marriages, Bordelaise was still "seriously" looking for love.

"So, how's it going?" she asked. I knew she was lighting a cigarette and heard her coughing, holding the phone away from her face hoping I wouldn't hear and tell her off. It was my turn to sigh. I'd told her so often about not smoking, but her impish answer was always "But what on earth do you do *after* if you don't light up?"

"You want to go on a cruise?" I threw it out to her as a surprise.

"Are you kidding me? You have to be sixty-five or older for cruising—that's the rule."

She yawned loudly again but fell silent as I explained what was going on and that it would be a private cruise on a very grand yacht. Then I read Bob's letter to her.

"He must have gone mad," she said bluntly when I'd finished. "What was he thinking of, sending you off on a cruise with these nutcases?"

"Montana will be there to protect me."

"Montana?"

"Harry Montana—he showed up at Bob's funeral. He's the P.I. Bob had looking into all the suspects' backgrounds to see what they were up to, and if any of them might have wanted to kill him."

"He sure didn't look too hard if one of them really killed Bob. Are you sure this Montana is on the up-and-up?"

I suddenly wondered. After all, I didn't know who Montana *really* was, only who he *said* he was. Yet he was on Bob's payroll and working with Bob's lawyer and seemed to know everyone and everything that was going on. "I guess he is," I said, a bit doubtfully. "Anyhow, he certainly looks the part."

"Maybe I'd better come on this cruise after all," she said, sounding worried and coughing some more. "E-mail me the dates and I'll meet you in London. Okay?"

"Okay," I said, relieved. "And Bordelaise . . . thanks."

"For what?" she said, still coughing. "I'm your friend, aren't I?"

# 22

*Montana*

When Montana was in London on business, he ate breakfast at Patisserie Valerie in Soho, where he kept an apartment. It was always the same, a croissant and strong coffee. He ate lunch wherever he happened to be when he felt hungry and had dinner most nights somewhere local, preferably Indian or Chinese. Tonight he decided to take Daisy to the Red Fort on Dean Street.

There were no taxis, and he decided to walk up Piccadilly, cutting through the side streets to Park Lane. He was ten minutes late when he gave his name to the doorman, waiting while the concierge called Daisy on the house phone. Given the go-ahead, the concierge escorted him to the elevator and pushed the call button.

The elevator doors opened directly into the penthouse. Daisy was standing there, arms folded over her chest. She wore a long-sleeved narrow black dress with a deep V neckline that fastened with a row of tiny buttons. The knee-length skirt showed off her slender legs and a string of emerald beads was wrapped around her long neck. The green brought out the color of her eyes and her long dark red hair swung luxuriantly over her shoulders. She looked, Montana thought appreciatively, better than a million bucks. Or even a hundred thousand. Rats sat next to her, his head cocked inquiringly to one side.

"You're late," she said by way of greeting.

"And you are beautiful tonight," he replied, adding that he was sorry.

"Sorry for the compliment? Or for being late?"

"Your choice," he said wearily. After a couple of nights with little or no sleep he was in no mood for verbal battles.

To his surprise, Daisy smiled. "Just testing," she said. "I promised myself I'd go easy on you tonight."

Montana was surprised again to see her blush. There was something endearing about Daisy despite her snippiness. He'd heard the story of her marriage from Bob and understood why she was perpetually on the defensive with men. He couldn't blame her but thought it was about time to put all that behind her and just get on with things.

"Come on in and let me get you a drink," she said in the low sweet voice that pleased him, walking him into the vast living area. Through the wall of windows was a view of the treetops, hazy in the glimpse of a half-moon and with a dazzle of red taillights in the street below.

Four large paintings hung on the wall, though none were by artists Montana knew. Ice tinkled against the glass as Daisy handed him his usual bourbon. "I wanted to ask you about Rosalia," he said.

"The woman who wanted a normal life with a husband who came home nights, and a family," she said. "I think I've found her." She told him about the letters from Spain.

"So why didn't you call me with this information right away?" he asked, irate.

She shrugged. "I didn't think it was that important. Besides, it's prying into Bob's personal life and after all she can hardly be a suspect. She loved him."

"So don't you think Bob would remember her in his will?"

"I suppose he might, but you can't seriously believe Rosalia came back for some sort of revenge. That she *killed* Bob? After all, *she* was the one who left *him*."

"We don't know that for sure. We have only Bob's side of the story. Who knows what really goes down between a man and a woman except the two of them? I don't see a motive for murder, but then I haven't spoken to Rosalia yet. I've no idea what she's like, or what she's capable of."

"But you found Davis Farrell. He called yesterday to accept my invitation. I liked him. He was the only one who talked about Bob."

"Farrell can be charming, especially with women. We found him selling insurance to Hispanic immigrants in Queens."

"Oh."

Daisy seemed so surprised that Montana smiled. "Come on, let's get some dinner."

The dog watched sad-eyed as the elevator doors began to close behind them and Montana promised a walk as soon as they got back.

# 23

---

*Montana*

Montana tucked Daisy's arm in his as they walked to the bottom of misty Park Lane where they got lucky and found a taxi. The wind had blown stands of her hair across her face, and he hooked them gently back with his finger. Her hair felt silken, heavy, as he ran his hand over it. She gave him a nervous sideways glance and they sat in silence until the taxi deposited them at the restaurant. Daisy's hand was cold as he took it to help her out.

"Cold hands, warm heart," she said flippantly, though he could tell she immediately wished she hadn't. "Actually, it's my feet that are always cold," she added, making him laugh as she again looked dismayed.

"What you need is some spicy Indian food to get your blood flowing again. Come on, baby, let's eat."

It had been so long since any man had called Daisy "baby"

that she practically melted. "I want *rogan josh* and *keema naan*," she said hungrily.

"And tandoori chicken and lamb masala . . ."

"All that!" she agreed as they took a corner table.

"Wine?" Montana asked.

"Beer. Kingfisher." She was an expert.

He gave the waiter their order, then reached for her hand again across the table. "Let's not fight," he said quietly.

"Okay," she said, but she looked apprehensive as he lifted her hand to his lips and kissed it.

The hand that had been so cold just minutes ago now surged with the heat of the blood rushing through Daisy's veins. She said, "Do you really think you should be doing that? I mean, kissing my hand?"

"The kiss was by way of apology. And now I want to talk business."

"Of course," she said, disappointed.

"So far we have four acceptances," Montana said briskly. "The ex-wife, the ex-mistress, the ex-friend, and the ex-partner. We're still missing the ex-scientist and the ex-lover."

"All those exes." Daisy picked gloomily at the tandoori chicken. "Why on earth did Bob have to dredge them all up anyway? Why not just leave well enough alone?"

"You know the reason. Whether Bob's suspicions are valid or not is up to us to find out."

The waiter brought the *keema naan*, a flatbread stuffed with spicy ground lamb, and Montana put some on her plate. "I'm off to Munich tomorrow," he said. "I have a lead on Marius

Dopplemann. He puzzles me, though. It seems one day he simply quit his very important job on some top-secret project, packed his bag, and was never heard from again. The FBI claims to know nothing, and so does every other official body I've contacted. I'm drawing a blank, and now I'm wondering what Bob knew that I don't, and why the hell he didn't tell me."

"Bob always loved to play games."

"I need to see those letters he wrote to Rosalia. Why don't I come back with you after dinner and take a look at them?"

Daisy sighed, but said okay. Montana smiled at her. "So? What did you buy for the cruise?"

"Did you really have someone following me?"

"You didn't notice the woman in the store going through the racks next to you? Or the man at the next table in the restaurant? He was right behind you when you arrived home."

Daisy was shocked. "I never knew stuff like this really happened!"

"That's what I'm paid for. Remember, I have to be careful with you, you're Bob's prize possession."

"He never owned me, you know," she said angrily.

Montana wondered if she would ever lose that defensive reflex. "And I doubt anyone ever will," he said softly.

"I asked Bordelaise to come on the cruise."

"Great. It'll be good to have a friend along. And I'll ask some other people Bob knew, plus a couple of my agents to keep watch on everyone. They'll be part of the crew and it's better you don't know who they are because then you'll always be looking."

"Sounds like fun," Daisy said bitterly.

Dinner over, they took a cab back to Park Lane where Daisy handed him the packet containing Rosalia's letters.

"I didn't read them," she said. "It's not right to read other people's love letters."

Montana nodded, then, remembering he'd promised Rats a walk, he took the dog down in the elevator and gave him a brisk trot around the damp park. Back upstairs again, he said good-bye to Daisy.

"I'll call you," he said. And then, again unable to resist her soft, vulnerable mouth, he kissed her lightly.

The last thing he saw as the elevator doors closed was Daisy standing there, a hand pressed to her lips where he'd kissed her. He hoped she wasn't regretting it.

# 24

## Marius Dopplemann

Ex–business Friend, Suspect No. 5

The most charming city in Germany is in the region of Bavaria, not too far from the snow-shrouded Austrian Alps, but today Munich was hidden under a heavy blanket of cloud that drizzled a thin, cold rain in nasty little squalls. No sooner did people put their umbrellas down than up they had to go again, causing men's faces to frown and women's hair to droop as they trudged miserably home through the evening rush. The weather also caused many to stop off at one of the hospitable terraced cafés where, safe from the rain behind plastic screens, they gratefully sipped a good München beer or a glass of wine or schnapps, putting off the moment when they would have to brave the weather again.

One of these men was Marius Dopplemann, aka Marcus Mann. Short, extremely thin, wrapped in an old beige raincoat and with no hat to protect his thinning brown hair, he slipped into the nearest café. Instead of the more convivial terrace area, he headed for the bar inside and took a seat. Immediately his rimless eyeglasses steamed up. He took them off and polished them with a paper napkin. The lenses were very thick and without them you could see his eyes were the ice green of bottle glass and with about as much expression.

Putting the glasses back on his beaky nose, Dopplemann, aka Mann, ran his hands through his wispy wet hair and ordered a glass of red wine. "A Bordeaux," he said in his hesitant, understated way, though in fact he knew exactly what he wanted. The bartender showed him the bottle and Dopplemann read the label carefully, then nodded his approval. It was not by any means a grand wine, just a pleasant red from a good wine-growing region, but it made him feel rich again just to order "a Bordeaux."

He'd learned a lot about wine from Bob Hardwick when he worked in the United States. Ten years had passed since that first meeting. He'd been just a shy young geek, a greenhorn to a life of fast living. But he'd learned fast and learned quickly that he liked it. He liked good wine and interesting food and fast cars and one special woman. He'd not thought about that woman for a long time and did not intend to do so now. Instead he took a folded newspaper clipping from his inner pocket, smoothed it out on the marble counter, and read—one more time—the glowing obituary for Sir Robert Waldo Hardwick.

Sitting back, he took a contemplative sip of the wine, remembering the way things used to be, when he was a young man and was said to be a genius, though all he knew was he was good at what he did. He was a scientist and an engineer and had a mind that knew no boundaries, something that enabled him to solve problem after problem and discover new methods in his research into space travel. "Ask Dopplemann" had become a byword joke in his circle, and a little insignificant man in every other aspect of his life, he'd basked in the sunshine of his peers' approval.

Dopplemann's name was not mentioned in Bob Hardwick's obituary however, though many others in the worlds of business and science and the arts were. In a way he was glad nobody mentioned him anymore. He was a forgotten man, yesterday's news, and that was exactly the way he liked it. He wanted no part of the past and had only a slender hold on the future. The present was what he dealt with, a day-to-day plod through a life that no longer held any promise.

Marcus Mann, formerly Marius Dopplemann and one of the best scientific brains in the world, now taught at a small private school in a suburb of Munich, attempting to drill the basic elements of science into indifferent young minds and facing defeat on a daily basis. It was not what he had envisioned from life, but with a terrible secret in his past, he was grateful for even this level of employment.

He folded the newspaper clipping and put it back in his pocket, sipping his wine and staring contemplatively into the patchy old mirror behind the bar. But it wasn't himself he was seeing reflected there: it was Bob Hardwick. Bob's wide, harsh face with its flinty blue eyes that could practically flay the skin off you when he was angry. As Dopplemann had good reason to know.

Finishing the drink, he paid his bill, counting out the coins scrupulously and adding exactly the right amount for the tip. Poor or not, he would never cheat on things like tips. He came from working-class roots and knew how much a tip meant. Turning up his coat collar, he pushed open the heavy engraved glass doors and stepped out to face the elements yet again.

He walked briskly to the station and was lucky enough to find a train about to leave. He leapt onboard just in time, almost knocking over Montana's agent, who leapt on behind him. They clung perilously for a few moments, then Dopplemann regained his balance, apologized to the stranger, and made his way to a seat where he stared out of the window at the passing scenery, never once looking around him.

Montana's agent took the seat behind, carefully keeping his gaze from meeting Dopplemann's reflected in the window. Instead he scanned the evening paper. When the car reached the end of the line, he followed Dopplemann off. He watched him walk to the bicycle chained to the railings, unlock it, then cycle off in the rain. A second man, who was also unchaining his bike, said he knew where Dopplemann lived, and the agent quickly dialed Montana at his hotel in Munich and gave him the information.

Whatever the weather, Dopplemann always enjoyed his bike ride home, out into the country lanes that led up and around a hillside, past a hamlet consisting of three small houses and a couple of barns, then on another couple of miles to a dead end and the tumbledown single-story building with a sagging tiled roof and a stout wooden door once painted green but now weathered gray from the wind and the rain and snow. One window was boarded up with a slab of fiberboard and the other was just big enough to let in some light. A wobbly chimney tilted east, like a tree in the prevailing wind.

A large dog, a mix of shepherd and Lord knows what else, came bounding toward Dopplemann as he propped his bike against the once-white stucco wall, then ran his hands through his wet hair. He bent to pat the dog, curbing its boisterousness. The dog was the one ray of light in his drab world. They had been together for three years now, and the shepherd guarded the tumbledown cottage as if it was a ducal palace. Not that there was anything to steal but it kept the vagrants away.

The two disappeared inside and soon a trail of smoke sputtered from the chimney and the smell of eggs frying in rancid lard stung the air. Dopplemann, aka Mann, was home.

Montana drove the rented car quickly and efficiently through Munich's clogged traffic until it finally petered out into suburbia and then into still-wild countryside. The road became narrower and the gravel turned to rutted mud. Dopplemann's cottage came into view through the now heavy rain washing over the woods green. Montana thought it looked like an illustration from "Hansel and Gretel"; all it needed was a woodcutter in lederhosen and a hat with a feather in it and he could be in a Grimms fairy tale.

As he parked, the door of the cottage flew open and a large dog ran at him, teeth bared in a growl that showed a healthy pair of fangs. Montana stayed inside the car as Dopplemann followed his dog.

"Who are you?" Dopplemann called when he was near enough.

Montana let the window down an inch or two. "A messenger from Bob Hardwick, Herr Dopplemann."

Dopplemann stopped dead in his tracks. His hissing voice lowered to a growl, like the dog's, he said, "Bob Hardwick is dead."

"This is a message from beyond the grave." Montana watched for a reaction. He did not get one. Dopplemann's face was inscrutable. "I have something for you from Bob. A gift. And an invitation."

Dopplemann hesitated, obviously torn between telling him to get lost and curiosity. Then, bidding Montana to wait, he led the dog back into the cottage and shut it inside.

He walked slowly back, looking like a man heading for the gallows, reluctant and terrified yet unable to run away.

Montana got out of the car to meet him. "Don't worry," he said in German, "it's a gesture of goodwill from Bob. I hope you'll recognize it as such and tell me you accept."

Dopplemann seemed to have gained control of his feelings. He took the envelope, opened it and scanned the invitation. Not a flicker of surprise, concern or fear crossed his face. Montana thought he would make a great poker player.

"Bob Hardwick always recognized a man's weaknesses," Dopplemann finally said. "He knew I would have to accept."

Montana nodded. He didn't know Dopplemann's story yet, but he would find out. "Obviously you'll need some financial help in order to get to Monte Carlo. I'll ask the lawyers to forward you an advance on your hundred thousand dollars, but your travel expenses will be paid."

"Thank you," Dopplemann said quietly. Then turning on his heel he went back into his house and closed the door.

## Montana

Driving back to Munich, Montana wondered what had happened in Dopplemann's past that had left him, one of the great scientific brains, isolated, barely eking out a living. He called his Munich contact and arranged to meet him for dinner at a restaurant that was light-years away with its ample good food and elegance from Dopplemann's eggs fried in stale lard in his dilapidated cottage. Montana would learn more about Dopplemann from the contact. Tomorrow he would take a plane to Málaga on Spain's Costa del Sol. And the final link in the chain of suspects.

# 25

## Rosalia Alonzo Ybarra

Bob's First True Love, Suspect No. 6

Rosalia sat quietly in the noontime silence of her hilltop home. Her eyes were half-closed, but she was aware of the scents of the star jasmine that grew in abundance over the white walls and of the lavender hedge beneath it. She glimpsed a hummingbird hovering over an orange hibiscus flower and saw the fountain spatter as another small bird took a quick cool bath. She saw all these things and smelled them, but she did not hear them because Rosalia was deaf.

It had come upon her suddenly. One month she could hear quite well, the next she heard sounds as though they were coming from a great distance: "Down a long tunnel," she'd told her doctor, mystified, expecting to hear him say it was merely some kind of virus that would disappear in time. But it was not and it had not, and within a year she was completely deaf. She had learned to adjust to her disability, though now she went out less and less. The biggest sadness was that, despite a hearing aid, she was no longer able properly to hear the voices of her family and retained them only in her memory, though she had become an expert lip-reader. And the biggest tragedy of all was not hearing her four-year-old granddaughter, whose voice was pitched too high for her even to catch the sound. But the two had learned early on to communicate and understood each other perfectly.

Still, Rosalia preferred to stay here, where she was safe, and also happy, where everyone understood about her deafness and where she was able to explain it carefully and calmly to the guests at her small pretty hotel, known as La Finca de los Pastores, the Ranch of the Shepherds.

The finca had been in Rosalia's family for generations, a poor place, barely more than a barn where the animals were kept, with a small living space above. In the old days, food was cooked by the shepherds in an iron pot in the big stone fireplace where the abandoned early spring lambs were also kept warm and hand-fed to save them from certain death. Land came with the finca, almond orchards and citrus and chestnut, and way beyond, in the foothills of the mountains, were forests of cork. All this was considered worthless when the family eked out their living hauling baskets of almonds or oranges onto the backs of their donkeys and selling them at the local market.

Those days were long gone, of course, but Rosalia still remembered those weary donkeys and their panniers filled with the fresh green-shelled almonds. She remembered the over-whelming fragrance when the almond trees blossomed, so strong it took your breath away, and the scent of orange blossom too, the kind that when you were young you planned to make a wreath out of and wear in your hair if you were lucky enough to marry in the spring. But even by then the finca had fallen into disrepair; it was no longer habitable and the shepherds were gone. Year by year it grew more dilapidated until finally the roof fell in and the winter rains and wild animals took over.

When she was seventeen, Rosalia had left her village for the coastal city of Málaga where she had apprenticed herself to a chef at the best hotel, and where she'd also met Bob Hardwick and fallen in love. But even true love had not been able to conquer the differences between them, and when Bob had left to seek his fortune elsewhere, she had not gone with him. It was her choice and she knew it was best for her.

She'd met an older man, Juan Delgado, who ran a small café. She married him and had three children but helped out cooking at the café. He had died quite suddenly, leaving her with no money and no home of her own, and she had no choice but to pick up her children and move back to the village she came from, and into the old Finca de los Pastores, which had come down to her through a series of deaths in the family.

In the beginning and with the help of her neighbors, she and her three children rebuilt a small part of it, just a couple of rooms, hauling, carrying, cementing. It was hard, bitter work, but at least they had a roof over their heads. In between times she worked at the village café, earning just enough to feed her small family, grateful for the charitable villagers who passed on their children's outgrown clothing to hers.

As she added a couple more rooms, she began taking in a few passing travelers, cooking for them in the evenings. Over the years she'd become famous for her cuisine, and with her guests' encouragement and much hard work, plus hard-won loans from the bank, she had built up the finca into a perfect Andalusian country house. Her tumbledown inheritance was now a delightful small hotel, patronized by people who enjoyed its elegant simplicity. Like her, they loved the gardens and the forested hills sheltered by towering mountains; they loved the absolute peace and quiet, and they loved the good wines from Rioja and the fine sherry from Jerez, especially the chilled amontillado, and the wonderful food that Rosalia continued to cook. Many returned year after year to be greeted by Rosalia's eldest daughter, Magdalena, who now ran the hotel.

Rosalia lived in her own house, linked to the finca by an arched arcade. A wall surrounded it, leading, as usual in Spain, into a flowery courtyard with a shaded columned patio, where Rosalia now sat, enjoying the peace. Except her mind was not peaceful because at the back of it still was Robert Hardwick. Her Roberto.

She had learned of his death via a newspaper article only a couple of weeks ago, and when she read it, it was as though a part of her life had finished with his. She had always fantasized she might see him again, that one day he would walk back into her life—big and brash, overwhelming her with his male presence, and she would show him her world and he would tell her about his. Rosalia sighed. It would never have worked. Roberto would not have understood her "burying" herself away in the countryside, though he would have admired her business acumen in running such a fine hotel. And she would never have understood his world, flying on his private plane to meetings in New York or Caracas or Sydney.

The heavy wooden gate crashed open, and her granddaughter, Isabella, always known as Bella, skipped through. Bella was wearing a sugar pink, black-spotted flamenco dress. Its stiff ruffled skirts were edged in black silk, and she wore the strapped black flamenco shoes with small heels that real flamenco dancers wore. Her cloud of dark curly hair fizzed around her pretty face and her round brown eyes sparkled.

"*Abuelita*, grandmother," she called. "This is my new dress for the *feria*." She spun on her heels, flouncing out her taffeta skirts. "Do you like it?"

Reading the child's lips, Rosalia hastily mopped her tears with a lace-edged handkerchief that, like all the finca's linens, smelled of their homegrown lavender. "But it's gorgeous, *guapa*, and so are you. You'll be the hit of the *feria*. You'll ride in the finca's cart pulled by two oxen with wreaths of flowers around their horns, and your mother and father will ride alongside you on their brave chestnut horses, shiny from all that brushing. You will help brush them, won't you?"

"Oh, I will, I will, I promise, and I'll polish the silver stirrups and the ornaments for the horses' heads . . ."

Bella was so excited, she flung herself into her grandmother's lap, beaming up at her. Her face changed to a look of concern. "*Abuelita*, are you crying?" she demanded, shocked.

She had never seen her grandmother cry; nobody cried here at the finca except herself when she fell or didn't get her own way, which it had to be said didn't happen too often either. She patted Rosalia's cheek tenderly, her brown eyes glossy with worry.

"It's allright, Bella," Rosalia said, smiling, "they were tears for an old friend who died. I'm crying because I'm sad for him."

"I see," Bella said, though she did not see at all, since death had not entered her life yet. And then she heard her mother calling and with a final kiss for her *abuelita,* she skipped off again, slamming the gate behind her as she always did, making Rosalia laugh. Bella always made her feel good. She wished Roberto could have known her.

# 26

## *Montana*

Montana had traced Rosalia's whereabouts from the old letters. Now he drove the small rented Renault west out of Málaga airport on Spain's sunny Andalusian coast and along the heavily trafficked road linking the tourist towns that were by now so built up they almost merged into one. Torremolinos . . . Fuengirola . . . Marbella . . .

He turned off before he reached Marbella, following a dusty road through sparkling white red-roofed pueblos newly built for foreigners from cold northern countries, who came here seeking the sun and cheap wine and the sweet life. On through ever-smaller villages, the real thing now, with narrow cobbled streets of flat-fronted whitewashed houses with iron-grilled windows and massive wooden front doors leading into the courtyards around which Spanish life revolved.

It was noon and an air of somnolence hung over the village where Montana finally pulled over opposite the local bar. Dogs lazed on doorsteps and men took their ease out of the heat of the sun, drinking cold San Miguel beer and passing the time of day.

The bar was basic, as all the bars in small Spanish villages seem to be. The terrazzo floor was littered with the shells of fava beans and nuts and the squares of paper that served as napkins, and a zinc counter held an array of tapas, the bite-size snacks that are a feature of Spain. Montana ordered a small dish of *boquerones*—tiny white anchovies marinated in oil and vinegar—as well as the pork with red peppers stewed to melting softness and the shrimp *pil pil*—small, garlicky, and spicy. With a hunk of crusty bread to scoop up the juices and a chilled San Miguel, he was perfectly happy.

He stood at the counter with half a dozen other guys, eavesdropping as they speculated about him and his tattoo. They didn't realize he spoke their language, and he didn't enlighten them. It always amused him to hear himself talked about like this. "A mystery man" was what they were saying, eyeing him covertly.

Finishing his beer, he paid his tab then asked in perfect Spanish if they could direct him to the La Finca de los Pastores. It was near the next village, they told him, astonished. Take the left turn past the cemetery, they said, then drive on up the hill, you can't miss it.

Montana drove on a road that wound around the hill where a massive billboard of a bull perched on the hillside advertised Soberano brandy, on past citrus groves and vineyards and woods of chestnut trees with glimpses of vast cork forests beyond. And then there was La Finca de los Pastores, shimmering in the sun atop its own hill.

A thick white wall ran around the property and the ten-foot-tall wooden doors were flanked by a pair of fountains tiled, Andalusian style, in patterns of cobalt blue and yellow, the colors of the sea and the sun.

Montana parked in the shade of a trellised overhang and walked into the courtyard. Flowers scented the air, crickets chirruped and another circular fountain splashed delicately. All was quiet, as if the whole world was taking a siesta. If he were lucky, he thought with a smile, he would find Sleeping Beauty here and wake her with a kiss. But what he found instead was a pretty little girl in a sugar pink flamenco dress, who ran around the corner and bumped into him.

"Oh!" She stared up at him with glossy brown eyes as he held her by the shoulders, steadying her. "Sorry," she added in Spanish. "I'm getting ready for the *feria* and I'm in a hurry. Mamaita wants me to take off the dress, she says it's too early, but I want to go now."

"I'll bet you do, and anyhow you look very pretty," Montana replied gallantly.

"Bella, where are you?" An exasperated voice preceded its owner into the hall; then she too came dashing around the corner. "Oh," she said, stopping short when she saw Montana. "I'm so sorry, I didn't know anyone was here."

"I only just arrived," Montana said. "I was met by your little girl on her way to the *feria*."

The woman laughed as she came forward, hand outstretched. "Wishful thinking," she said. "The *feria* is not until next week, so you could say she's a little early. Hello, I'm Magdalena Ruiz, the manager of the Finca de los Pastores. I'm not sure we were expecting you, Señor . . . ?"

"Harry Montana." He shook her hand. "And no, you weren't expecting me. I dropped in on the off chance you would have a room."

"Then you're lucky. We had a cancellation today and one of our nicest rooms is available."

Magdalena Ruiz told him the story of how the Finca de los Pastores came about as they walked through cool hallways, then out into a leafy garden.

"And Doña Rosalia still lives here?" Montana asked the question casually.

"Indeed she does." Magdalena opened the door of a guest cottage overlooking a cool green pool. "Dinner is served from eight-thirty on," she told him. "The bar is always open. I'm sure you'll find your way around quite easily."

His cottage was dominated by an ebony-colored four-poster draped in white muslin. The floors were the classic polished terra-cotta Spanish tiles scattered with traditional Andalusian rugs. A rustic white-painted desk stood under one window and French doors led onto a wisteria-scented patio.

Smiling, Montana dialed Daisy's London number on his cell phone. She picked it up on the first ring and said hello rather breathlessly.

"Caught you on the run, have I?" he asked, imagining her green eyes flashing as she answered haughtily that of course he had not.

"I'm in Andalusia," he said, "in a beautiful old finca turned into a hotel, and it's so peaceful I think I can hear my own heart beating."

"I didn't think you had one," Daisy said, which made him laugh.

"A cheap shot," he said, "when in fact what I was going to say was it's the perfect place for a honeymoon. You might want to bear that in mind when the time comes."

"Montana," she said severely, "I'm not thinking of marriages and honeymoons, and anyway, I thought Rosalia lived in Málaga."

"She used to. She was married and ran a little café there, doing the cooking herself, even though she had three children."

"She had three children? Oh, Montana, you don't think they might be *Bob's*?"

"We checked. The dates don't match, and besides, all the birth certificates state that their father was her husband, Juan Delgado. When he died, she moved up here into the backlands. She and her children rebuilt this place from scratch, and it's now a very successful small hotel. I haven't tried the food yet, but you can bet dinner is going to be great. Don't you wish you were here with me?" He grinned as he said it; he knew which of her buttons to push.

Daisy ignored him. "So what about Rosalia?"

"I'm hoping I'll get to see her tonight."

"She's going to be so shocked to hear about Bob, and getting the invitation to his . . . you know, his *wake*." She spoke in a horrified whisper. "First love is something you never forget," she added.

"Have you forgotten yours?"

"Of course not," she said, taken by surprise, and then she laughed, remembering. "I was sixteen and he was my prom date. He gave me an orchid for my wrist, and I wore a pale green silk dress that rustled when I walked. He had blond hair and blue eyes and looked like a California surfer adrift on the shores of Lake Michigan, and he was the handsomest guy I'd ever seen. We danced every dance together, then made out in the back of somebody's Buick Monte Carlo. I thought I'd die of happiness with that first kiss."

"And how long did this great love last?"

"About three weeks," she admitted with a sudden giggle. "Anyhow, what about you?"

"I'm not telling," Montana said over her outraged protests. "I'll be back in London in a couple of days," he added. "Will you still be there?" She told him she would and that Bordelaise was flying over to join her.

As they said good-bye, Montana was surprised by how Daisy lingered in his memory. As if to banish her, he went outside and swam fifty laps of the long pale green pool, then took a shower and headed off to explore Doña Rosalia's world.

The bar was a shadowy vaulted room with a curved marble counter. The walls were half-tiled in colorful Andalusian patterns that owed much to their Moroccan heritage and tile-topped tables were set out in another jewel of a courtyard where yet another fountain bubbled. Crickets hummed in the background and small cheeky birds twittered on the backs of the chairs, begging for crumbs.

Montana sat in a high-backed white wicker armchair, sipping a glass of cold, pale amontillado sherry and nibbling on small sweet biscuits, contemplating the darkening blue of the sky. La Finca de los Pastores was the kind of place where you felt at home; it was an ideal world, even if only temporary.

Other guests began to arrive; they smiled and nodded a good evening, and a young man played Rodrigo's haunting Concierto de Aranjuez very softly on the guitar.

A woman entered, tall, erect, stately in that Spanish way, with her shiny black hair pulled into a knot at the nape of her long neck. She wore an ankle-length red skirt, very gypsyish with a white shirt and a heavy necklace of coral beads, and with a fringed red silk shawl thrown over her shoulders.

Montana knew instantly this had to be Rosalia. She looked every inch the aristocratic Spanish lady as she smiled a greeting to her guests.

At her side was a man with a heavy-jowled face, piercing dark eyes, a mustache, and slick dark hair. He wore a shirt that Montana recognized as being custom-made and narrow black pants tucked into Spanish riding boots. He looked like an elegant gypsy.

The two walked over to him. "Señor Montana, I am Doña Rosalia. Welcome to La Finca des los Pastores," she said, giving him a smile of such sweetness he understood why Bob had been so smitten. Rosalia was not a beauty, but she was special; she had her own look, and even though Montana knew she must be around sixty, there were few lines on her face. With her large dark eyes under perfectly arched brows, her arrogant nose, and her tall, rounded body, she resembled the portraits of Spanish grandees in the Prado, and with her slightly old-fashioned look and her gentle demeanor, she made every guest feel she was their friend.

"This is my good friend Hector Gonzalez," Rosalia introduced him. "Hector looks after all my business," she said, then with a wry smile, "He's also my interpreter. You see, I'm deaf." She sighed. "It's odd how the world treats a deaf person. If you're blind, people can understand, but deafness is hidden and people think you're stupid when you don't respond. So, now my Hector takes care of me. I can read lips, but Hector will tell me every word you say, Señor, so best be careful," she added with a laugh as she excused herself to greet more arriving guests.

Before he went in to dinner, Montana wrote Rosalia a note asking if she would see him—alone—afterward. She must not be alarmed, he said, but he had an important message for her. He asked one of the young women servers, crisply smart in a simple pale blue cotton dress, to deliver it personally to her; then he went and ate one of the best meals of his life, alone under the stars at a table for two.

# 27

*Montana*

Rosalia was waiting for him on her patio, sitting in a carved wooden chair. "Welcome, again, Señor Montana," she said.

He stepped closer. "Can you understand me, Señora? Or would you prefer me to write down what I have to say?"

"You speak good Castilian Spanish, I can read your lips perfectly."

"Thank you for agreeing to see me, Señora Ybarra."

"It's Ybarra Delgado," she corrected him, "though somehow I have the feeling you already know that."

Her brown eyes met Montana's and he saw she was nervous. "I'm a messenger from a man you once knew," he said. "A man who loved you dearly. A man who missed you to the end of his days."

"Of course you mean Roberto."

"Sir Robert Hardwick. Yes."

"I read about the accident," she said quietly. "I knew he died."

"I'm sorry."

"This is the second time I've lost Roberto," she said. "It doesn't get any easier, which just goes to prove the old saying 'Time heals all things' is quite wrong."

"Bob was a remarkable man."

"You knew him well?"

"For more than ten years. I admired him, and I respected his honesty."

"He was a Yorkshireman; he was always true to his roots and to his code of honor." She looked steadily at Montana. "We were very much in love, all those years ago. You never lose that feeling for a man, not even when you're an older woman like me. But there was no way we could stay together. Roberto had this terrible ambition, and I was a simple girl from an Andalusian hill village. All I wanted was what every other girl I knew wanted. A husband who loved her, children of her own . . . to be 'a family.'" Rosalia sighed. "It became obvious it would never work."

"This may sound strange," Montana said, "but I come bearing an invitation from Robert." He handed her the envelope. "He hoped you would join a cruise on a private yacht. It's to celebrate Robert's life, and he asked only people whose lives he had touched. You were the most important name on that short list."

She looked bewildered. "On a yacht? To celebrate Roberto's life?"

"He left a letter saying he wished he could be there, but he wanted everyone to have a good time and to remember him."

She shook her head, sighing. "I don't know. I really don't know if I can . . ."

"He wanted you to be there for the reading of his will at his villa in Capri," Montana added. "He will make you a gift of one hundred thousand dollars if you will take the cruise—to remember him."

She got to her feet, and he could see she was disturbed. "I must think about it," she said. "It's late . . ." She held out her hand and Montana bent respectfully over it.

"Thank you for listening to me, Señora," he said. She smiled as she turned away. "It was Roberto I was listening to," she said as she walked back into her house.

# 28

*Daisy*

Bordelaise was supposed to have arrived yesterday. I'd sent a car to the airport to meet her, only to be told by the driver she was not on the flight. And not a word from her since. I paced the apartment, wondering where she'd gotten to. The house phone rang, and I grabbed it, angry as a hornet.

"You could at least have called!" I yelled.

"You missed me that much?" Montana said. Sighing, I apologized. He said he was downstairs and I told him to come on up.

"Sorry," I said again as he stepped from the elevator. "I thought it was Bordelaise. She was supposed to be on yesterday's Continental flight, but she's gone missing somewhere between Chicago and London. And she doesn't answer any of her phones."

"Has she ever done this before?"

I said she had. "She's a creature of impulse, a spur-of-the-moment gal. If anything more exciting comes along, she'll take it. Regardless."

"Want me to do anything about it?"

"She'll show up," I said, hoping I was right.

We sat side by side on the white sofa in front of the tall windows overlooking the gray park. It was late afternoon, and I asked Montana if he would like tea, coffee, a drink. He shook his head and said he wanted to get down to business.

"I met Dopplemann," he said, and my eyes opened wide in surprise.

"Oh, you really *are* good," I said. "You found him after all."

I listened while he filled me in on their meeting.

"But why did he run away?"

"That's what I need to find out. I have a meeting in Washington tomorrow with a man who claims to have known him well."

"An old friend?"

"I doubt it. Dopplemann's a very inward person; it would be hard to be 'friends' with him."

"And what about Rosalia and the Andalusian honeymoon hotel?"

"You could do worse than spend a honeymoon there."

"I could do nothing worse than be condemned to go on another honeymoon. My first one was hell—ten days in Hawaii with half of L.A. and their noisy offspring and my new husband on the cell phone all the time, calling God knows who— probably some other twenty-year-old blonde he wished he was with. *And* I got food poisoning from bad shrimp and spent two of those days in bed—alone—while he went out fishing with the guys. At least that's what he told me. Now I wonder."

"You can't hang on to the bad memories for the rest of your life. Get past it."

"Trouble is, I still don't know what I did wrong."

"You did nothing *wrong* except marry a bad guy."

I looked Montana in the eyes. "Seriously, though," I said, "do you believe I did nothing to cause a husband to walk out on me?"

"I'd guess he was just a walking-out kind of guy. I'm willing to bet he's already walked out on the twenty-year-old he left you for and is on to the next, or maybe even the one after that."

"He's a jerk," I said.

He agreed; then to my surprise, he took my hand in both of his and brushed his lips across it. Heat swept up my arm. I told myself it was only a little kiss on the hand and that of course it meant nothing, that there was nothing between us but a failed marriage and a lonely childhood. "We're both walking wounded," I said in a voice that trembled as he let go of my hand.

"Then let's make a deal. I promise to protect you from the bad guys of the world, and you promise to keep me company so I won't feel lonely."

"It's a deal." We stared solemnly at each other for a long moment, then he took my chin in his hand, tilted my face up to his, and this time he gave me a proper, though gentle, kiss. I had an urge to clasp him to me, to give him the other, harder kind of kiss, but I pulled myself together and, eyes lowered, cheeks pink, moved away.

Montana was all business again. "So now we've located all the suspects on Bob's list, plus we have motives for each of them. I've also invited the red herrings; a guy Bob knew by the name of Brandon van Zelder, in his forties, good-looking, knows everybody who counts, good backgammon player, and women love him. He's bringing along a young woman singer. I know her well. I thought she'd create a good diversion, entertain us when things got a little sticky. Then there's Reg Blunt."

"*Reg?* From the Ram's Head?"

"Bob wanted to invite him. He said he was a true friend, and believe me, Bob didn't have many. He also wanted to invite Ginny Bunn. So, that's our little cruise group," he said.

Before I could comment, the house phone rang. It was Bordelaise, and she was downstairs.

She breezed in wearing skintight jeans, stiletto boots, and a Chanel tweed jacket, smelling delightfully of Arpège, the scent she'd used since we were both in our teens.

"Sweetie," she yelled, dumping her Chanel tote and skidding across the parquet, flinging her arms around me in a giant hug that almost sent me sprawling. "I missed you," she added, holding me at arm's length and peering worriedly at me from under her thick blond fringe.

"I'm okay," I said, not sounding too confident about it. "Where were you?"

She gave me a familiar grin that lit up her elfin face. "I made a small detour to Paris, darling, somebody I met in the departure lounge at O'Hare. He was young and hot and"—she shrugged—"well, you know, I've never been one to resist temptation."

I sighed. "Bordelaise, this is Harry Montana. I told you about him."

She took in his lean, cool length. Out of the side of her mouth she whispered, "Yours or mine, sweetie, just let me know," then she sauntered up to Montana, who was standing by the window looking very Darth Vader in his black, kind of sinister in a way that was catnip to a woman like Bordelaise.

"Harry," she said, offering him her hand and a challenging smile.

He grasped her hand and gave her a little bow. "I've heard all about you from Daisy."

She threw me a look over her shoulder. "I do hope not *all*."

"I told him you're coming on the cruise with us."

Bordelaise widened her eyes as she smiled up at him. "I always wanted to go cruising."

"Then I'm sure you'll enjoy the *Blue Boat*." Montana looked across at me. "You two have a lot to catch up on. Nice meeting you, Bordelaise."

"Likewise," she said, watching his narrow butt appreciatively as he walked away. "See you onboard, Harry," she called, grinning that wicked little grin.

"Well." She beamed as the door closed behind him. "You kept him a nice little secret, girlfriend, didn't you? Anything going on between the two of you, might I ask?"

"Not a thing," I said firmly. "And I'm sure he's never even thought about it. He's not interested, nor am I."

"Then you certainly *have* lost your touch, sweetie. We'll have to see what we can do about getting it back again."

"We'll catch up on everything," I said, showing her to my room, which course we would share, the way we always had. "And I want to hear all about the Paris interlude." Still remembering her with Montana, I found myself having to push back a niggling feeling of something that just might have been the green-eyed monster.

# 29

## *Daisy*

Time passed quickly with Bordelaise to keep me company. In the few days before leaving for the cruise, we shopped, we lunched, we got our hair and our nails done. We behaved like a couple of real girly girls, and we enjoyed it. We took Rats on long treks on Hampstead Heath in the rain and the wind; then, teeth chattering, we finished up in the pub for a restorative drink and a bag of salt and vinegar crisps. We lunched at Le Gavroche in memory of Bob, and dined at the Bombay Brasserie, where I introduced her to good Indian cooking. We flipped pancakes for breakfast and doused them in Mrs. Wainwright's homemade strawberry jam with dollops of heavy cream, washed down with gallons of hot coffee. The night before we were to leave for the cruise, we ended up side by side in the twin beds in my room, she in unexpectedly childish flowered flannel pj's with Victoria's Secret written in sparkles across her bosom, and I in my virginal white granny nightie with bed socks for my perpetually cold feet. Our bags were packed and ready, out in the hall. We were flying to Nice the next morning, prior to boarding the *Blue Boat* in Monte Carlo.

"So, what's really with you and Montana then?" Bordelaise cradled a cup of hot cocoa in both coral-nailed hands, blowing on it to cool it. She peered at me over the tops of her glasses. "You two interested in each other or what?"

"I don't know." I shrugged away the question she'd been asking more obliquely for the past few days, rubbing in hand cream and inspecting my own French-manicured nails, so prettily tipped with white. "He's different," I admitted. "He's a bit wounded, like I am, only his was a bad childhood."

"So what does the mysterious Chinese tattoo mean, anyway?"

"I never asked."

Bordelaise rolled her eyes. "Lord, I'd have asked on the first date."

"We've never had a date. It's always been business."

She gave me a long tell-me-another-one look. "You mean to say all you talked about was Bob and the suspects and the cruise and if the butler really did it?"

"Pretty much."

"Well then, sweetie, you really have lost your touch. Where's the woman I used to know? The one who knew what she wanted from life, and *who* she wanted and went out and got him, even if he did dump you later." Frowning, she slurped a mouthful of cocoa impatiently. "Montana's sexy as hell, Daisy. And he's available. And I'll bet my boots he's interested."

"I thought you two were interested," I said, avoiding her eyes.

"Hah! And exactly how long have you known me, Daisy Keane? Thirty years? More? Don't you know by now I never go after my friends' men? And I never date anybody else's husband. Not that yours didn't try," she added, taking another gulp of the cocoa.

I gaped at her. "He *didn't*!"

"Of course he did, the creep. And he got a mouthful of the truth about himself from me that he'll never forget." She eyed me in a conciliatory fashion. "I didn't tell you before because I didn't want to hurt you, but if you're still carrying a torch for him I figured it was time you knew the truth."

I slithered under the duvet, eyes shut. "How could he?" I moaned.

"Because that's the way he is. But not every man is like him, you know. For God's sake, get over him, give yourself a chance, why don't you?"

"Okay. So Montana kissed me," I admitted.

Bordelaise was alert in a second, sitting up straight, gazing interestedly at me. "And?"

"It was nice."

She threw back her head and groaned. "You're impossible. How many times has he kissed you?"

I thought about it. "Well, if you count hands and cheeks as well as lips, I think about four or five."

"Hmmm, that's *definite* interest. So, where do you plan to take it from here?"

"I'm attracted to him," I admitted. "He's exciting . . ."

"And *hooray* for that. What a relief, you're a woman after all."

"But I haven't anything planned, if that's what you mean."

"And has he?"

"Of course not." Any thoughts in that direction were pure fantasy. "He's like you. He tells me I have to get over it, move on. He said he'll protect me from the bad guys of the world if I will keep him company and stop him feeling lonely, though I have the feeling he hasn't minded being lonely until now," I added thoughtfully.

"Well, there you go then." Bordelaise raked her fingers triumphantly through her shaggy hair. "He's interested all right. You'll see on the cruise: moonlight on the water, champagne, soft Mediterranean nights . . ."

I could almost see her plotting. Still, her scenario sounded pretty romantic, even to me.

"Maybe," I said, cautious as ever, making her groan again and sending Rats, who was sprawling on my bed, running anxiously to make sure she was okay.

She sleeked back his ears and peered through her glasses into his soulful brown eyes. "My, you are a good dog, aren't you?"

But Rats had turned away. He was staring hard at the door. It was half-closed; nevertheless, I felt that sudden cool breeze blow over me.

"Did you feel that?" I asked.

"Feel what?"

"That sort of breeze that just blew through the room."

Bordelaise shrugged. "I didn't feel anything."

"I don't know what it is," I said, "but it's been happening quite a lot lately. It's like a wind blowing around me, but the doors and windows are always closed. I thought it might be Bob—you know, sort of coming back to check on me and Rats . . ."

Bordelaise's eyes popped. "You're *crazy*." She stared nervously at the door and the empty hallway outside. Don't tell me you believe in *ghosts*?"

"Maybe," I said, because I was beginning to think that, after all, maybe I did.

But Bordelaise made me get up and check the apartment, then lock the bedroom door before we went to sleep. I knew it was all right though, because Rats was back on my bed and already sleeping. He would never do that if Bob was around. Still, it was a long time before we fell asleep that night.

# PART III

---

# DAY ONE.
# ARRIVAL AT THE
# *BLUE BOAT.*

---

## The Suspects

*Many a woman has a past,
but I am told that she has at least a dozen,
and that they all fit.*

—OSCAR WILDE,
*LADY WINDERMERE'S FAN*

# 30

*Daisy*

At three hundred feet long with a forty-five-foot beam, *Blue Boat* was one of the larger yachts afloat. Built in the Bremen shipyards of the great German yacht builder Lürssen, she could correctly be described as a megayacht. Technically, with her sleek steel hull and two powerful KHD-MWM diesel engines, she could reach a speed of twenty knots, with a range of six thousand nautical miles. She could easily cross the Atlantic but was most often based in Mediterranean waters, where her owner, an American woman friend of Bob's, an oil heiress, liked to spend her summers.

Towering five decks high, with wide side decks and with a thirty-foot cigarette boat invisibly tucked in the tank deck to port and a pair of vintage wooden Chris-Craft tenders tucked starboard, there was nothing to spoil the yacht's beautiful lines, not even the eight-seat silver-blue helicopter perched on top.

A swimming platform aft could be lowered hydraulically,

and the yacht's "toys"—Jet Skis, water skis, scuba tanks, and snorkel gear—were stowed there.

Above the lowest deck—the tank deck—were accommodations for the thirty-six crew members, with their own dining room and lounge. On the deck above were the guest accommodations, with four lavish suites and nine staterooms. Above that was the main deck, with its soaring central atrium, inlaid marble floors, soft ivory couches, and ebony tables banked with flowers, and a glass elevator and a crystal staircase behind. There were comfortable lounges, a library, a media room/theater, and a spacious dining room. A hair salon and a small gym and spa were cantilevered over the top deck.

The large afterdeck was equipped for sunbathing, with big square padded lounges, a plunge pool, and a long oval table that could seat twenty for dining under the stars. The foredeck had informal seating and a bar, and shady areas for just sitting and talking or reading.

On the very top, behind the bridge, which of course was equipped with the very latest technology, was a glass-enclosed piano bar, which slowly revolved to take in the view.

The palatial bedroom of the owners' suite had wide-window views and a fireplace for those chilly, or perhaps just romantic, nights. The adjoining sitting room was paneled in dark walnut to match the overhead beams set in an ivory ceiling, with creamy carpeting and rich fabrics.

The yacht itself was not painted your usual naval cobalt blue. Her color had been personally chosen by the owner—a woman in love with the Mediterranean—and was the palest aquamarine, the exact shade of the shallow sea where it curved inshore, just before the tiny waves hit the sand. This color scheme was carried throughout the ship: pale aquas, a tawny sand color, ivory, and taupe. On deck the soft furnishings and awnings were blue, and even the towels were that same pale aqua, embroidered with seashells in sand color.

No detail had been forgotten, either in the construction of the yacht, the cost of which was rumored to be close to a hundred million dollars, or in the interior design, by one of the world's best in the yacht trade. And needless to say, *Blue Boat* was the apple of not only her owner's eye but also her captain's.

Captain Jurgen Anders was Norwegian and had lived near or on the water all his life. He'd attended Naval Academy and served his apprenticeship first in the Navy, then on cruise liners. He was proud to be the master of one of the best and most beautiful yachts afloat, proud to work for a woman whom he admired and who treated him as a friend, and he was proud to show off his ship to those who were privileged to charter it, at what was said to be almost half a million dollars for a single week. But of course, if you had to ask the price, you couldn't afford it.

Today, he had personally inspected the yacht to make sure everything was shipshape, and now he marshaled his officers and crew on deck to await the arrival of the guests.

The sun blazed down on Monte Carlo, and the air smelled of mimosa and jet fuel. A sleek mahogany-and-steel vintage Chris-Craft was waiting to take us to the ship, manned by pair of good-looking young officers who saluted us, then helped us onboard.

Our luggage was loaded onto another tender, and we set off at a fast clip across the harbor to where *Blue Boat* lay at anchor.

The captain and his officers and crew were lined up to greet us. "Royalty must feel like this every day," I whispered to Bordelaise.

Captain Anders was blond and good-looking and I noticed Bordelaise's appreciative glances at him as he showed us the heart of his ship, the bridge, gleaming with screens and instruments and radar and all things nautical, about which I knew nothing.

We met the master chef and saw his immaculate steel kitchen and the wine cellar with every major château represented, as well as my favorite simple rosé from Saint-Tropez. The chef told us he shopped the local markets at every port of call for the freshest and the best, and the local fishermen knew to call him about the latest catch.

We were shown to the flower-filled owners' suite; the spacious sitting room had windows all around, and the bedroom had walk-in closets and his and hers bathrooms. I noticed a Picasso nude on one wall and a Matisse on another, but when I was told this suite was for me, I said I thought Bob would have liked Rosalia to have it.

We took the glass elevator down to the other guests' accommodations, and I was given a forward suite, smaller but equally lovely, with a large window that looked onto the deck. It was filled with roses and Casablanca lilies, and this time there was a Klimt on the wall, of a tall woman in what looked like a patchwork dress made up of scraps of lace and silks and velvet.

Bordelaise was given a stateroom farther down the hall, smaller but perfect. The furniture was built in around the walls in pale woods, and there were no angles and corners, everything curved.

I left her to unpack with the help of a pretty Scandinavian stewardess called Camille, combed my hair, put on lipstick and straightened my rather creased yellow linen dress. Then I took the glass elevator up to the main deck to find Montana and greet my guests.

There he was, cool in black pants and a white linen shirt open at the neck, sleeves rolled to below the elbow showing the mysterious tattoo, slightly sinister with his hawklike face and cropped hairdo. I realized anew how much I fancied him.

Smoothing my creased yellow linen, I wished I'd changed into something fresher, but it was too late now, he'd spotted me in the glass elevator.

"Like an angel from above," he said mockingly. But then he took my face in both his hands and planted a firm kiss on my lips.

"Good to see you," he said. "I don't know why, but I missed you."

"Are you always going to mix a compliment with a put-down?"

"Not always." He grinned. "Anyhow, you look pretty good for a detective."

"Hah, Daisy Keane, Girl Detective. That'll be the day."

"Trust me, sweetheart, that day has arrived. Or it will with the arrival of our first guest."

We didn't have to wait long, and the first was Lady Diane Hardwick.

# 31

## Diane

Diane stood on the dock, eagle-eyed, watching the porters manhandling her Vuitton luggage, groaning as they dropped the heaviest piece. She proceeded to tell them exactly what she thought of them and their clumsiness, in the same colloquial working-class French they spoke.

She stared approvingly at *Blue Boat* as the tender swept her toward her destiny. It was a pity this was going to be Bob's wake and she was going to have to put up with the Keane woman, who anyway she suspected of being her husband's mistress, and with whom she therefore did not intend to spend any more time than absolutely necessary for appearances' sake. She wondered who her fellow passengers were. If they were friends of Bob's then they were sure to be rich and that suited her just fine.

She'd dressed carefully for departure, correct in a white linen suit with a straw hat, wedge rope-soled espadrilles, and an expensive Bottega Veneta tote, and when she stepped from the tender onto the yacht, the smiling captain greeted her like royalty. He escorted her himself to the atrium where he said Miss Keane was waiting. Captain Anders was rather handsome and she gave him her most charming smile. Satisfied, she felt she was back where she belonged.

## *Daisy*

The beautiful atrium was filled with light; it smelled of the lilies bunched in vases around the room, and I was standing in the middle of it when Diane entered. I knew she recognized me from that humiliating evening at the Hôtel du Cap when she'd bearded the lion—namely, Bob—in his den and demanded he give her more money, and now she tried to put me at a disadvantage by speaking in French. "Miss Keane, *comment ça va?*"

"*Bien, merci, et vous,* Lady Hardwick?" I said. "Welcome aboard *Blue Boat,* and thank you so much for agreeing to come on this little cruise. I know how pleased Bob would have been."

Still in French, Diane said, "Bob was a very difficult man to please."

"Allow me to introduce Harry Montana," I said. "He was Bob's friend too, and he'll be sharing my duties as host of this cruise."

Montana bent gallantly over Diane's hand. "Champagne, Lady Hardwick?" he asked, beckoning the steward over.

There was a sudden flurry of activity behind them, then a loud female voice exclaimed in Italian, "*Dio mio,* this is gorgeous. Did Bob Hardwick buy this boat all for himself?"

Diane swung round and came face-to-face with Filomena Algardi.

"*You!*" she spat accusingly.

"*You!*" Filomena spat back.

Both whirled on me. "What's *she* doing here?" they demanded in shrill unison.

"This is Bob's cruise and he invited both of you," I said quickly, but Diane's face was red with anger.

"How dare he? How *dare* my husband invite his mistress to celebrate his life. How *dare* he?"

"Lady Hardwick," I said quietly, "this was Bob's last wish. You have to respect that. Or not take the cruise."

I had played my trump card and Diane knew it. A check for one hundred thousand dollars awaited her and she wasn't getting off the ship without it, nor was she leaving until the will was read and she was declared the winner.

Ignoring Filomena, she beckoned a steward. "Show me to my suite, young man," she said haughtily as she stalked away.

"Dinner will be at eight-thirty, Lady Hardwick," Montana called after her.

She turned to look at him. "Of course," she said, sighing because she knew she had no choice.

Filomena was wearing a Pucci silk jersey shift that slid over her lithe body like a second skin. Its turquoises and blues brought out the blue of her eyes and set off her golden coloring perfectly. Her blond hair was pulled back in a rough knot and skewered with amber pins and her gold thong sandals were embellished with turquoise stones. She carried a dark orange soft leather tote, "borrowed" from the boutique where she worked.

"I didn't know poor old Lady Hardwick was invited," she said sulkily, inspecting me from head to toe. I could tell she knew to the euro how much my yellow linen dress had cost and she was not impressed.

"Bob invited quite a few of his old friends," I said. "Including Harry Montana, who'll be helping me host this cruise."

Filomena shifted her attention to Montana. Her smile was pearly with pointed little eyeteeth, like a beautiful cat. "Well of course, any friend of Bob's is a friend of mine," she purred as he took her hand. "Did I hear you say we would be having dinner together, Harry?"

"At eight-thirty, Signorina. I'll look forward to it."

Filomena leaned closer and said something in a breathy whisper I knew I was not meant to catch.

"Maybe then, Harry, you can tell me why Bob invited so many other 'friends,'" she was saying. "He couldn't have been thinking of leaving them *all* something in his will, could he?" She gave a little shrug and added, "Maybe I can understand about Diane; after all, she was once his wife. And of course I'm almost in that same category. You know that Bob and I really loved each other, we were together for so many years, far longer than with Diane. If only circumstances hadn't forced us apart we would have been together to this day. If he were alive, that is," she added, crossing herself.

Montana was saved from replying by the arrival of Reg

Blunt, who strode into the atrium aiming for me like a heat-seeking missile, arms outstretched to embrace me. His dark blue blazer bore the crest of the Sneadley Cricket Club, his gray flannels were well-pressed and his square face was wreathed in smiles.

"Daisy lass, there you are!"

Hard on his heels came Ginny Bunn, yellow hair upswept under a jaunty yachting cap. In white stretch capris, mules, and a navy-and-white-striped T-shirt, she beamed like a ray of sunshine.

"Can you believe this boat?" Ginny marveled, taking her turn after Reg to engulf me in a giant hug. "It's just gorgeous, I can't believe I'm really here." She stopped to check out Filomena, then grabbed her hand and pumped it enthusiastically. "It's Filomena, isn't it?" she said. "Remember me? I'm Ginny, the barmaid from the Ram's Head in Sneadley. You came in a few times with Bob."

Filomena give her a cautious smile, obviously wondering why Ginny was on the cruise, probably wondering if she'd also been Bob's mistress, and probably also wondering the same about me.

Reg was telling me how glad he was to see me. "The chauffeur brought old Rags back to Sneadley Hall all right," he said. "The poor little bugger didn't know which end was up, he was so confused, he's missing you and Bob that bad. Not to worry, though, he'll get over it. Mrs. W brings him down to the pub for his usual banger, and we told him you'd soon be back for him."

He shook Montana's hand, slapping him heartily on the shoulder. "Good to see you too, Mr. Montana. I was hoping we might get you back up to Sneadley, recruit you for our cricket team. I'll bet you'll make a good batsman."

"It's Harry, and the only batting I've done is in baseball."

"Not much different, lad. Come back up why don't yer and give it a try."

Reg turned, still beaming, to Filomena. "Miss Filomena, how are yer? I remember Bob bringing you into my pub."

Filomena looked past him. "Do you?" she said distantly, obviously wondering how many more strange "friends" Bob had invited, and exactly what they meant to him.

"Champagne, Ginny?" Montana snagged a glass and handed it to her. Ginny's eyes sparkled like the fizz of the champagne as she looked up at him with a flirty little smile. "Mmm, this is good. Tell me, is it going to be like this all the time?"

"As much champagne as you like," Montana promised. "Bob wanted to be sure his friends had a good time."

Ginny heaved a sigh. "I'm only sorry the poor old bastard can't be here to enjoy it with us," she said. Then, "Oops, of course I didn't mean it like that—*poor old bastard!* It's just a term of endearment, if you know what I mean."

Montana laughed and passed her and Reg over to the steward who would show them their staterooms.

Just then Charlie Clement strode in, looking every inch the successful businessman on holiday in a white shirt and beige silk pants, sockless in soft suede loafers and carrying a blazer.

"Too damn hot out there," he grumbled by way of greeting. "*And* they kept me waiting. It's not good enough, simply not good enough."

"Welcome aboard *Blue Boat*, Mr. Clement." I was unable to keep the note of sarcasm out of my voice. "I'm sure Bob would have been glad to see you here in the company of his friends, heat or no heat."

"Exactly how many of Bob's *friends* are on this boat anyway?"

"About a dozen. Let me introduce one. This is Harry Montana, he's helping me with the arrangements."

Charlie shook hands, taking Harry in from head to toe. "I'll push off if you don't mind," he said, edging away. "I need to cool off in the shower."

"Dinner's at eight-thirty, Clement," Montana said as he turned to go.

He swung around. "You mean *all* of us? *Together?* Jesus, what kind of cruise is this? I *choose* who I dine with."

"Those were Bob's conditions. He requested you all abide by them. If you don't approve, you are free to leave."

Clement stared at him for a long moment. Then, "Hah," he said. "Damn it, I'll do it your way," and he strode off, an angry man.

Brandon van Zelder was next to arrive, an old acquaintance of Bob's, Montana told me quickly, as was the woman with him. Tall and handsome, with thick dark hair and piercing dark eyes, van Zelder was immaculate in a Brioni blazer and preppy Bermuda shorts. He waved cheerily at Montana. The woman was almost as tall, with a fall of pale blond hair and eyes as brilliant as ten-carat sapphires. Model-slim with legs that went on forever, she was a golden tan apparition in a simple gray shift dress that stopped well above her very pretty knees.

"Just thought I'd add a little spice to the game," Montana said to me over his shoulder before wrapping his arms around the blonde, who kissed him soundly on the lips.

My mouth pinched into a tight line and I looked determinedly away.

"Hi, I'm Brandon van Zelder." The Brioni-clad aristocrat spoke to me. "I understand you're my hostess. Awfully good of you to invite me. I love little jaunts like this, gives me a chance to find a good backgammon game, y'know. I'm pretty good at it, though I say so myself. Do you play?"

"Hello, and yes I do, or rather I did occasionally, with Bob—"

"Brandon, how are you, man?" Montana came over, and they embraced, slapping each other on the shoulder and grinning. Then Montana said, "Let me introduce Texas Jones."

I groaned inwardly; of course the beauty with her hooks into Montana would be called something wild, like *Texas*.

"Pleased to meet you, Daisy." Texas had an appealing southern twang. "And thanks for invitin' me on this cruise. I don't get much opportunity to do anythin' like this, not unless I'm workin', that is. You know, singin'. I'm a cabaret artist. I work occasionally on the cruise ships, but nothin' as gorgeous as this yacht. And this is the first time I've ever been a guest."

"Then I hope you enjoy it," I said, warming up a little.

Montana told them about dinner, and they went off to their staterooms just as Davis Farrell arrived.

Davis was in his hippie outfit: rumpled shorts, a T-shirt, denim jacket, and brown leather sandals. His long hair was pulled back in a ponytail, and he had a rough, stubbly beard. Nevertheless, there was no disguising he was a good-looking man.

He looked around the superluxurious marble atrium, the inlaid floors, the white-uniformed stewards with their silver trays of champagne, the enormous displays of flowers, and the ambience of pampered wealth and power. It was obvious he felt quite at home.

"You must be Daisy Keane," he said, taking in my creased yellow dress and probably also wondering if I'd been Bob's mistress. "Davis Farrell," he said, shaking hands.

"Welcome to *Blue Boat*," I said, sounding very formal. "I'm only sorry Bob isn't here to say that to you himself."

"I doubt he would have," Davis said. "Still, it's a nice thought."

Taken aback, I quickly introduced Montana. "Another friend of Bob's," I said.

"So, exactly how many 'friends' are attending Bob's wake anyhow?" Davis asked, frowning.

"A dozen or more," Montana said.

Davis gave a bitter little half laugh. "Who knew old Hardwick had that many 'friends'?"

Montana told him of the dinner arrangements, and he shrugged moodily. "If I have to, I have to," he said as he went off to find his stateroom.

Hard on Davis's heels came Rosalia and Hector, with Magdalena and little Bella and the nanny.

## Rosalia

Looking at Rosalia, no one would have guessed she was nervous. She had long ago perfected the smile that hid a thousand hurts, and she'd always had that regal carriage, like that of a dancer, which had first attracted Roberto to her. Today she wore her glossy black hair the way she always did, in a knot at the nape of her neck. She had on the crisp long-sleeved white cotton shirt that had almost become her trademark, a dark blue linen skirt, and comfortably heeled shoes, and she carried a wide-brimmed straw hat and the woven straw bag she'd bought in the local village store. Rosalia had found herself long ago; she had no need to flaunt designer labels and try to impress.

What she was wondering, though, as she had so many times before, was exactly why she had agreed to this. After all, she had not been able to keep Roberto with her when he was alive, and she certainly could not hope to bring him back from the dead by participating in the cruise.

Sighing regretfully, she turned to look for the rest of her small party. Her daughter and granddaughter were still talking with Captain Anders, and Hector, *dear Hector,* was walking toward her, smiling encouragingly. With a little buzz of pleasure, she thought how very Spanish he looked. Like her, Hector never changed: he was who he was, and she liked that about him. Hector made her feel secure, though he was not, and never had been, her lover. Rosalia was not a promiscuous woman. She'd had two lovers in her life: The first was Roberto and the last her husband.

It was only because Hector had insisted that she'd agreed to come on Roberto's farewell cruise. "Roberto loved you," Hector had said firmly. "You refused to see him all these years. Now he's asked you for one final favor. Besides, you have to see what he's going to leave you in his will. He was a very rich man, it could be a great deal of money."

She'd been astonished when Hector had said that. Of course Roberto wouldn't leave her anything, she was simply a lover he remembered from long ago.

Spotting Montana, she thought how attractive he was, so very . . . *masculino*. There was a sort of strength about him, the same kind of strength Roberto had. She was sure Montana, like Roberto, was a man of principle.

He took her hand in both of his, smiling warmly at her. "I'm so glad you decided to come," he said. "I know how pleased Bob would have been."

## *Daisy*

Standing in the background, I thought how lovely Rosalia was. You chose well, Bob, I thought. This one is a true lady. Now if only you had been different, she would have stayed with you, given you children, a real family life, and I've no doubt she would have made you a very happy man.

I found Hector's flamboyant gypsy looks a bit startling but noticed how considerate he was of Rosalia, anxious for her not to be embarrassed by her deafness. Still, I thought Rosalia couldn't have chosen anyone more different from Bob. Magdalena, the daughter, was tall and rangy, with her mother's winning smile, and the little granddaughter was enchanting. I shook hands and greeted them all. *If only, if only* was going through my mind, but there was never any going back.

When the steward came to escort them to their rooms, I said to Montana, "Now I know why Bob couldn't get Rosalia out of his mind. And don't even begin to suggest she might have killed him because I refuse to believe it. My money's still on Dopplemann. Anyway, where *is* Dopplemann?" I glanced at my watch. "It's five o'clock, and we're supposed to sail at six. Do you suppose he's still coming?"

"He made it to New York the week Bob died so I'm sure he'll make it here from Munich."

"He *what*?" My eyes almost popped from my head, and I sank into the nearest sofa. "Now I'm *certain* he did it. All you have to do is prove it, Montana."

"Don't be too sure. Charlie Clement was also in New York, and so was Davis Farrell."

I groaned, thinking of the luxury yacht full of suspected murderers. "Why didn't you tell me this before?"

"We're only just getting the information. It takes time, you know."

"So what about the women suspects?"

"I've got nothing on them. Yet."

"What does that mean?"

Montana lifted his shoulder in a shrug. "I guess we'll have to find out," he said, just as Dopplemann lumbered into the atrium.

# 32

## Dopplemann

Dopplemann was sweating. He hadn't realized it would be so hot and he was wearing his loden green wool jacket with the pleated back and the half belt. Pushing his brand-new Panama from his perspiring forehead, he looked around. He'd never seen such a dazzling display of luxury and it crossed his mind—just for a moment—that if Bob had not done what he'd done to him, he himself might have owned a yacht like this.

His bottle-thick glasses misted over and he took them off and polished them on a new cotton handkerchief, gradually becoming aware of the man and the woman standing opposite him. He put the glasses back on and they swam into focus.

## Daisy

"Welcome to *Blue Boat*," I said to Dopplemann. "I'm Daisy Keane, Bob's friend and your hostess. I believe you know Harry Montana." For the life of me I couldn't offer him my hand. I stared astonished at him, pale and sweaty and peering back at me through his thick lenses. "We were afraid you'd miss the sailing."

"I caught the wrong bus," Dopplemann said in his strange hissing voice. "It took me a mile or so out of my way and I had to walk back."

"You should have taken a taxi," Montana said severely. "You might have delayed the sailing."

Dopplemann merely shrugged. "I apologize," he muttered, and taking off his glasses he polished them again. He darted a quick glance at me from his cold watery green eyes, then clicked his heels and made a formal little bow as the steward came to show him to his room.

"Dinner's at eight-thirty," Montana called after him. "Try not to be late."

I sank into the sofa again. I couldn't believe how strange Dopplemann was. "He looks like Dirk Bogarde in the final scenes of *Death in Venice*," I said. "All he needed was the dribbling mascara. Poor little man," I added, suddenly overcome with a feeling of pity.

"That 'poor little man' has one of the best scientific brains in the world," Montana reminded me. "Spacecraft might not be heading for Mars if it were not for him. He's perfectly capable of planning a murder."

"Oh, God," I said. "Just promise me I don't have to sit next to him at dinner."

Montana grinned as he took my hand. "I've got it all worked out. You're sitting next to me. How about we meet in the piano bar at seven-thirty?"

"I'll buy you a drink," I teased. Then, with an impulsive kiss on the cheek, I left him and hurried back to my suite, relieved not to have to confront any more potential killers—at least for a couple of hours, while I snatched some sleep.

# PART IV

## ON BOARD.
## THE FIRST NIGHT

*The Book of Life begins with*
*a man and a woman in a garden.*
*It ends with Revelations.*

—OSCAR WILDE,
*A WOMAN OF NO IMPORTANCE*

# 33

*Daisy*

The throb of the ship's engines woke me. I got up and opened the window, watching the palm trees and Prince Rainier's palace recede into the distance and then the long green pine-filled coastline of the Côte d'Azur slide into view. The yacht slipped smoothly through the water leaving a creamy wake in which dolphins darted, and I tried to fasten the memory in my mind so that later I could close my eyes and live it over again. Regrets swept over me as I thought of Bob, and I realized how important it was to safeguard the memories of the time we had spent together. I knew how much he would have enjoyed this cruise, and the Villa Belkiss, but Bob had not expected to die; he'd thought he had all the time in the world.

I looked around my peaceful suite, glowing in the rosy sunset and filled with flowers. In a way, this cruise on a luxury yacht was Bob's final gift to me, and my final gift to him would be to help Montana find his killer.

I showered and dressed quickly in an apple green pleated chiffon shirt and narrow cream silk pants, adding my emerald beads and earrings and the big, flashy princess-cut yellow diamond ring Bob had given me last Christmas and that I almost never wore. Gold sandals and a whiff of the Hermès Rouge scent I'd bought because I'd thought, erroneously it transpired, it was meant only for redheads, and I was on my way to the bar to meet Montana.

I was the first to arrive; there was just the bartender and a nice man named Melvyn, who told me he hailed from Oklahoma, playing standards on the white baby grand.

The lighting in the bar was soft and outside the windows the last of the sunset streaked the sky with rose and pale green. Deep curved banquettes were piled with cushions and the walls were of dark wood inlaid with intricate designs. I hitched myself onto a barstool and ordered a cosmo. As if by magic, a steward appeared bearing hot hors d'oeuvres. And right behind him came Montana.

"You're early," he said, touching my arm lightly and giving me that half smile.

"And *you* are late. Do you always keep women waiting?"

"Not if I can help it, and certainly not when they look like you. Would you take it as an insult if I tell you you look beautiful tonight?"

I eyed him warily, uncertain whether he was making fun of me. "Okay," I said grudgingly, "even though it's not true."

"Who gave you the diamond?" He picked up my hand to inspect it.

"Would you believe me if I told you I bought it myself?"

He let go of my hand and looked into my eyes. "No."

Despite myself, or maybe it was the cosmo since I'd now had more than a few sips, I giggled. "Of course I didn't, it was a Christmas present from Bob."

"A generous man."

"Among other fine qualities, yes, he was." I closed my eyes and saw Bob's face in front of me: my ogre, my Shrek, my beloved friend and mentor. "Listen, Montana," I said, suddenly very serious, "I promise to do everything I can to help you nail Bob's killer. Just tell me—and I'll do it."

"Okay, fine. . . . I appreciate your cooperation—it's easier than fighting all the time. And anyhow, here they come," he added softly.

They arrived all at once, looking, I thought, as mixed a bunch of suspects as you could envision. Filomena was every inch the South of France woman in a tangerine silk slip dress. She said hello then took a seat at the bar and soon had a martini and a plate of olives in front of her as she chatted to the bartender. Texas was sexy as all get-out in another jersey shift, lavender this time, sweeping her long blond hair to one side as she talked music with Melvyn at the piano.

Dopplemann sidled in, still wearing his heavy loden green jacket with the half belt and the little pleat in the back, only now he had matching pants and a gray-checked shirt. He looked like an escaped convict. He nodded good evening to us as he made his way purposefully to the bar, where we heard him ordering a glass of good Bordeaux. He certainly had fine taste in wines.

He took a barstool next to Filomena, bidding her a gruff

*Guten Tag.* She gave him a shocked stare, then looked around for an escape. Spotting us, she came over.

"*Amici,* save me from that strange man," she said nervously. "What's he doing on this ship?"

"He's one of your fellow guests," Montana said, explaining who Dopplemann was. She stole another glance at him, wanting to be impressed but failing.

Meanwhile Melvyn was playing "Body and Soul," which I couldn't help thinking was appropriate. After all this was a wake.

Captain Anders arrived, smart in his white uniform. All the officers and crew seemed to have been chosen for their looks as much as their abilities.

"Just came to check everyone was comfortable," the captain said. "I hope you all enjoyed the sunset, it was spectacular tonight."

Montana went off to speak to him alone while I attempted a conversation with Filomena. I said I liked her dress, a safe subject, I thought; and she told me in her halting English that the designer was Roberto Cavalli, her favorite of the moment. She asked "who" I was wearing, and I admitted I had no idea; it was just something I'd bought in a hurry at Harvey Nichols.

"A good store," she said approvingly. "I shopped there when I was with Bob too."

I wondered what she meant by *too.* Was she putting me in the mistress category? I suddenly realized that probably all my suspects thought I had been Bob's mistress and hastened to tell her I was merely his employee. "And his friend," I added.

She gave me a long shrewd look. "I believe you tell the truth," she said, sounding surprised.

"Of course I tell the truth!" I turned pink with indignation, and she laughed.

Just then Bordelaise swept in, blond fringe bouncing over her sparkling eyes. She had on a discreet cream pantsuit with about a dozen pearl necklaces, and Brandon van Zelder was on her heels, movie-star handsome in a white dinner jacket.

"*Dio mio,*" Filomena murmured, clutching a hand to her cleavage. "Who is this man?" And without waiting for an answer, she slipped off the barstool and headed his way.

"You're looking gorgeous," I said to Bordelaise.

"You're not so bad yourself—when you make the effort," she retorted, and we grinned at each other.

Montana was now at the other end of the bar, talking to Dopplemann. He wiggled his eyebrows at me to come join them. Unable to bring myself to smile at Dopplemann, I said a stiff good evening and that I hoped he was enjoying his wine.

"Please, call me Marius," he said, in his quiet, hissing voice. "And this is a very good wine, an Haut-Brion. It never fails to amaze me that such a perfect wine comes from a mere four acres in the middle of a rather shabby suburb of Bordeaux. I learned much of what I know about good wines from Bob, Miss Keane. He was a good teacher in the finer things of life," he added.

Astonished that he had said so much, I managed a smile and Montana gave my hand an encouraging squeeze. Then Charlie Clement showed up.

He prowled over to the bar, leaning against it, one hand in his pocket as he ordered a double Jack Daniel's on the rocks. He nodded a curt good evening at us.

"Evening, Clement," Montana said, intent, I thought, on spreading goodwill to all tonight. In the background Melvyn had switched to Lennon and McCartney. "Let me introduce Marius Dopplemann," Montana added.

Clement's face registered surprise, then shock as he looked the little man up and down. "The scientist?" he asked, but Dopplemann looked away and did not answer.

Clement glanced inquiringly at Montana, but Montana merely signaled the waiter to bring more canapés. Dopplemann took a half dozen, then ate them so quickly I thought he must be really hungry. I drained my cosmo and contemplated a second. This was going to be a long night.

"Hiya all!" Ginny's exuberant voice cut through the bar as she elbowed her way in, all done up in black pants, an off-the-shoulder black top, and stilettos, and with a bunch of dark feathers tucked into her yellow hair. Grinning, she slid onto the barstool next to Montana and ordered a gin and tonic on the rocks.

"I like my drinks classy, like my men," she added with a naughty wink, inspecting Charlie Clement as she did so. "And who might you be then?" she demanded, unfazed by his sullen demeanor.

"Charles Clement," he said stiffly, acknowledging her with the brief nod that seemed to be his customary greeting.

"And I'm Ginny Bunn. You a friend of Bob's then?"

"Ex-friend."

I thought he'd gotten right to the point.

Ginny was unfazed by his attitude. "Wait a minute, I remember you. You came to Sneadley a few times, to the Ram's Head. I'm the barmaid there." She tasted her gin and tonic and gave a nod of professional approval at the bartender. "I always remember faces," she added, looking thoughtfully at Charlie. Then she suddenly shut up, her face closed. She turned away and began to talk to Montana.

I glanced around to see who else had shown up. Still no Diane, no Rosalia, no Davis Farrell.

I watched Dopplemann down another dozen or so hors d'oeuvres and took my second cosmo over to where Bordelaise was still talking with Texas.

"So what d'you think, girls?" I parked myself on the next barstool.

"I think it's pretty good, especially since I don't have to pay for it," Texas said in her southern twang. "I'm just a workin' girl, y'know. I can't afford trips on yachts."

"You don't have to work. You could get any guy you wanted, any guy in the South of France," Bordelaise said. "Rich guys, I mean."

Texas downed her vodka. "Not my style, honey. I'm the kind that falls for a man head over heels before I even find out if he's rich or poor. So far, he's always turned out poor." She laughed. "Luck of the game, I guess."

Texas was not at all the calculating chick I'd expected from her appearance; she seemed really nice. It was just that her looks misled you into thinking she'd be a man-eater. Thinking of men, I looked for Montana. He was still talking to Ginny. I wondered if I would ever get over this jealousy thing for a man who only wanted to be buddies with me. A man who wanted me to keep him company so he wouldn't be lonely, and so he could keep the bad guys of the world away from me.

I was wondering if this night would ever be over when the steward announced that dinner was about to be served.

# 34

*Daisy*

The long table in the oval dining room looked beautiful. Blue-green hydrangeas were banked in low silver tubs down the center of the table, the wall sconces shed a perfect pinkish light, and candles flickered everywhere. Stewards waited to serve us, and champagne and wines cooled in crystal buckets.

Rosalia came in with Hector and Magdalena, followed by Reg Blunt. Only Diane and Davis Farrell were still missing.

Montana had planned the seating and everyone milled around peering at the place cards, looking to see who was next to them. Montana and I were at the head of the table, with Reg and Diane, who hurried in after us, at the other end. Next to Montana was Rosalia, then Charlie Clement, Ginny, and the empty chair for the missing Davis. Then came Filomena and Brandon. On Reg's left was Texas, then Dopplemann, Bordelaise, Magdalena, and Hector. I thought it unfortunate that we were a man short and had had to place two girls together, and also that poor Bordelaise had drawn Dopplemann.

Diane arrived and stood, posing in the doorway long enough for us all to notice her, the grieving widow in black chiffon. Her red hair was upswept, her long, smooth neck was wrapped in a thin strand of very sparkly diamonds, and she wore matching diamond earrings. I had to admit she looked lovely in a hard sort of way. Her face tightened though when she found she was seated next to Reg, who was already downing a bottle of Kronenbourg beer.

"Thought I'd be the last one to show up for dinner," Reg said jovially to Diane, getting to his feet. "I was running in low gear after that plane journey. Haven't flown much, y'know, and I'm not that good a traveler. Anyhow, not unless it's in style, like this. This boat is grand, isn't it?" He smiled at us. "Lady Hardwick'll keep me company, won't you, luv?" He gave Diane a friendly nudge. "We go back a bit, Lady Hardwick and me, y'know. Bob used to bring her up to Sneadley when they were still just courtin'. And that's some time ago now, isn't it, lass? A few years under the old bridge now, I'd say."

Diane flinched, then proceeded to ignore him.

Waiters wafted napkins over our laps and poured pink champagne. *Amuses bouches,* as Bob liked to call them, were served. And still Davis Farrell had not joined us. I wondered worriedly if he'd opted out and decided to go home tomorrow.

Filomena was not missing Davis. She'd latched on to Brandon van Zelder in a torrent of Italian-accented English, speaking so softly he had to bend his head closer to hers, which of course was exactly what she'd intended.

Ginny did not look happy. She had turned pointedly away from Charlie and was staring forlornly at Davis's empty seat. She had no one to talk to and heaven knows Ginny loved to talk. Sitting next to Dopplemann, Bordelaise rolled her eyes helplessly at me.

Across the table, Hector asked Charlie what he did for a living, which earned him a dismissive glance and the curt reply that he was in the entertainment business. Tension crackled like lightning and I wondered uneasily how we were going to make it through the next five days.

Davis Farrell finally arrived with the first course. He'd cleaned up a bit for dinner in a good jacket and an expensive blue shirt, and despite the ponytail suddenly looked every inch the successful Wall Street man. Apologizing, he explained that he'd had a phone call from New York that had to be dealt with right away. "They're not used to me not being there," he added.

"Who's not?" Ginny asked as he took the seat next to her. She was surprised when he told her about the young immigrants who were his clients.

"Funny, I thought everybody here was going to be rich and successful," she said.

"How do you know I'm not?"

She eyed him up and down. "The jacket's okay. It's the beard and the ponytail that give the wrong impression."

Davis laughed, then he asked where she was from and they fell into a conversation about Sneadley and the Ram's Head.

Bordelaise was giving it a good try with Dopplemann. "How was your flight, Herr Dopplemann?" I heard her say.

He glanced sideways at her and the light reflected strangely off his thick lenses. "I found it adequate and fast, despite the great security that now prevails," he said.

Bordelaise took a deep breath. He was hard going

Out of the blue Dopplemann said, "I like your hair, Fräulein Maguire. It is very blond, very"—he seemed to hunt for the word he wanted—"very *charming*."

Accepting his clumsy compliment, Bordelaise gave him her sunniest smile and told him to call her Bordelaise.

Rosalia was telling Charlie Clement about her hearing problem, saying she hoped he would excuse her if she didn't grasp what he said right away. She spoke halting English and Charlie looked impatient, but then he seemed to have culti-vated impatience, made it part of his persona as a means of putting other people on the defensive, forcing them to talk faster, act hurriedly. Not Rosalia, though. She asked what Charlie thought of the yacht, then went on to say how good it was of "Roberto" Hardwick to treat his old friends to such a wonderful cruise. Charlie harrumphed a bit and said vaguely he guessed so. And that was that.

Raising surprised eyebrows, Rosalia smiled across the table at Hector, asking him in Spanish how he was doing. He smoothed back his too-long hair, shined like spit-and-polished army boots, stroked his mustache, and said aloofly he was fine.

Obviously it was my turn to say something. "Hector, I've heard so much about the Finca de los Pastores and how beauti-ful it is. It must be wonderful living there."

He inclined his head graciously. "Indeed, Señorita, I wouldn't live anywhere else."

"Oh please, call me Daisy," I said, then drew him out until he began to tell me about the hotel.

Dinner was served, a lobster salad followed by individual beef Wellingtons. We'd ordered the kind of good old-fashioned food Bob would have enjoyed. Wines were poured, conversation stumbled on and the tension grew. There was cheese and salad and a half dozen desserts and with them we served a special champagne, Pol Roger's Cuvée Winston Churchill.

Montana had barely spoken to me all night. Now he whispered it was time for the toast. Ringing his fork against a glass he asked for silence. "Daisy has something she wants to say to you all."

He glanced expectantly up at me as I got to my feet. I had a little speech planned but I cleared my throat nervously, looking around the table at the guests.

"First I want to bid you welcome on Bob's behalf. You know by now he chose you all specially, he wanted all of you together for a final celebration of his life. Actually, 'I want them all to have a damned good time,' was what he said. But there's something else you might want to think about. He believed that by bringing you together you might take another look at how he personally affected your lives. If you did, he said you might surprise yourselves."

They looked back at me. Charlie's face was noncommittal and an ironic smile lifted one corner of Davis's mouth. Diane looked angry, Filomena puzzled. Ignoring the champagne, Dopplemann continued to sip his Bordeaux, staring deep into his glass as though he might find an answer in there. Rosalia, understanding from Montana what I had said, was the only one to comment.

"Roberto was always a wise man," she said quietly.

"He was," I agreed. "And now we'll drink to him in Winston Churchill's favorite champagne, which is why it was named after him. Churchill was also Bob's hero, 'A man amongst men,' he called him, 'a lion-heart.' Bob wished he could be like him, and in so many ways—courage, integrity, strength—he was." I lifted my glass. "So let us drink to Sir Robert Waldo Hardwick, a wise man and a good friend to us all."

"Here, here." Reg was the first to raise his glass, followed by sullen murmurs of "To Bob."

Diane's face had closed into a mask. Now she glared at Filomena. "The Italian should not be here. She's nothing but a whore."

*"Dio mio."* Filomena was on her feet. "How *dare* you call me *that*! Bob left you because you were such a bitch and now I see it's true. Bob told me himself that you didn't deserve his name and that I did. It was *me* he loved, not you . . . I was the one who made him happy."

An embarrassed silence fell. Around us the stewards began to clear the dishes.

"We'll see how much he cared when the will is read," Diane hissed back. "Then you'll find where old mistresses end up. In the garbage can. Don't forget *I was his wife*—"

I said quickly, "Please, Diane, Filomena, this is meant to be a civilized dinner. Bob wanted us all to have a good time."

"Since we're on the subject of the will, might I ask exactly *why* we are all here?" Charlie, who had continued to drink Jack

Daniel's, said. "I'm not sure any of us could have been called Bob's friends. For instance, that man." He pointed at Dopplemann. "My God, he looks like a farm laborer. Nobody has heard of him for years. Why on earth would Bob invite *him*?" He stared at Dopplemann as though he was an insect under his microscope. "Come on, Herr Dopplemann," he said, "tell us how you knew the great Sir Robert Hardwick. What's your real story, eh?"

"Stop it, Clement," Montana ordered. But Dopplemann had shriveled under Charlie's attack, curling over his wineglass, head bowed. After a moment he muttered something, then he got up and walked out.

Montana went after him. He grabbed him by the shoulder but Dopplemann shrugged him off and continued on his way. Montana watched him worriedly, then came back to the table.

"I think that's about enough for tonight," he said coldly. "Diane, you were invited because you are Bob's ex-wife. I don't know what, if anything, he's left you in his will, but I'm asking you to be civil for his sake. As for you, Clement, if you don't want to be on this voyage you can leave tomorrow. We'll be in Saint-Tropez around seven; the choice is yours. But I'm warning you, any more insulting behavior and I will personally have you removed. Have I made myself clear?"

"Who the hell are *you*, telling me what I can and cannot do?" Charlie pushed back his chair and followed Dopplemann out the door. "Fuck you all," we heard him say as he left.

I glanced at my stunned guests. Then Diane got up and without a word flounced off.

Filomena's eyes followed her. "It's true I was Bob's mistress," she said, "but we loved each other, truly we did. And I'm sad he's dead." She turned piteous eyes on Brandon. "How could Diane say such bad things?" Giant tears rolled down her cheeks and Brandon pulled a silk handkerchief from his top pocket and began to mop them.

"It's all right. No damage done," he said comfortingly.

Horrified, my eyes met Montana's. "I think we'd better call it a night," he said. "Hopefully tomorrow will be better."

"Jeez," Bordelaise whispered. "I'm heading for the bar! And I certainly hope Charlie and Diane won't be there."

"I'm worried about Dopplemann," Montana said after they'd gone. "I'd better go look for him. I'll meet you in the bar later."

"Poor Dopplemann," Bordelaise said as we nursed a good-night glass of champagne. "That Charlie is a real bastard, I knew it the moment I saw him. Men like that usually have something to hide, trust me."

Several of the young officers showed up to socialize, and Bordelaise was in her element. Melvyn played "Smoke Gets in Your Eyes" and Texas sang along in a husky smoldering voice that left them rapt. Even Filomena, recovered from her tears, smiled bravely, sitting very close to Brandon.

Fifteen minutes later, Montana showed up. "There's no sign of Dopplemann," he said worriedly. "I had the steward check and he's not in his cabin. I also checked the decks, no sign of him there. I'm hoping Clement didn't goad him into doing something stupid."

Realizing what he meant, Bordelaise and I stared at him, horrified.

"You never know with a man like that," Montana said. "He's capable of anything. I'm going to have to tell Captain Anders." He called over one of the young officers and they went off together. Minutes later the yacht started to slow down; then it made a half circle and began slowly to retrace its path.

"Oh, my God," I said. "He really thinks Dopplemann might have jumped."

There was a few seconds' silence while everyone gathered their wits, then we all ran onto the deck. Hanging over the rail, we searched the blue-black sea, now illuminated by a glaring light. The side of the lower deck lifted hydraulically, the tenders were put out and the officers began their search.

"Oh, no," Filomena moaned. "It's that dreadful man's fault. . . . But that little Dopplemann is so strange."

"It'll be all right," I said, trying to sound positive while still looking for a body in the water.

"Don't bet on it," Bordelaise said. "A man like that, humiliated in public . . ."

The rest of the crew were combing each deck, searching every room. The barman said Dopplemann had ordered another bottle of the Haut-Brion. He'd thought he must be taking it to his room, and Montana said he didn't believe he'd kill himself when there was still a full bottle of good wine to be drunk.

Searchlights played over the water, turning it a rather pretty milky blue. Looking at it, I thought it might not be a bad way for the killer to go.

Everyone except Charlie and Diane was on deck, peering over the rail. The wind blew the women's evening dresses against their bodies and in the half-light they looked like a beautiful carved frieze: hair blown back, faces uptilted. Reg and Davis, Brandon and Hector stood watching and waiting.

"Surely Clement's insult wasn't enough to send a man to his death," Reg said. "Clement was obviously pissed out of his mind and everybody knows men say things they shouldn't when they're like that."

Hector paced the deck, back and forth, back and forth, and Texas, Filomena and Bordelaise huddled silently together.

## Montana

Montana had returned to the lower deck. The giant steel fuel tanks gleamed under the lights and the throb of the yacht's engines sent small shudders through the ship. Over the noise he caught another sound; a buzzing, like a hacksaw on wood. Ducking around the tanks he followed it to its source.

Dopplemann lay sprawled on his back, the empty wine bottle still clutched in his hand. He was passed out and snoring.

Montana informed Captain Anders, the medical officer was summoned and Montana went back up on deck to tell the others.

The panic was over, but not the fear. The guests slowly drifted off to their rooms, relieved that they didn't have a dead body on their hands and that the cruise would continue and the will would still be read on Capri.

# PART V

# LOVES ME/
# LOVES ME NOT

*All love, all liking, all delight*
*Lies drowned with us in endless night.*

—ROBERT MERRICK

# 35

*Daisy*

Now that we were alone, Montana looked at me. My mind was still a blank from fright and I gripped the deck rail, still shaky. The breeze played with my hair as I watched the creamy curve of the ship's wake and the little phosphorescent fish jumping, smelling the sea and the piney scent coming from the land as we hugged the coast en route to nearby Saint-Tropez. For once I had nothing to say.

Montana said gently, "They're taking good care of him. He'll live."

"I almost wish he wouldn't," I said bitterly. "It would have been the easy way out, then we could all have just gone home."

"You're being judgmental. Dopplemann was humiliated in front of us all, so he went off to hide and got drunk. The man has lived alone so long it probably never occurred to him anyone would go looking for him."

I was still reluctant to forgive Dopplemann for what he'd

put us through. "Anyhow, how's he going to face everybody tomorrow? Knowing we all know."

"He'll get over it, and so will you. Come on, Daisy, let it go why don't you?"

He uncurled my hand from the rail and held it to his lips. Like magic, Dopplemann disappeared from my mind. My knees trembled. I hadn't felt like this since I was a teenager, and certainly not with "the husband." Maybe the bad sex with him was my fault but I still blamed it on him; despite his promiscuous-lover-boy image, the husband had not been a great lover. And now I was wondering if Montana was. Wrong of me, I know, but sometimes the mind just takes over and anyhow it beat worrying about Dopplemann.

Montana let go of my hand and stared out to sea. I wondered what he was thinking. He looked a hard man, with his hawklike profile, cropped head and tight lean body; a man who would always keep himself in tip-top shape, ready for whatever danger might be around the next corner. Then why, I asked myself, did I fancy him? Was it the whiff of danger that accompanied him, as well as that hard-toned body and the way he looked in a white terry bathrobe—I remembered him when he came into my room at Sneadley with the tray of tea and gingersnaps—kind of sexy and relaxed. I heaved a sigh that made him turn his head and look at me.

"You still here?" he added with an amused twinkle in his ohh-so-s-e-x-y charcoal gray eyes.

"Penny for your thoughts?" I said.

"They're worth more than that."

"So a quarter then."

"More."

"Fifty bucks."

He held out his hand. "I'll take it. Pay up."

"You have to tell me first."

He shook his head. "It doesn't work that way. You have to pay for the goods before you can take them home."

I sighed again, exasperated. "You're an ornery man, y'know that?"

"Funny, I thought you were the ornery one."

Running out of steam, I slumped back against the rail. I felt his hand on my cheek and turned to look at him. His fingers stroked the curve of my cheekbone then smoothed their way down to my mouth, traced my lips. He took my chin in his hand and tilted my face up to his. For a long instant our eyes locked, then I shut mine tight as his face moved over me and his mouth closed in on mine. It was the kind of kiss I never wanted to end and when he finally took his mouth away and I gasped in the few necessary jolts of air, that's exactly what I told him.

"I don't want to stop," I said breathlessly. "I've wanted you to kiss me like that for so long."

He stroked my face again, his eyes on mine, our shaky breaths linked; then he moved his hands to the nape of my neck sending jolts of lightning through my eager body.

"What now?" I murmured, moving my neck under his hand like a purring cat. "Wanna come to my place?"

I heard his rumble of choked laughter. "Oh, Daisy, you may be the only truly honest woman I've ever met. Do you always say exactly what you feel?"

I nodded. "And it never fails to get me into trouble." I eyed him up and down lasciviously. "Which is what I'm hoping it will do now."

He moved away. Taking my hand, he walked me along the deserted deck. "I'd better escort you to your cabin," he said, disappointing me.

We stood silently in the elevator, then, side by side but no longer holding hands, we walked along the corridor to my suite.

Outside my door I turned to face him, aware of every inch of him next to me, every nerve ending raised and expectant. "Well?" I asked, still breathless with sexual longing.

"Daisy." He tilted my face up to his with a finger. "Are you sure about this?"

I smiled, radiant with delight. "Let me show you how sure I am," I said, and unlocking my door, I took his hand and led him inside.

Was it that I thought I could steal his strength, make myself invincible through him? Was it that I was curious about his body, and about the secrets of his life he had so far kept from me? Like for instance the meaning of the tattoo on his right forearm? And what the *C* in Harry *C.* Montana stood for. And *who* he was, because of course I knew almost nothing about this man except the few words about his lonely childhood and the fact that he had once worked in a diner in Galveston and was a "kind of a friend" of Bob Hardwick.

Montana was a mystery man in more ways than one and now at least I was about to solve the mystery of his body and his lovemaking. Would it be the way I thought it might? Would

I fall into his arms, swooning like a lovesick maiden, trembling as I waited for his touch? Not *me*. I wasted no time. Shameless in my need, I had my dress unzipped in half a second and he was helping me off with it in another second more.

"Daisy, Daisy . . . sweet, perfect Daisy," he said, admiring my breasts, which pointed upward, longing for his touch. Then, like a knight in shining armor, he picked me up and carried me to my bed.

Pushing the turn-down chocolates out of the way, I lay back against the pillows, watching as he stripped then stood before me, as beautiful as any man could be. I beckoned him closer, sitting up as he came to me and took me in his arms, naked body against naked body, flaming with heat, sinking under his small tender kisses, reeling under his touch, kissing him back as though I couldn't bear to ever let him go.

"*Touch me,*" I whispered, drunk with the sensation of his fingers on my skin. "Touch me," I murmured again . . . and again . . . as his lips caressed me . . . And "Ah, Montana, *Montana* . . ."

"Don't you think you should at least call me Harry?"

I opened my eyes and looked at him. "Oh. Yes. Right. *Harry*. Do it some more . . . *Harry* . . . "

Much later, my legs still wrapped around him, arms flung out across the bed, I lay like a spent firework, all my stars and shimmering spangles shot into the night sky.

I ran my hand over the mysterious tattoo. "What does this mean?" I asked.

"It's a Tibetan saying. It means 'Love and kindness.' Three

of us buddies in Delta Force had it done. They were the best men you'd ever meet in your life. Both were killed in Afghanistan." He paused, thinking. "I miss them," he said.

Untangling himself, he lay back. Eyes closed, he said, "The time I spent with them was the best of my life; they were like the brothers I never had."

The hard man was showing his soft underbelly, suddenly vulnerable, suddenly human. I stroked the tattoo gently with a finger, wishing I'd never asked. "I'm so sorry."

He looked at me and seeing the sympathy in my eyes he said, "The other great event in my life was meeting the man I called my father. He wasn't my real father, of course, I had no relationship with *him* from the day I was born to the day he died. But this man saved my life. This man raised me—because before I met him I was just another tough kid heading for trouble. His name was Phineas Cloudwalker, and he was a Native American of the Comanche tribe. He was sixty-seven years old then, whip-thin, with a body hard as nails. He picked me up on a dirt road in the Texas backlands, driving a Ford pickup so old it looked as though he might have inherited it from Grandpa Clampett. I was hitchhiking, thumbing a lift on a cold forsaken night when no person with any options would have been outside. Rain was slicing down and I was soaked to the skin, but Cloudwalker had a sick dog and he'd taken him to the vet. He cried as he told me that the dog had been put down, and I remember marveling that a grown man was actually brave enough to cry. I'd never seen anyone show emotion before."

Montana was quiet and I held my breath, waiting for what

might come next. I could almost hear the hard shell I'd grown around my broken heart when the husband left me cracking. Montana, this tough man, had opened himself to me, shown me his deepest feelings, his sorrow at the tragic loss of his buddies and his true father. I thought his Cloudwalker had meant what Bob had meant to me: salvation. They were men who had taken us, broken as we were, and fixed us, made us whole again; living, breathing, feeling human beings.

"And now there's you," Montana said softly. "The kind of woman a man likes to love."

I didn't dare to ask, Well then, do you love me? It was too early to talk of love. After all, what we had going here was just a physical connection. Instead I said, "Would you cry in front of me, Harry Montana?"

"I cried at Bob's funeral." He surprised me. "I'd lost a great man. A friend."

"I cried too," I admitted. "And I've cried so much since I don't know where all the tears come from."

He twined a strand of my hair around his finger. "Daisy?"

"Yes?"

"I don't want you to be afraid."

What did he mean? Should I be afraid of falling for him? Or afraid of what Dopplemann might do next?

"Oh, I'm not, really I'm not," I said, sounding much more confident than I felt.

"Good girl." He put his arms around me and pulled me to him. "You're very beautiful, you know that?"

"Well, nobody much has told me that lately," I admitted.

"Then listen to me now. Take notes. Imprint it in your brain. You are *beautiful*. I want you to repeat that to yourself thirty times a day. Promise?"

I laughed. "I'll try."

Pushing me away, he got up, took the bottle of champagne from the ice bucket and opened it. He poured two glasses and handed me one.

"Let's drink to us," he said, smiling. So we did, and then I ate all the bedtime chocolate, suddenly ravenous from all that lovemaking.

"There's twenty-four-hour room service," he reminded me.

"But what would they think if they saw you in my room?" I asked, shocked.

He shook his head, laughing. "Come here, you silly, proper prudish woman," he said and dragged me onto his lap. Forgetting all about champagne and room service, I started kissing him all over again.

# PART VI

# DAY TWO.
# SAINT-TROPEZ

*Life is a foreign language:*
*All men mispronounce it.*

—CHRISTOPHER MORLEY

# 36

*Daisy*

I slept the sleep of angels, fitting into Montana's body like it was meant to be. The next morning, vaguely aware of daylight behind the closed curtains, I finally surfaced from beneath contented layers of drowsiness, opened my eyes, and looked for him. He wasn't there. I searched for a note, checked the sitting room and the bathroom. Empty. I stared around, stunned. Montana had left me and without even a good-bye.

It's foolish I suppose but the pain of rejection hit me one more time, the same awful agony I'd felt when the husband had left. Those cracks in the shell around my crusted heart I'd experienced last night when Montana had revealed his more vulnerable side to me, sealed up again with the finality of superglue. I told myself I was a fool and men were men, only after sex and nothing more. Yet hadn't *I* seduced *him*? He'd asked if I knew what I was doing, and I had, so blithely, said yes. Now I'd gotten what I'd asked for. Nothing more, nothing less. It wouldn't happen again, though; this one was over before it even began.

It slowly dawned on me that outside the big picture window lay the magical little port of Saint-Tropez. I could see the pine-clad hills of Ramatuelle curving into a clear blue sky, I could hear gulls calling and when I opened the window there was the scent of flowers and the sea. I needed a beach and the warmth of the sun dappling my love-bruised body; I needed to cool my pain in that cool blue sea, to breathe close up the refreshing scent of those flowers. I needed rosé wine and fresh-caught fish and those tiny wild strawberries called *fraises des bois*. Of course I did not need Harry Montana.

In the shower I let the water flow over me, washing away all traces of our lovemaking. Squeaky clean, I emerged wrapped in a soft cotton robe, just as my stewardess, Camille, arrived with breakfast. I poured a cup of coffee and took a bite of the buttery flaky croissant, baked the way only the French can. Then I rang Bordelaise's room.

"What?" she answered.

"You awake?"

"I am now."

"Open the curtains and take a look outside."

I heard her grumbling as she got out of bed, and the sound of the curtains being pulled back. Then "*Ohh!* Will you just take a look at *that!*"

"Awake now?" I asked, grinning.

"You betcha. What have you got planned?"

"Beach. Swimming. Lunch. Wine drinking. People watching. Maybe a little light shopping later . . ."

"Give me half an hour, babe, and I'm all yours. Oh, wait a minute, what about the suspects? Are you just going to let them go off on their own?"

"Well, do *you* want to go swimming with Dopplemann? *Or* Charlie Clement?" I heard her groan. "Of course you don't and neither do I. The hell with it, Bordelaise, I'm going to leave Montana to deal with them."

"Hmmm." I could almost hear her brain clicking. "So, *exactly* where *are* you with Montana? I thought you looked pretty chummy last night. And don't bother to tell me I'm wrong. I can smell the start of a love affair at fifty paces."

"Well, this time you *are* wrong. It's all over."

"*Over?* I thought you were going to tell me it had just begun?"

Sighing, I gave her a quick summary of the events of the past few hours. Finally I said, "So when a man picks up and leaves without so much as a good-bye, not even a note—not even a phone call—what's a woman supposed to think?"

"The worst," Bordelaise agreed.

Sighing, I slipped into a turquoise bikini and a gauzy light blue caftan—part of my Harvey Nick's London purchases. I called Patrice de Colmont, Club 55's owner, and made reservations for lunch at two o'clock, grabbed my straw tote and went and hammered on Bordelaise's door. She flung it open, beaming.

"Quick, let's make a run for it before Dopplemann finds us," she said in a loud whisper, already scampering along the corridor with me behind her, giggling like naughty children as we trotted down the gangway onto the dock.

We strolled about in the sun, inspecting the stalls selling

jewelry and belts, T-shirts and scarves, sunglasses and souvenirs. Getting a taxi is not easy in small crowded Saint-Tropez and there only ever seem to be about two of them anyway, but I knew where to call and we waited by the port for it to arrive.

The taxi driver was cute and his name was Paul. He chatted us up in French as we wound our way through the fifteenth-century town's narrow streets and alleys and out onto the main road. He turned at the sign that read "Plages," driving past endless vineyards, the source of the delicious local rosé wine, and turned again at the sign that read "Pampelonne," all the way to the end of the road and, at last, the beautiful beach. Paul told us to call him when we wanted to return and took off, leaving us staring at the Bentleys and Ferraris in the parking lot.

Despite its chic clientele, Le Club 55 is a simple place. The entrance is a boardwalk shaded by tall bamboos. It leads to a terrace and the outdoor restaurant and popular bar. Woven reeds and white canvas awnings are slung like overhead sails, and the place is awash in bougainvillea, oleander, and tamarisk. In front is the golden, umbrella-dotted beach and the sea, and a lot of "beautiful" people.

In the shady dining area, the tables are set with pale blue cloths and fresh flowers and the breeze blows from the beach, bringing in with it a slew of small motorboats from the grand yachts moored offshore. On them are the designer-clad rich folk and pretty young things in the tiniest of bikinis, all heading for lunch at the classiest and most popular beach club in Saint-Tropez.

Patrice took my hand and kissed it, commiserating gently with me about Bob. He'd known him for many years and said he would be missed. The club had been in Patrice de Colmont's family since 1955, when his mother and father had bought a beach shack and started cooking for Brigitte Bardot and her film crew, who were then shooting *And God Created Woman*. At that moment Saint-Tropez was "born," and so was Le Club 55.

We established ourselves on beach mattresses under an umbrella, but I couldn't wait to get into the water. It slid over me like a soft silk gown, just cool enough and just warm enough. I dived then broke the surface spluttering, shaking my hair from my eyes. I wasn't thinking about Montana. I wasn't thinking about Dopplemann. I wasn't even thinking about Bob. I was thinking only of my own sensual pleasure at being immersed in this smooth crystalline water and of the strength of my own body as I dived through the waves and streaked for the horizon. Bordelaise matched me, stroke for stroke. We hadn't been on the school swim team for nothing.

Cool at last, we floated serenely back to shore. Shaking off the drops of water like the pair of Labradors who had swum alongside us, we strode back up the beach to our little sanctuary and sat for a while, letting the sun dry us before adding more Hawaiian Tropic.

I lay back on my mattress and closed my eyes. For the first time since I'd left London I felt completely relaxed. Half asleep under the thatched umbrella, I was aware of the sound of laughter and the tinkle of ice in glasses, of the soft rustle of the breeze in the tamarisks and the flop of tiny waves onshore. I wished I could stay here forever and never have to face reality or Montana or the suspects again.

"*Madame*, your table is ready." A smiling young attendant in a blue T-shirt interrupted my thoughts, and Bordelaise and I put on cover-ups and wended our way through the now-thronged tables. I ordered a bottle of the house rosé, and we sipped it in delighted silence, nibbling on crunchy sweet radishes and nuggets of cauliflower and strips of red peppers, each fresh as the dawn, dipping them in a pungent aioli. A feeling of well-being swept over me like the calm after the storm.

We commented lazily on the gorgeous bodies, the jewels; the outrageous flaunting and preening; the tanned girls and bronzed tattooed guys; on the plump titans of industry in bathing shorts and baseball caps inscribed with the names of their own yachts, the famous models and the movie stars. Of course there were other, regular people who came here year after year, not to see and be seen but simply because they loved it.

We had just finished our striped sea bass and a delicious salad and were on to our second bottle of wine, waiting for the wild strawberries, when Bordelaise said in a whisper, "Don't look now, but guess who's coming our way."

So of course I looked. It was Diane. I heard her exasperated sigh. "Damn it, Daisy, now she's seen us and she's coming over."

She was right. Diane had spotted us and was heading our way.

She glared indignantly at us. "What are *you* doing here? It's impossible to get a reservation."

"Turned down, were you?" Bordelaise could patronize with the best when she wanted. "Too bad. Of course Daisy and I enjoyed an excellent lunch, and a lovely day on the beach."

"Then you won't mind if I sit here with you." Diane had parked herself before we had a chance to object. She fussed with her white leather tote, smoothed her hair, which she wore pulled back in a knot and adjusted the bustier top of her blue sundress. She poured herself a glass of our rosé and drank deeply. Her eyes met mine over the rim of the glass.

"Were you fucking my ex-husband?" she said to me.

I gasped. Next to me, I heard Bordelaise's snort of laughter.

"I always suspected you were," Diane said. "You were so close to him, always there, always answering the phones, always on the plane with him, always at that dreadful place. Sneadley Hall. Even here in Saint-Tropez, and at the Hôtel du Cap."

"I remember you at the Hôtel du Cap," I said, knowing she recalled all too well the scene she'd created when Bob had told her that the coffers were empty as far as she was concerned.

"Of course you do," she said, sounding suddenly weary. "What you didn't know was how much I needed that money. And why." Her long emerald eyes reflected back the sunlight as she glanced at me. "But then there was no reason you should know the truth, was there? I never told Bob then, so why should I tell you now?"

"What truth?" I asked, but she turned her head away, obviously deciding she'd said too much.

She waved an arm clanking with gold bracelets to summon a waiter. "Bob is dead and gone and I'm sure he's taken good care of me in his will." She flashed her eyes keenly my way again. "Hasn't he?"

"I really don't know what's in Bob's will," I said. "You'll have to wait until Capri to find out."

I thought I caught a desperate glint in her eyes but then she quickly turned to the waiter and ordered the grilled turbot and another bottle of the rosé. Then she switched on her smile and asked Bordelaise where she was from, and what she was doing here, and how she was liking the cruise.

In an instant Diane changed from a frightened desperate woman to the accomplished social charmer, enjoying herself at the finest beach club in Saint-Tropez, a place she obviously belonged, since people kept coming over and kissing her on both cheeks and asking why they hadn't seen so much of her.

Her reply to each of them was that her husband had died recently and she was just recovering from the shock.

And maybe she was, I thought, surprised. I'd learned quickly, you never knew with Diane.

## 37

*Daisy*

We called Paul, the taxi driver, to pick us up and left Diane enjoying her lunch with her friends.

Still puzzling over what she could have meant, we drove back into Saint-Tropez and set out to troll the boutiques, just reopening at four o'clock after the noontime siesta. And wandering the cobblestoned back alleys, who should we come across but Filomena, toting several large shopping bags bearing the names of Hermès and Erès and Blanc-Bleu. She'd obviously been making quiet inroads into her hundred thousand. Immaculate and gorgeous in expensively simple white linen, she strode along as though she owned the place.

"*Ciao, amici,*" she called, waving her free hand and beaming at us from across the street. "Look what I got." She hoisted the bags. "I haven't had this much fun in years. Shopping sprees always make me feel good."

Without looking, she darted across the narrow street directly in front of a blue Mercedes convertible driven by a good-looking blond man. He blasted his horn angrily, then did a quick double-take and stopped.

"I almost killed you," he said in French, throwing up his hands in mock despair.

"If I had to die I would have been happy it was at your hands," Filomena called back, laughing.

He leaned an elbow over the car door, looking interestedly at her. "So what are you doing tonight? I know where there's a good party. On Paul Allen's yacht."

Bordelaise and I exchanged meaningful glances. Paul Allen was the Microsoft billionaire and his yacht, *Octopus*, was the biggest and grandest in Saint-Tropez, way bigger than *Blue Boat*, a towering gray-blue hulk topped with *two* helicopters.

Filomena sauntered over to him; cards and smiles were exchanged along with a lingering handshake while irate drivers piled up behind them, honking and shouting. Unfazed, Filomena waved good-bye. She smiled nicely for the angry drivers, then strolled back across the street to where we stood, open-mouthed at her cool.

"Silly young man," she said dismissively. "He thought I would be impressed when he dropped Paul Allen's name and his yacht."

"Well I certainly was," Bordelaise said.

"Hah! Of course he doesn't know Paul Allen. He's like me, cruising on the fringes, hoping to get lucky and break into it, make contact, get some of the perks from the rich man's table."

Filomena was mixing her metaphors but we got what she

meant, and like Diane, she surprised us, only this time it was by her frankness.

"I look rich, he looks rich," she said with a shrug of her elegant brown shoulders. "But we're both just faking it, hoping we get lucky."

Just then Texas came around the corner, also clutching a slew of bags, though not Hermès. "Hi," she yelled. "You gals doin' some shoppin' too?" Her shoe heel caught in the cobblestones and she almost fell. "Oh, shoot." She hopped on one foot, clutching her ankle. "Is that ever painful."

Brandon came around the corner after her. He smiled at us then glanced, alarmed, at Texas. "What happened?" She wobbled on one leg and he put his arm around her waist to support her, but she groaned some more.

"She caught her heel," I told him. "It's probably a sprain. Better get her back to the ship and let the doctor take a look."

"Of course. Yes, certainly. The ship." Brandon seemed to talk only in short sharp bursts.

"I'll come too." Filomena slid her arm around Texas's waist.

"Okay, it's the doc for me then." Texas moaned. "Sorry to miss more shopping though."

As she hopped off we saw Filomena holding Brandon's hand behind Texas's back and we laughed.

We bought apple turnovers at a bakery and munched them happily, gazing in the window at the fun costume jewelry in a tiny shop called Alix's. Then Bordelaise bought a bracelet encrusted with turquoise flowers while I went for a splendid necklace—a collar or *collier* as the French saleswoman called it, of five strands of peridot droplets threaded on thin golden links.

It was now five o'clock and we were to sail at six. We emerged onto the quai right next to the Café Sénéquier, where we spotted Dopplemann, drinking wine and staring blankly at the parade of yachts lined up, stern-in, across the street. Their flags flew and their crews, in white shorts and shirts, stood ready to serve cocktails or set sail at a moment's notice. As always, Dopplemann seemed oblivious to the passing of time and I reluctantly decided I'd better remind him before he got drunk again and missed the boat.

He jumped when I said his name, sending his wineglass crashing to the floor.

"Fräulein Daisy. And Beaujolais." Getting her name wrong, he gave her a hesitant smile and scrambled to his feet. His spindly legs stuck out of his shorts like a pair of bleached twigs and he wore a loden green T-shirt; it seemed to be his favorite color. Around his neck was strung a pair of powerful-looking binoculars.

"It's time to get back to the ship, we sail at six," I said curtly.

"Ah, yes. Yes, of course." He quickly picked up the guidebook from the table and added some coins to the tip saucer. "Yes, well, I'd better hurry along."

He ambled silently alongside us, glancing from time to time at the art show several blocks long. He stopped in front of a small but detailed painting of a fisherman's cottage: whitewashed walls, blue tiled roof, an open window, yellow curtains blowing in the breeze, a pile of fishing nets and a black dog, snoozing in the sun.

Dopplemann took off his glasses and polished them. He put them back on again and peered even closer at the painting. I glanced at my watch then at Bordelaise, brows raised impatiently, but we couldn't just leave him.

"I will buy this painting," he announced loudly. The vendor stated his price and Dopplemann took out a shabby leather wallet that looked as though he'd owned it for about a hundred years.

"I think you're supposed to bargain," Bordelaise said, but he shook his head.

"The artist works for his living. He sells. I buy. Is a fair price."

With the painting clutched tightly under his arm, seemingly as precious to him as a Rembrandt to a museum, we hurried off again. Around the corner we came across Davis Farrell taking a panoramic photo of the yachts.

"Got to get some pictures, otherwise people will never believe I was here," he said, falling into step with us. "You guys have a good day?"

"Terrific," I said, thinking that the beach and the lovely winey lunch seemed an awfully long time ago.

"Exactly what era is that hairdo?" Bordelaise asked, frowning at his ponytail.

"Late sixties, I'd guess." Davis tweaked his shaggy ponytail. "You mean you don't like it?"

"Let's put it this way: like an old rug, it's seen better days."

We were laughing as, with Dopplemann trailing behind, we boarded our yacht.

"Remember, dinner's at eight-thirty," I reminded them.

Then, oh so casually, I asked, "By the way, has anyone seen Montana around?" No one had.

"That's the first time you've mentioned him since this morning," Bordelaise said. "Not bottling it all up, are you?"

"All what?"

"All that anger you're feeling toward him. It's not good. Anger never achieves anything. Think rationally. Montana wouldn't seduce you then disappear and never want to see you again."

"He didn't seduce me. I seduced him."

"Ah, well . . . I see. . . . Still, the same applies." Bordelaise was trying her best to make me feel better and failing. "No doubt he'll be in the bar at seven-thirty along with the rest of us," she said cheerfully as we parted at my door.

# PART VII

# Day Three. Revelations

*We seldom confide in those*
*who are better than ourselves.*

—ALBERT CAMUS

# 38

## Montana

It was raining in northern France, slicing down sideways, turn-ing the narrow country road into a slick roller-coaster ride. Montana handled the rented Peugeot 460 as smoothly as a rac-ing car, speeding back to the local airport at Tours.

The small town near Le Mans he had just left was a desolate place, made even more desolate by the heavy gray skies and the cold rain. The shuttered dark brick houses offered none of the delights foreigners expect from France, and he had no doubt the inhabitants of the town felt the same way. They probably longed to escape the treeless roads and the flat fields where only turnips and root vegetables grew, and the soulless arcades of the cement mall dominated by the ugly hypermarket that would be called a blot on the landscape if the landscape were not already so terrible.

The name de Valentinois was the clue that had led Montana first to the château area of the Loire and then to a small town near Le Mans. And now he knew all there was to know about Diane.

Driving through the rain, he finally had time to think about Daisy. He'd received a phone call from his second in command at four that morning. There had been no time to lose if he was to take care of events in the Loire, fly on to New York to investigate that scene, and still get back to the ship before it reached Capri. Before it was even light, he'd flown by helicopter to Nice where Bob's Gulfstream was waiting, then to Tours, and now he was to continue on to New York. He hadn't forgotten about Daisy, but there had simply been no time to make contact with her, no time to change from investigator to the lover, no time to think about the right thing to say. All he could do now was call and hope she would understand.

Daisy delighted him, she charmed him, she made him laugh. She was a mischievous minx in a prude's clothing, a seductress, and a hurt and troubled woman who hid her wounds successfully. That is, she had until she met Bob Hardwick. Bob had soon seen through her façade, and now so had Montana.

Arriving at the small airport he gave the rental car to a valet in the private sector and quickly headed toward the plane, stopping on the tarmac to make his call. The plane's engines were revving and the rain was still slicing down. It was difficult to hear but Daisy was not answering her cell phone anyhow.

Checking his watch, Montana guessed the *Blue Boat* had sailed. Daisy was probably at dinner, entertaining the suspects and cursing him for leaving her alone with them.

Even though he'd left her on the yacht with a probable murderer, he knew Daisy was safe for the moment. But if Bob had left her all his money, she would become a target. Meanwhile, the two agents onboard kept constant watch over her; nobody could threaten Daisy without the agents being all over them in a second.

He left a message saying, "I'm here in rainy, lonely northern France without you. You can guess where I'd rather be. I apologize but there was no time to tell you anything, and besides you were sleeping so peacefully it wouldn't have been right to wake you. I'm on my way to New York. I'll call from there. Meanwhile, baby, keep up the good work."

He did not mention the word *love*, or even say a casual "love you." He wasn't sure she would have wanted him to. And anyhow, he never said he loved anybody.

# 39

## *Montana*

The scorched mass of twisted black metal that was all that was left of Bob Hardwick's canary yellow Lamborghini had been uncrated and was up on blocks in the New Jersey garage where Montana had had it transported after the accident. A team of forensics experts hovered over it, examining the pattern of the fractures, poking into the melted morass that had been the engine. Strangely, two things had survived. The frame of the driver's seat was intact, along with its seat belt; and the roll bar was not even dented.

"Odd how these things happen. Sorry it took so long," Len Glazer said. He was the expert who analyzed wrecks of planes and vehicles, applying his science to find out how the accidents happened. "But it was more complicated than it looks. You might almost have thought he could have walked away from this."

Hands thrust in his pockets, Montana stared at the wreckage, thinking, If only he had. But Bob had died and now Len was here to tell him exactly how it had happened.

"We took samples from what remains of the engine and sent them on to the lab. They came back positive for an explosive. There's no doubt that this wreck was caused by a bomb planted directly under the engine. It was ignited by a remote control device—most probably a planted cell phone set on tremble. All the bomber had to do was dial the number. And bingo. Bob should have been blown to bits. But here's what I believe happened. Bob had stopped the car and gotten out to take a leak or stretch his legs. As he walked along the road, someone dialed the planted cell phone's number, the bomb detonated and the car exploded. Bob was caught in the blast and thrown over the edge of the cliff. He wasn't killed directly by the bomb. That's why he wasn't a burned-out piece of wreckage like his car."

"You mean if he'd walked a few yards farther he might still be alive?"

Len nodded. "The cell phone was probably hidden under his seat."

Montana shook his old pal's hand. They'd worked together before and knew each other well. "Thanks, Len. Sorry I can't stop and have a drink with you but I have to get to work." He slapped Len's shoulder, already on his way out the door to where his chief assistant waited at the wheel of a black Ford F-250 twin-cab pickup.

"It's as we thought," Montana said tersely, and he told him what had happened. "What we need to do now," he said, "is check all calls made from the suspects' cell phones on that day."

The assistant threw him a skeptical glance. "That's all, huh?"

Montana grinned. "Hey, you've done it before, man. Let's do it again, even if we have to raid the phone company's offices. But why not start with our suspects' home turf? They're all on-board the *Blue Boat*, so we have a free run. Farrell's offices are right here in New York and his apartment is close by. Dopplemann was here too, staying at a Motel 6 out by the airport. And Charlie Clement was at the Waldorf Towers. Any one of them could have done it."

"So could one of the women. You can dial from abroad y'-know."

Montana nodded. Of course he knew. What he didn't know was which of the women would have been able to find some-one to plant the bomb for her. Still, the old saying "Where there's a will there's a way" applied to murder too. Anything could have happened.

Bob's Lamborghini had been in the shop for a week before the accident and then driven to a parking garage at his office building. There was not enough room to park all three of Bob's cars at his apartment and he often left one or another in the of-fice garage. Whoever had it done it had observed the luggage placed in the car and had known Bob would use the sports car. It would have been easy for someone to enter the garage. It would take less than a minute to plant the explosive and the phone. Death by the second.

Montana heaved a sigh, grieving for what might have been. "You get onto it here," he said. "I'll take care of the European end. And now, old pal, I have a plane to catch."

Bob's Gulfstream was waiting on the tarmac at Teterboro. Montana called and told the pilot to ready it for take off, he would be there in ten. He had solved the first part of the puzzle. It was no longer merely probable . . . it was definitely murder.

# 40

## Daisy

It was the next morning and I was out on the afterdeck taking deep breaths of the pure briny air. We would spend the day at sea en route to Sorrento. The yacht slid so smoothly through the waves I might have been in a hotel on land; the sky was a cloudless blue, the sun was shining and Montana was still not here. I'd checked my phone but there was no message, just some garbled buzzing.

Dinner had been a nightmare last night. Filomena and Diane were not speaking, Charlie Clement never left the bar and Dopplemann disappeared again, only this time he went to his room. Rosalia seemed worried and Hector demanded to know where Montana was, he needed to speak to him. Davis beat Brandon at his own game of backgammon, taking him for a few hundred dollars I knew Brandon couldn't afford and Texas limped around on crutches, downing painkillers and looking miserable. And still Montana hadn't shown up.

"Screw it," Bordelaise had said gloomily, calling for another drink in the bar after dinner. "I'll be glad when this cruise is over." And so, I thought angrily, would I.

Now, though, Bordelaise showed up in a brief pink bikini. I thought she looked really good in it too. She said hi, and I said hi back, still glowering over the suspects and Montana. She took out a book and began to read. I flung myself into the chair next to her and put my hands behind my head, staring up at the sky. It made a change from the sea, though both were the same damn blue.

Bordelaise put down the book—*The Last Time I Saw Paris*—I noted its title. "I guess you haven't heard from him," she said.

"Nope."

"And it bothers you."

"Yup."

"How about a glass of champagne?"

"Too early."

Bordelaise sighed and sat up. "My oh my, but aren't we the spoiled brat? You'd think you were the first woman to have been left by a man. Either give him the benefit of the doubt or just get over it."

I swiveled my eyes indignantly at her. "I thought you were on my side."

"Not when your side is a pain in the neck."

"Oh, thanks!"

"I could have been unladylike and said 'pain in the butt,' but you'll notice I didn't," Bordelaise said.

"You still could. It's true, I know." Suddenly repentant, I

reached out and took her hand. "The truth is I do care. I know I shouldn't, I know it was only meant to be a fling, a quick affair over with in a week probably, but now I'm caught in my own trap. *Me*, Bordelaise, who never wanted to fall for a man again. And when I do—just look what happens. He leaves me without so much as a thank you it was nice knowing you."

"Sometimes that's the way it goes. But my bet is this time it's not. He'll be back."

I picked up her book and riffled through the pages. "What's this about anyway?"

"Man meets woman. Man leaves woman. Woman leaves man. Only it all takes place in Paris and on a drive through France, stopping at romantic little inns and eating up a storm, loving and hating and loving all over again. It's about a woman finding herself, Daisy. You might want to read it."

I threw her a suspicious glance. "Maybe I will. Meanwhile I swore I was never going to eat again, but how about an early lunch?"

With *The Last Time I Saw Paris* tucked under my arm instead of Bordelaise's, we stuffed ourselves with burgers and fries and Cokes and enjoyed the guilt.

At four o'clock I took myself to the spa on the top deck, where I planned to revive my spirits and my looks with a little massage. I bumped into Ginny in the changing room and impulsively gave her a hug, pleased to see a face I could trust. "Hey, how're you doing?"

"Great . . . good . . . ," she said, but she didn't seem too sure. "Do you know where Montana is?" she asked. "I need to talk to him."

It was beginning to seem like everyone needed to talk to Montana. "He left the ship yesterday. I don't know where he went."

Ginny frowned. "It's actually quite urgent."

My ears pricked up. Did she know something? "Can I help? Montana and I are working together for Bob, you know."

She gave me a worried glance from under her spiky black lashes. She seemed about to tell me, then suddenly changed her mind. "No, no, I can't tell you, it wouldn't be right. I have to speak to Montana."

"Okay, then we'll wait for him to get back. I expect he'll show up before we get to Capri." I wished I was as confident about that as I sounded.

"Enjoy your massage, love," I said, falling into the Yorkshire vernacular. "I'm having one too."

Ginny beamed at me, quickly back to her old perky self. "Eh, Daisy luv, you almost sounded Yorkshire yerself then," she said. "It's funny, isn't it," she added, "how you miss it? Even here on this grand yacht, seeing all these lovely places, I keep thinking about Sneadley and how the azaleas'll soon be out in the Hall's grounds and how much we'll miss having the village fete there this year. I love listening to the Old Mills Silver Band play in the twilight afterwards, even though there's no more mills or collieries and the lads in the band are too young to have played when they still existed."

I reassured her that until Sneadley Hall was sold off we would still hold the village fete on its front lawns, then I'd personally inform the new owners of the tradition and get them to agree to carry it on. "So you'll have your fete *and* the silver band

and the coconut shy and the jumble sale, and the jam sponge
cake competition that anyway Mrs. Wainwright always wins.
And I promise I'll come every year just to be there with you all.
*My friends,*" I added, a little teary eyed now.

A short while later, lying on the massage table having the
living daylights thumped out of me by a strong smiling Scandinavian, I was still wondering what Ginny had to say that was
so important and that she could only tell Montana. My massage switched to New Age music, hot stones were placed along
my spine, infusing me with warmth and a feeling of well-
being, and I dozed dreamlessly, my mind for once a blank slate.

Later, I was having a moisturizing facial. I was lying on my
back, my muscles had turned to liquid, my eyes were hidden
under slices of cucumber, and my hair was swathed in a white
towel. Indolence had taken over. I wanted to see no one, go
nowhere—especially to another dinner with the suspects. All I
really wanted was a sandwich in my bathrobe in front of the
TV with Rats on my lap trying to steal bits of it. I wanted so
bad to be back at Sneadley with everything the way it used to
be before I even heard of Harry Montana.

"Daisy."

I shifted a slice of cucumber and saw Filomena hovering
over me, wrapped in a bath towel and nothing else.

"I envy you, Daisy, you look so relaxed," she said.

She looked tired and worried. Something was up.

She gave me a long look, then shrugged the way only an
Italian woman can, shaking back her hair, lifting one graceful
shoulder, tilting her chin over it and looking petulantly down

her nose. "I'm so very tired," she complained. "Exhausted in fact. I never knew a cruise could be so tiring."

"It's all the excitement, I suppose. And all those meals and dressing up. I'm beginning to long for a sandwich in my bathrobe in front of the TV."

Her face lit up and she clapped her hands, endangering the bath towel and her modesty. "Daisy, what a brilliant idea. Why don't we do that? I'll come and have a sandwich with you. I'd so much enjoy that."

Oh my God, I thought, now what have I done! "Well, I don't know, I'm the hostess, I really should be at dinner," I said cautiously.

"Oh, poof to being the hostess. And dinner was torture last night. Let's just ask the girls; the men can take care of themselves for once. Why not, Daisy? It'll be fun."

She was so eager for me to say yes, I gave in, and we set a time of seven-thirty in my suite, in our bathrobes, and no makeup. "But I have to ask Diane," I warned.

"Oh, poof to Diane." She tossed her hair. "I don't have to speak to her."

"Okay them, I'll arrange it," I said.

## 41

## Daisy

To my surprise all the women came, all in their white waffle-cotton bathrobes *and* without makeup—well, except perhaps for a hint of blusher and definitely eyebrow pencil (Diane) and a bronze glow (Filomena). Other than that, we were pretty much as God made us, plus a few years. Rosalia surprised me by showing up with Magdalena and little Bella, who we planted in front of the TV with a Disney video on low and a slice of pizza—her favorite food. She looked so adorable in baby blue pajamas that for a minute I thought longingly of what I'd missed by not having a child.

Texas hobbled in on her crutches, looking even more lovely with a naked face. Ginny came, scrubbed and pink-cheeked, yellow hair tied up on top with a red ribbon, buxom in her white robe and looking not unlike a Kewpie doll on top of the Christmas tree. Diane had let her long, flame red hair fall free and appeared years younger, except for her eyes. They had a world-weary look that not even the thought of a ham sandwich could take away.

She pointedly ignored Filomena, who looked like Bardot in the early years, blond hair in a ponytail, a poster girl for a Mediterranean beach. Bordelaise looked about sixteen, and I— Well, I guess I just looked haggard.

I hadn't had a pajama party since I was a kid—long enough ago to be a distant memory. But anyhow, here onboard *Blue Boat*, things were different. One waiter poured chilled rosé while another served delicious hors d'oeuvres. There were platters of sandwiches—ham and cheese, egg salad, tuna salad, BLT, Italian sausage . . . When you asked for sandwiches on *Blue Boat*, you got *sandwiches*, and we fell on them with such cries of delight you'd have thought we hadn't eaten in a week.

We moved out onto the deck to watch the sunset, sprawling in lounge chairs, plates on our laps, glasses of wine by our sides. Ginny came and perched at the foot of Diane's chair and Diane gave her a long look then took a Handi Wipe from her bag and pointedly cleaned off the chair. Filomena was sitting as far as possible from Diane. She'd piled her plate with sandwiches and was eating ravenously. Texas said she loved Serrano ham and just nibbled on that and some cheese with no bread, which I said must be how she kept her lovely figure.

"Sometimes that, sometimes it's involuntary starvation," Texas replied.

Filomena looked up from her plate. "Involuntary? What do you mean?"

Texas shrugged. "Sometimes work is hard to come by, money is short, and I don't have enough for much more than a McDonald's ninety-nine-cent burger. If that."

Silenced, we stared guiltily at our piled plates. "I know what you mean," Rosalia said gently. "I was poor when I was young and I had three children to feed." She smiled as she looked at Magdalena, who was in the cabin, sitting on the floor watching the video with Bella. "It's lucky children don't really under-stand that they are poor. Where we lived, everyone was the same, it was just the way life was. They all ate the same things, rice and the half-spoiled vegetables given away at the end of the market, with perhaps a bone from the butcher to make a soup." She smiled. "That's where I really learned my cooking skills, making the most out of what little we had."

I stared at her, baffled. This was Bob Hardwick's woman, *his love*! All she would have had to do was call and Bob would have given her everything she needed. Anything she *wanted*. Even to the end of his days he would have done that. I remembered the packet of letters tucked into the wall safe in my room and decided to get her alone later and return them. One thing I knew for sure: this woman had not murdered Bob.

"I grew up poor as well," Filomena said from the corner by the deck rail where she was sitting. "Papa was the local baker so we never lacked for food, but there was never enough money for Mama to buy pretty new clothes and nice shoes." She sighed. "Maybe that's why I have a cupboard full of them, some I've never even worn." She gave that Italian shrug again. "When I see pretty shoes I have to have them, I just can't resist."

"Freud would give you full marks for that analysis," Diane said nastily.

Filomena's eyes flashed. "So what's your background then, Diane? Come on, tell the truth now, it's just us girls together."

Diane leveled a hard stare at her then looked around at the rest of us, perched on the edges of our chairs, waiting for what she was going to say.

"Of course I was fortunate enough to be born into a noble family," she said proudly. "I was an only child, and my parents spoiled me, but . . ." She heaved a theatrical sigh. "I wanted more than life in a château, the debutante balls, the parties. I wanted to be a movie actress like Catherine Deneuve, or a singer living a bohemian life with a lover in Paris, a Jane Birkin. . . . But then I met Bob Hardwick and he fell madly in love with me." Balancing her glass on her plate, she shifted her glance to Filomena. "*I* was the love of Bob's life, you know. He was devastated when I left him." She heaved another sigh and I thought what a bad actress she would have made. "But I could no longer stand being merely the chattel of a rich man."

"And so what did you become when you left him?" Filomena's pearly little cat teeth gleamed in a wicked smile. "A famous actress? A singer like Jane Birkin? The wife of another rich man? Or just a divorced woman with a gambling problem?"

Out of the calm cobalt blue night an angry gust of wind suddenly slammed into the deck, sending Diane's glass flying and spilling wine all over her. The wind died as quickly as it had come and Diane gasped. Alarmed, she took her Handi Wipes from her bag and dabbed at the mess. "Is there going to be a storm?" she asked, but the sea was calm and the evening sky a clear blue.

I summoned a steward to clean the mess, poured more wine and handed around the sandwiches. Everyone took at least two more. "Well after all they are small," Bordelaise said, excusing herself with a grin. I could tell she was enjoying herself.

"The trouble is," Filomena said, looking sad, "I don't know if I'll get that lucky again. I don't know if I'll ever meet another rich man like Bob."

I couldn't help asking if that was what she wanted, to find another rich man to look after her.

"It's all I know how to do," she said simply. "Be the girl-friend of a rich man. I was nineteen when I met Bob. I never went to college, never had a job, never had the chance to learn how to do anything else. All I know is clothes and shopping and jewelry. You've no idea how much I regret those wasted years."

"With your looks you could have been a movie star," Bordelaise said, but Filomena shook her head.

"I'm a klutz in front of a camera. 'Hopeless' one director called me when I auditioned for him." She frowned. "I thought that was a little unkind."

We agreed it was, all except Diane, who drank more wine, staring balefully at her rival.

"I can't believe you two," Ginny said. "You have everything: looks, glamorous lives in glamorous places, opportunity. All I had was a simple life in a Yorkshire village, but I'm beginning to think you should envy *me*. I had a lovely childhood; we had pigs in our field and a rough-and-tumble pony in the shed behind Dad's greenhouses. We had a couple of dogs that slept on the sofa, and a few black cats that shed all over everything. The house was too small and it was always a mess and my brothers and sisters were always fighting, but they smacked up the school bully when she started on me and told her never to do it again—or else. I've never taken money from a man, and I've never been married, but not for the want of the askin', and it was my choice. I'll know when I meet Mr. Right, and if I don't, well, I'll always be Ginny Bunn, the best barmaid Sneadley's Ram's Head's ever had."

Rosalia, who'd managed to follow most of this, said, "*Bravo*, Ginny, you're right to love who you are and what you are. It's the way a woman should feel about herself. What a pity more of us don't," she added. "You shouldn't underestimate yourself, Filomena. You're beautiful and you're still young, but those aren't your only assets."

Filomena had let her guard down. I knew she felt inadequate and thought she had nothing to offer, and quite suddenly I felt sorry for her. I was sure she hadn't killed Bob, no matter how desperate she was for the money.

Magdalena came and said it was time Bella was in bed. I kissed her good night, and with a final wink from Bella, they departed. I caught Rosalia before she left, though. I took the manila envelope from the safe and handed it to her. She looked at the packet of letters.

"You'll never know how hard it was for me to send them back," she said. "I don't blame Bob, I never have. A man should follow the path he's chosen. But then, my dear Daisy, so should a woman."

I waited hopefully for her to say more, but with the letters clutched to her breast and tears glistening in her eyes, she kissed me on either cheek. "Thank you for taking such good care of Roberto in his last years," she murmured as she left. "I know he must have loved you too."

# 42

## Daisy

Ginny peeked into the bedroom and seeing I was alone, she said, "I can't keep this thing to myself any longer. I was going to tell Montana but I'm bursting with it. I just can't go on looking at that man any longer, knowing what I know about him." Her mouth tightened and her eyes flashed angrily. "The bastard," she snarled.

"Who?"

"Charles Clement. Charlie everybody calls him, as though it makes him nicer."

I sat down on the bed and patted the space next to me. "Come, sit here, Ginny, and tell me all about it."

"It's really Mrs. Wainwright's story, not mine," she said, "but everybody in the village knew about it. You know how Bob was, always inviting folk to the Hall. Some weekends it was just men."

"I remember. I'd make all the arrangements then go back down to London and leave them to their boyish devices."

"Hah, boyish!" Ginny said bitterly. "So Bob invites this Charlie Clement a couple of times, for the shooting and the like. Then another time Charlie brings a girl with him. Mrs. Wainwright was in the hall when they arrived, and Charlie introduced the girl. Mrs. W said she could see Bob disapproved, he thought she was too young, and so did she. Well, you know Mrs. W, she's a bit of a nosey-parker, and later she asked the girl how old she was. She told her she was eighteen but Mrs. W didn't believe her.

"Oh, God, Ginny," I said, "you're telling me she was underage?"

Ginny nodded. "She mentioned it to Bob and he took the girl aside, asked what she was doing. She cried and said she wasn't a prostitute, she only did this with men like Charlie who liked schoolgirls, and that he paid good money. Then she admitted she was only thirteen."

"Oh . . . my . . . God . . ."

"Bob went berserk. He punched Charlie, knocked him flat right in front of the girl, and she just stood there, giggling like a child. Mrs. W said she'd never felt so sorry for anyone in her life. And she heard Charlie Clement vow to get back at Bob. 'Don't think I'm alone in this,' Charlie said in a nasty tone of voice. 'You're only like the rest of us, Bob Hardwick.' So Bob hit him again, and this time he knocked him out.

"Bob had Charlie's things packed in minutes, and he was driven off to the station sporting a big black eye and no doubt with a bad headache. I believe Bob found out where the girl came from, her home I mean, not where she'd been living in London. Mrs. W said he drove her back there and talked to her parents, and she thinks he offered to help them.

"She also said she got the distinct impression Charlie Clement had brought the girl as a sort of gift for Bob. Can you just imagine such a thing?" Ginny added.

I shook my head. Now I understood why Charlie might have misled Bob. He wanted revenge.

I promised to tell Montana when he got back, and just then Texas limped into the bedroom. "We thought we might go to the bar," she said cheerfully. "Maybe I'll even sing for you tonight."

Ginny perked up, thrilled. "Then I'm off to get dressed," she said. "Can't go to that posh bar in my dressing gown, now can I?"

I showed my guests out, powdered my nose, put on some lipstick and slipped into my old "uniform" of black pants, black top, black ballet flats.

Bob was right; the suspects were beginning to reveal themselves. It was like peeling away the skins of an onion until at the heart we would find the truth.

In the bar, I saw that Texas had also slipped into a "little something" but hers was a little something glamorous: a cool gray chiffon that flashed silver when she moved. Leaning against the black baby grand, she sang silky sultry songs about love and broken hearts: "Smoke Gets in Your Eyes," "My Funny Valentine," "Spring Is Here." And, finally, "Body and Soul." It seemed a fitting way to end the evening.

# 43

## Dopplemann

It was late, and everyone had left the bar except Dopplemann.
Alone in the dark and the silence, with only the soft throbbing
of the engines as the yacht slid through the waves making for
Sorrento by early morning, he wondered again why Bob Hardwick had invited him on his "farewell" cruise, especially since
he'd recently made the tremendous effort and returned to New
York with the intention of having things out with him. But
Bob had refused to see him. "Sir Robert is busy," an assistant
had informed him. "He'll be in meetings all day."

Dopplemann had said he would wait. "Sir Robert will be in
meetings far into the night," the male assistant had said curtly.
He obviously didn't know who Dopplemann was, but then
Dopplemann had been gone a long time.

He didn't know if the man had even bothered to tell Bob he
was there; to him he was just an eccentric shabby man who

looked like nothing. A man who *was* nothing, thanks, of course, to Bob.

He heard a woman's footsteps and glanced nervously up. She hesitated, peering into the dark as though looking for somebody; then she took a step forward and the light caught her. It was Daisy.

Dopplemann shrank back into his dark corner. She didn't see him and went and knelt on a sofa by the window. She rested her head on her arms, gazing out at the nighttime sea.

"Daisy," he said quietly. She swung around.

"Oh my God," she whispered, sounding scared. "Herr Dopplemann."

"I'm sorry I startled you," he said. "And please, my name is Marius. It was given to me by my mother after a great deal of argument. My father complained it was too romantic; he said it was a name for composers and artists, not for men like us. Anyhow, 'Mutti' prevailed and Marius I became, though for most of my life I seem to have been addressed by my patrimonial name."

She was staring at him, eyes bugging.

"I couldn't sleep," he said. "And I assume neither could you." Uninvited, he sat on the sofa next to her and felt her shrink from him. "Is something troubling you?" he asked gently.

"No. . . . Well, yes. . . . Many things. . . . Bob . . ."

He clicked his tongue sympathetically. "It's distressing to celebrate someone's death, but isn't it what Bob himself wished?"

Daisy slumped into the sofa cushions. She turned to look at him. "There's more than just that . . ."

"Do you wish to tell me?"

Daisy was puzzled. Dopplemann was acting like a human being. Maybe it was because they were alone in the dark in the middle of the sea, cut off from reality. She decided to play him along.

"Herr Dopplemann . . ."

"Marius," he corrected her.

"Marius," she said, "have you ever been in love?"

"Yes, I've been in love. It was the most painful time of my life."

"But *why* was it so painful?"

Dopplemann took off his glasses and with his usual nervous gesture, began to polish them with the soft cloth he kept in his jacket pocket. "Because she betrayed me." He put the glasses back on and surprisingly, he smiled at her. "Women are like that sometimes, so I've heard. Her name was Magali, and she was Hungarian. They're a passionate race, you know, always making war or making love, whichever is more important at the moment." He shrugged. "I asked her to marry me. I was crazy with love, ready to give her every penny I had, everything I owned. But when she asked for what she really wanted, I told her the price was too high, I couldn't do it. She begged, she threatened, she cajoled. She promised to marry me the next day if I gave her what she'd asked for. 'You'll be rich for life,' she told me, but I told her riches were not what I wanted."

He took off his glasses again and polished them agitatedly. "Of course, I should have realized that she was working for a foreign power and that all she really wanted was my knowledge. They wanted me to spy for them. To trade America's secrets." Dopplemann paused. "And in return I would get the woman I wanted."

He put the glasses back on. He was twisting his hands together so tightly the veins popped. "Bob had always kept a friendly eye on me; he said he didn't think I was a practical man, I was too caught up in my scientific daydreams. He'd met Magali, and like everyone, he wondered why a shrewd, beautiful woman of the world was courting me." He shrugged again. "Magali arranged a rendezvous with an agent in a park in Washington. Somehow Bob got to know about it. He followed me, guessed what was going on.

"'Scum,' he called me. 'This country has been bloody good to you,' he said, 'and now you'll turn her in for a cheap woman who's got you wrapped around her little finger and doesn't give a shit about you, a woman who'll dump you as soon as she's got what she wants. You're a brilliant scientist,' he told me, 'but you're an idiot. Any man who'll contemplate selling out the country that gave him every accolade, every chance . . . is no friend of mine. And I'll see that you are no friend of anyone else's.'"

From behind the glasses, Dopplemann's glassy green eyes met Daisy's stunned ones. "Because I had not actually committed the crime, Bob gave me an option. Leave immediately and he would say nothing. Make some excuse, he said, health, family . . . anything. Just leave. If not, he would turn me in to the FBI."

"So of course you left," Daisy said, breathing a sigh of relief.

Dopplemann lifted his empty eyes to Daisy's. "I asked Magali to come with me. She laughed at me, said I was worthless, that she had no use for me anymore, no one had, and I was as good as dead. I've prayed many times over these past years to find it in my heart to forgive her, and to forgive Bob, because between them they ruined my life. Bob could have overlooked it, he could have let me stay, let me do the job I'm trained for. After all, I was the best in the world . . ."

"So you've never forgiven him." Daisy understood now what Dopplemann's motive for murder was.

"I had been the best. Now, because of Bob, I was nobody. It's impossible to forgive that." Dopplemann got to his feet. He pulled at his jacket, straightened his tie, coughing nervously as he once again adjusted his glasses. "I've never spoken about this to anyone. It's been a long time inside me, but here, on the ship, away from everything, and because you knew Bob so well, I found I could talk to you."

Daisy scrambled to her feet. "Thank you for confiding in me," she said, suddenly frightened again. Desperate to get away, she almost ran to the door, but he followed her. "I won't wait for the elevator," she said, making a dash for the stairs. "Good night, Herr Dopplemann."

"Marius," she heard him correct her as she ran up the stairs and back to the safety of her cabin.

She locked the door and stood with her back against it, breathing heavily. She didn't know how she'd managed to sit there with a murderer while he poured his heart out about his lost love and about how Bob had betrayed him. *Dopplemann was truly crazy.*

She sat on the edge of the bed, kicked off her shoes and sank back against the pillows. A red light blinked on the phone. A message! It had to be from Montana. She grabbed the phone, but it was only Texas asking her to call her first thing in the morning, she had something important to tell her about Charlie Clement.

Daisy thought it would never end. It was just as Bob had said in his letter to her. All the suspects were beginning to reveal their true selves. And their motives for murder.

# PART VIII

# Day Four.
# Sorrento and Capri
# Before the Storm.

*A man cannot be too careful*
*in the choice of his enemies.*

—OSCAR WILDE,
THE PICTURE OF DORIAN GRAY

# 44

## Montana

Montana was on his third espresso at a café at the marina in Sorrento when, like a summer mirage, *Blue Boat* appeared on the horizon. He felt like hell and was desperate for a good night's sleep. Rubbing a weary hand across his stubbled jaw, he wondered if Daisy would be glad to see him or if she was so pissed off by now she'd give him the ice treatment women were so good at.

Daisy had been on his mind a lot on those long flights on Bob Hardwick's Gulfstream jet, cocooned at thirty thousand feet in silver-gray leather, ears buzzing from too much plane travel in too short a time. He was beyond eating, beyond sleeping; he'd simply covered his eyes with a mask and tried to relax, getting up every now and again to pace. And to think.

He had most of the pieces of the puzzle together now, and the answers were surprising, as was the motive for the murder. He didn't yet have sufficient proof to accuse the killer, but back in New York at his high-tech headquarters, which these days was where a great part of investigations took place, men were working on it. They were checking computers for documents, financial statements, real estate transactions, birth certificates, identifications and prison records. Right now, Montana thought life was full of surprises, some of which came at you from left field.

He watched *Blue Boat* put down her anchor. He could see some of her passengers lining the rails, gazing at the pale golden cliffs of Sorrento, getting their first whiff of the aromatic scent of lemon and orange trees. Vineyards sprawled over the hills and rococo Belle Époque hotels perched on the very edges of the cliffs. Brightly colored fishing boats chugged into port, bringing in their catch, promising good fresh seafood for lunch, and hanging over the marina was an excited buzz of rapid-fire Italian.

At any other time, Montana would have been charmed by this, but right now he had Daisy on his mind. Today he was going to put her first, make up to her for deserting her without explanation. He hoped she'd gotten his phone message and understood, but he wasn't betting on it.

A Chris-Craft emerged from the tank deck, and some of the passengers climbed into it. He punched in Daisy's number.

"That you?" he said when she answered.

"Shouldn't I be asking that question?" Her voice was frigid as an igloo in winter.

"You should. But do you really want to know the answer?"

"It's a matter of complete indifference to me."

"On a business or a personal level?"

There was a silence, then she said, "I'm working for Bob, so I'll discuss business with you. The personal level does not exist between us."

"What if I apologized and said it was unavoidable?"

"I don't need apologies," she said abruptly. "I need to talk to you. There's a lot going on here you need to know about."

"I'm at the marina waiting for you," he said, and she rang off.

He paced the quai, hands thrust in his pockets. Things did not bode well. He'd have given anything not to have hurt Daisy but he'd had no choice. And he would not allow a woman to come in the way of his work. Work came first and it always would.

# 45

*Daisy*

I climbed into the tender and we set off for the quai. Bordelaise was coming along as my reinforcement. I knew Montana couldn't say anything too personal in front of her, and anyhow, I wasn't going to allow him to apologize. Men seemed to think they could get away with anything and I was about to prove that at least this one could not. From now on it would be all business.

I spotted him waiting on the jetty. Damn it, he looked good. I wondered again where he'd gotten the suntan—not from chasing killers across continents, I knew that. I choked back a sigh. From now on it was all business, and besides, my mind was so stuffed with information on the suspects, I had no choice but to speak to him.

"Doesn't he melt your heart, even just a little?" Bordelaise murmured in my ear as we disembarked and he came toward us.

"No," I lied, but I couldn't fool my oldest friend. I arranged a cool smile on my face for Montana's benefit, but my heart was thumping and I was dying inside. When he took my hand, it was like an electric shock and my cool attitude melted instantly.

"How are you?" I said, snatching my hand back.

"Better, now I've seen you." He looked me over. "You look tired, though."

I shrugged. "Couldn't sleep. And neither could Dopplemann. We met up in the empty bar at two A.M."

His smile disappeared. "What were you doing out alone at that time in the morning?"

I gaped at him. "I told you, I couldn't sleep so I got up and took a walk—"

"Jesus." He let go of me. "You must have fooled the agents keeping an eye on you. They'd have assumed you'd gone to bed and that was that."

"So much for professional surveillance tactics," Bordelaise said. "And hello to you too, Harry, how are you?"

He turned to her. "Good to see you, Bordelaise. How are you enjoying the cruise?"

"So far, it's terrific. You wouldn't believe the undercurrents and the plotting and planning, to say nothing of the confessions and then those late-night confrontations in the bar."

Montana hailed a taxi, and we climbed in and headed up the steep hill into town, to the Albergo Lorelei et Londres, which he said had the best view in all of Sorrento.

I didn't bother to ask how Montana knew that. He was the kind of man you could put in any town in the world and he'd know the best places to go. And he wasn't wrong about the tiny nineteenth-century inn, with its terrace overhanging the infinite blue of the Bay of Naples with a view of the isle of Capri on the horizon and of Vesuvius to the north. The inn was swagged in purple bougainvillea with lemon trees in pots and tables under shady red awnings. There was a bustle of laughter and talk and everyone but me seemed to be having a good time.

We took a table under the red awning where the sweet sea breeze lifted my hair and my mood and I began to feel a little better. Suffering from an overkill of cosmos and champagne, I ordered Pellegrino with lemon, while Bordelaise and Montana had Peroni beers. A platter of *calamari fritti* was brought, still sizzling from the pan, with a bowl of lemony aioli to dip them in. We picked silently at them and after a while I relaxed. I wasn't ready to forgive Montana, but at least now I could look him in the eye without wanting to kill him.

"Want me to start, or do you want to tell me *your* news first?" he asked.

"You go first." I popped another aioli-laden calamari into my mouth. At this rate I was going home ten pounds heavier but who cared?

"I'm sorry I left you so abruptly, but I got a call at four in the morning. You were fast asleep. I didn't want to wake you."

I held up my hand for him to stop. "This meeting is purely business."

"Okay. The call was from my assistant in New York. We had a forensics team working on Bob's car and they'd come up with some interesting conclusions."

I took another calamari, and he leaned across the table and put his hand on mine. "*Listen,* Daisy," he said, "this is *important.*" And then he told me how Bob died.

In the hot sun of Sorrento I turned to ice. I looked at Bordelaise's shocked eyes, then back at Montana.

He said, "I'm sorry," and stroked my cold hands.

Anger flared. I was ready to personally strangle the killer; he'd taken Bob away from me, taken a good man's life while his own despicable life went on. "Of course it's Dopplemann," I said. "He told me last night how he felt about Bob." I filled Montana in. "So you see," I said, "revenge was Dopplemann's motive. It *was* him, I *know* it."

"We'll have to wait until I have positive proof," Montana warned.

"Then what about Charlie Clement?" Bordelaise asked.

I'd brought her up-to-date on Ginny's story about Charlie, and now I told Montana about Texas's having seen him at the notorious École de Nuit. She'd been working in Paris a while ago and had gone to a club with a man she'd met, an "exclusive" club, he'd told her. It turned out to be one of those anything goes places: sex for anyone who wanted it any way they wanted it, even with children. The guy she was with told her it was Charlie Clement's place and pointed him out to her. She had left immediately when she saw what kind of place it was, but it was Charlie's club, all right.

"So Bob was right," Montana said, "and they are all showing their true colors."

"Rosalia's the only one who doesn't care what's in Bob's will," I said. "She doesn't want anything from him, she never has."

"I wonder," Montana said thoughtfully.

Bordelaise waved at someone at another table. "Got to go," she said, grabbing her bag.

I saw Captain Anders get to his feet as she walked toward him. They looked pleased as Punch with each other.

"Bordelaise is back on form," I said, smiling.

Montana must have mistaken the smile for a chink in my armor because he said, "And what about us, Daisy? Are we to go on fighting about nothing?"

*"Nothing!"* My cheeks were hot with indignation. "I fall asleep with a man next to me. Next morning he's gone and no explanation. That's *nothing*?"

"Of course it's not, but there's a reasonable explanation. Besides, I called and left you a message. Didn't you get it?"

I stared at him. "What message?"

"Do you want to hear it?"

Looking at his anxious face, I thought if I kept on pouting and said no he might leave and I didn't want him to do that. "Okay. Go on then, tell me," I said sulkily.

"So what do you think?" he said when he'd finished his explanation.

I got to my feet and gave him a long look. Without another word he took my arm and led me down to the marina, onto the tender and back to *Blue Boat*.

Everyone was ashore and the ship was quiet. My suite was cool; the air-conditioning purred and the curtains were drawn against the afternoon sun. I tossed my bag onto a chair and walked to the bedroom. I turned and beckoned him.

"Come here, Montana," I said. And to his credit, he walked, laughing, into my open arms.

It wasn't a repeat performance, it was a whole new scenario. His kisses were more tender, mine more demanding. His hands felt new to me, his lips hot and familiar. His body fitted mine, his caresses made me tremble and his mouth made me beg for more. I wanted Harry Montana more than I ever knew I could want a man. And Harry Montana fulfilled every one of my needs.

We were still in bed at seven o'clock that evening, showered and naked. "Just catching our breath," he said, nuzzling my neck.

I moaned, burying my face in his chest hair and taking little bites. "I can't face the suspects tonight. I don't want to think about murder and money and who did it. Can't we just stay here, be alone?" I begged.

At the back of my mind I was thinking this might be all there was for us: tonight and no more. You never knew with a man like Montana; never knew when he might disappear again, and this time for keeps. I wanted all I could get of him. Now.

"Then let's not see them," he said, surprising me. "We'll send for room service."

"But then you'll have to hide in the bathroom," I objected.

"Do you really think they'll believe you're going to eat *two* dinners? Come on, Daisy, get real, nobody cares except you and me."

I gave him a cautious sideways glance. "And *do* you care?"

"Yes," he said, suddenly serious. "I care about you, Daisy."

He hadn't said "I love you," but for now I was content. This wasn't just a brief sexual fling; I was with a man I was growing to care deeply about, a man who cared about me.

"Let's send for that room service," I said, beaming.

# PART IX

## Day Five.
## The Villa Belkiss.
## The Reading of
## the Will.
## Time for the Truth.

*We owe respect to the living;*
*to the dead we only owe the truth.*

—Voltaire

# 46

## Daisy

It was early the next morning, and Montana was on the veranda sipping a cup of coffee. "Come on out here, Daisy," he called.

Still in bed, I yawned lazily and gave a long luxurious stretch. My body felt as relaxed and supple as a kitten's. "No, you come back here," I answered, thinking that making love in the morning might be even nicer than at night. But instead he came and hauled me up by my arms and led me to the ship's rail.

"Look," he commanded.

The island of Capri rose in front of us, a tiny jewel on the sapphire sea. The little town was a tangle of brilliant blossoms and greenery studded with white houses. It lay between a pair of towering limestone cliffs where small boats puttered and caves and grottoes lurked and giant rocks sprouted from the depths. I recalled the legend about the Roman emperor Tiberius, who so loved the island he built a villa there and refused ever to return to Rome. Looking at the scene before us, I could understand why.

Naked and with Montana's arm around me, I leaned my elbows on the rail. I wished that we were just a pair of ordinary tourists ready to explore the beauty Capri had to offer and that today did not have to happen.

Montana guessed my thoughts and said, "Maybe one day we'll come back again."

Knowing his busy life, I wasn't betting on it. Deciding I'd better make the most of the time I had, I took his hand and led him back to bed. For now, our date with destiny in Capri could wait.

A couple of hours later we emerged on deck. We took the tender to the Marina Grande and rode the funicular up to the Piazzetta, the little square and the hub of Capri town, ringed with pretty cafés and boutiques and dominated by a tall clock tower with a beautifully decorated majolica face. The hands on the clock pointed to noon. Our rendezvous was at two o'clock at the Villa Belkiss. We had a couple of precious hours to ourselves.

Hand in hand we strolled the cobbled streets, stopping to peer into the tiny boutique where the famous Capri sandals were handmade, and at the jewelry stores and the fashion boutiques. Tempted by the aromas coming from the Ristorante Pizzeria Aurora on the Via Fuorlovado, we sat on the terrace sipping fortifying glasses of red wine and watching the Caprese world go by, sharing a *pizza all'acqua,* topped with mozzarella and *peperoncino* chilies in the Neapolitan style. Heaven on a thin crust.

I was enjoying myself so much I almost forgot why we were here, but then Montana's cell phone beeped. He answered quickly. A look of concern crossed his face and he ran a hand over his stubbly dark head.

"Are you sure?" he asked finally. Then he nodded. "Okay. Right. Got it."

He rang off and his eyes met my anxious ones. He said nothing, but I guessed he knew who the killer was.

*"Tell me,"* I demanded.

"You'll know soon enough" was all he would say.

I slugged down the last of my wine and called for another, but Montana ordered espressos instead.

"You'll need to keep your wits about you," he warned. "There'll be a couple of guards at the door, but they'll be unarmed. I can't take a risk of weapons with all those people in the room. You'll be safe, don't worry."

I nodded, wishing Bob hadn't set this up but if he hadn't then I wouldn't have met Montana. I guessed I had to take the good with the bad.

We strolled slowly up the beautiful Via Tragara, peering at the intriguing arched stone stairways set between the pale stucco buildings, and at villas behind tall iron gates, flanked with giant oleanders like bridal bouquets. The lane was bordered with high garden walls and the sounds of summer were all around us: the chatter of the birds, the crackle of crickets, the hum of dragonflies. Sunlight sparkled in diamond points off the sea, slicing through trellises dripping with vines and anointing the bunches of small, tight, opalescent green grapes, beating down as we turned gratefully in to a narrow shady lane that led up the hill. At the end was a high white wall and a pair of massive blue wooden gates. A tiled plaque with the name THE VILLA BELKISS was set into the wall.

Montana gave me a long look as he rang the bell. We were finally here.

## 47

## Daisy

A white-jacketed servant, an older man with a wrinkled walnut brown face and dark hair sprinkled with gray, flung open the gates.

"Welcome to the Villa Belkiss. I am Enrico," he said. "I worked for the Signore Vassily for almost twenty years. Signorina, Signore, the Villa Belkiss welcomes you. Refreshments are waiting. Please come in."

We stepped into a courtyard. Twin bluish gray pools bordered the sides, lit with the flash of small golden fish. The path between led to broad steps with risers tiled in blue and turquoise. Narrow columns flanked the portico, and the front door stood open. Beyond it I could see a great room running the full width of the house. And beyond that, through open French doors, was the sea.

The ceiling soared two stories high and its wide beams were painted a soft blue. A mezzanine jutted over one end, and the terra-cotta floors were studded with cobalt blue stars. The white walls were hung with old silver mirrors and muted artworks, and there were white sofas deep enough to sink into.

Lured by the view, as everyone who ever came here must have been, Montana and I walked out onto the terrace. An infinity pool seemed to spill into the horizon, and a narrow waterfall cascaded from above us into a lower deep green pool, where the sea surged over the rocks. Under a vine-covered pergola was a long wooden table, the perfect place to dine on a hot summer night, and comfortable chairs were grouped around a large outdoor fireplace. Another blue wooden door set in the garden wall led out onto the rugged limestone cliffs, but in the Villa Belkiss's garden, all was soft and gentle.

Roses and honeysuckle, bougainvillea and hibiscus, morning glory and jasmine climbed trellises and flowed over the low stucco walls. There was the murmur of the brook and trickle of the waterfall, and the cooing of doves and the soft hum of cicadas.

"It's so peaceful," I whispered to Montana. "So tranquil. Did you know that Vassily designed it himself?" I added.

Vassily was the son of a Russian mother and a Turkish father, famous for the ethereal lightness of his dancing and his ability to lift prima ballerinas like feathers. When he first found the villa, it was a mere two-bedroom, flat-roofed, whitewashed cube surrounded by scrubland, but it had the magical view, and of course he fell in love with it. He spent years designing the house and its gardens, and when it was finished he gave lavish parties with musicians on the terrace or the mezzanine, to which all the European haut monde came. He served lobster and champagne and caviar, as well as the local flinty white wine he was fond of, and later he would dance for his guests.

He brought all his lovers here, men as well as women, because that was how he was. Then when he was old—well, old for a ballet dancer—around fifty—he wrote the tell-all autobiography that scandalized the world and lost him a great many friends, and he returned to live here in near seclusion with the dog he adored.

He had the blue door carved into the garden wall so he could walk the dog on the cliffs. He knew those cliffs like the back of his own hand, knew where all the dangerous fissures and indents were, hidden by the scrub grass.

"He died right on this terrace," I told Montana. "Sitting in his favorite chair with his dog by his side, sipping his favorite white wine and looking out at his favorite view."

My eyes met Montana's and I knew we were both thinking of Bob and how much better it would have been for him to die peacefully here, like Vassily.

Enrico appeared with glasses of iced tea and the little almond cakes he said were the specialty of the villa. I checked my watch. It was almost two o'clock.

# 48

## Daisy

Dark clouds were gathering on the horizon as the murder suspects straggled into the courtyard, looking like any other bunch of tourists in shorts and skirts and sandals, sunglasses and straw hats. As usual, Davis had a camera slung around his neck, and Dopplemann was carrying the expensive pair of binoculars, bought, I assumed with Bob's money, somewhere on this trip.

Charlie Clement stalked in wearing the wraparound shades that conveniently hid his eyes. Magdalena had left Bella aboard the *Blue Boat* with her nanny and come with Rosalia and Hector, dapper as always in a white jacket, his hair groomed to within an inch of its life.

Diane wore black, to suit her "widow" image and was put out at having to walk, while Filomena strode in, glamorous as a showgirl in short shorts, newly purchased Capri sandals and a skimpy halter top. She was with Brandon, of course, while

Bordelaise, ever the cheerleader in a suntan, shorts and a white tee, was with Texas, exquisite as always in a plain cotton shift. A wind rattled the trees, sending Dopplemann's Panana spinning along the terrace and he scrambled quickly after it, looking like an ungainly stick insect in his shorts.

Reg and Ginny exclaimed admiringly about the villa, drifting out onto the terrace for the view. Reg said he'd never in his life seen anything like it, and he thanked Bob out loud for inviting him because he could have gone through life not knowing places like this existed. Ginny talked to Enrico, who was offering glasses of the famous flinty white wine or cold beer, iced tea or Pellegrino. The old man seemed pleased with all the activity, happy to see the villa come to life again I supposed. Of course, he was completely unaware of the real reason we were here.

Across the bay, the dark clouds piled closer and in the distance thunder rumbled. I caught Montana's eye and he nodded. It was time. I got everyone in the great room, arranging the suspects on the first row of chairs in front of the grand ebony desk where Montana stood, with the red herrings in the row behind.

My work done, I went to sit behind the desk next to Montana. A clap of thunder shattered the expectant silence and the women glanced nervously at each other.

I thought the scene was exactly as Bob had outlined it in his letter to me: the country house, the impending storm, the suspects all gathered, waiting for the will to be read.

The women crossed their legs, put their purses on the floor next to them, smoothed their linen skirts, hitched down their shorts and folded their hands on their knees. The men leaned back in their chairs, arms across their chests, looking, I thought, aggressive, except for Dopplemann, who sank into his oversized chair looking like the White Rabbit caught in Alice's Wonderland. Charlie snapped his fingers at Enrico for another drink and Davis stared straight ahead at Montana.

There were a few nervous coughs as Montana picked up his file of papers and told them Bob's will was in the form of letters, one to each of them.

And then he began to read.

# 49

*Sir Robert Hardwick's Will*

*"Friends,"* Bob began his first letter,

*"If I may still call you that. I hope you've enjoyed my cruise and that you celebrated my life as though you really meant it. But what we are here for now is to find out which one of you killed me."*

Shocked indrawn breaths hissed around the room and everyone glanced nervously at everyone else.

*"Before we get to that, though, I want to remind you that it's not often anyone gets a second chance in life, yet today I'm offering each one of you that chance. Let's begin with you, Diane."*

Diane leaned eagerly forward in her chair.

*"I can't say for sure whether you killed me, Diane, but you thought you had good reason. I saw the anger and the desire to hurt me in your eyes many times. I wondered Why? Was I not generous enough? Did I not give you more than the prenup specified? As Lady Hardwick, you had everything you wanted, and yet you still wanted more. What is it with this thing called Money? Lord knows, as a kid I had none, just like you, Diane."*

Diane's mouth clamped into a thin line. She glanced around trying to read her neighbors' faces, but they were looking at Montana, waiting for what was to come next and somehow Diane knew she was not going to like it.

*"At first I fell for all your family château and family tree nonsense, because you looked the aristocratic role. But later I took a look at French history. I thought your name sounded familiar, and that's because it originally belonged to Diane de Poitiers, the Duchesse de Valentinois, mistress of King Henry II of France. Diane de Valentinois dominated French court life until the King died, and then his wife, Catherine de' Medicis, forced her into 'seclusion.' Not to her glorious château at Chenonceaux but to the cheaper and much plainer Chaumont.*

   *"But of course, Diane, I'm sure you already know all this."*

Diane stared at Montana, seething with anger at being caught out in her lie, but she said nothing and he read on:

*"In keeping with this story, a château awaits your 'retirement.' It's smaller to be sure than Chenonceaux or even Chaumont but entirely suitable for my lady.*

"You may remember it, up in the hills above Saint-Tropez? We once visited it together. A charming, pleasant place set in its own pine-filled acreage with a view of the sea and excellent for entertaining. So good, in fact, that I've left you enough to 'entertain' properly while at last also earning your own living. Plans are already approved to turn the property into a hotel, which I've renamed for you—the Château de Valentinois. Finally, my dear Diane, your background will match your story. And all your old friends will come and stay. Think what pleasure you'll get from being able to charge them this time.

"This is your 'second chance.' There'll be enough money to cover the cost of the renovations, plus setting up in business and a reasonable 'pension' of ten million dollars to get you through life, payable monthly so you don't blow it all at the Casino. The rest is up to you. There's an old saying, 'Empty hands will find mischief.' Well, this will give you something to do. Make no mistake, it will be work, work, work. I wonder if you are up to it? We shall see.

"What I don't understand, though, is what happened to all the money I gave you? What happened to the jewelry? The property? I don't believe your gambling problem is that severe, so what exactly did you do with it?

"And no, dear Diane, I don't really think you murdered me. For one thing, I don't believe you're clever enough to pull off something as complicated as murder—unless it was a crime passionnel, sticking a knife into a cheating lover's back, that sort of thing.

"I think in your own way you loved me. And for a while there I was in love with you. I treasure those moments, despite the aftermath. So, chère Diane, I bid you good-bye, and wish you bonne chance.

"There's just one caveat. In order to have your very own château, you must now tell the truth. So stand up, my dear. Admit who you were *then, and who you are now, and where my money went and why. Leave nothing out, for I can assure you that by now, Montana will know it all."*

Every head turned to Diane, who sat stony-eyed, face flaming. After a few moments, she got up. Looking at Montana, she said, "Since you know everything there's nothing else for me to say."

"But Bob wants *you* to tell us, Diane."

She shrugged impatiently. "So you can gloat, I suppose."

"We're not here to gloat over another's misfortune. We're here for a second chance. Remember?"

She lifted her chin defiantly. "All right. I'm no aristocrat. I reinvented myself, like so many other women have done. I was born Diane Lenclos on a poor, miserable little farm with a father who beat me and my sister, and a mother who drank herself to death because it seemed a better option than her life. Our farm was so near—and yet so far from—the beautiful châteaus of the Loire, which were about as accessible to me as the moon. That's the reason I took the name Diane de Valentinois. As a girl, I longed to be like her." She shrugged. "And I almost made it, didn't I?

"When Maman died, my younger sister, Alice, and I were left alone with Papa, and he continued to vent his rage on us. We ran the house and helped on the farm, avoiding his backhanders across the face as much as we could, but we showed up for school once too often with bruises and the teacher called the child welfare services. Papa was put in jail for six months. I don't know what happened to him after that, I never saw him again.

"I was thirteen and Alice was nine when they put us in the cold red-brick 'home' along with forty or so other homeless children. We each had a bed to call our own and a small chest of drawers in which to keep our possessions, except Alice and I didn't own any. We got three just-bearable meals a day, schooling six days a week and church every morning and twice on Sunday. I felt as though my soul was wearing a straitjacket. It was squeezing the life out of me. I waited until I was sixteen before I ran away. I promised Alice I'd come back for her when I was successful. Like every other teenager, I was going to be a movie star. I looked good enough, all I needed was the money and to know the right people. I thought it would be easy."

Diane stopped. She stared at the floor, biting her lower lip as though what she was going to say next was too painful to bear.

"There's no need to go into detail about my life then," she said finally, "so I'll skip a few years. Let's just say I married a rich man and became Lady Hardwick and a different person.

"I'd promised Alice I'd be a success, and when at first I wasn't, I was too ashamed to admit it to her. Wait, just wait, I said, it'll be all right, I'll come for you soon. But now I was a society lady and all wrapped up in my new life, in the clothes and the parties and the jewels and my houses. I had my new image to live up to and Alice was a country mouse, all she knew was our deprived childhood and the children's home. Bringing Alice to live with me would have given my game away, so I put her off. I gave her money, said I'd send for her when I could.

But Alice couldn't wait any longer. She decided to rent a car and come to Monte Carlo to see me. She was near Lyon when the car hit a tree. They got her out using the Jaws of Life and took her to the hospital. In her handbag they found a letter from me.

"I was giving a party when the phone call came. I was terrified for Alice, but my guests were important people, I couldn't just leave them. So to my shame, I just carried on. I flew to Lyon the next morning. Alice was in a coma. She was wrapped in so many bandages she looked like a mummy. They said the windshield had shattered in her face. They said there was brain damage."

Diane lifted her head and looked at her audience. Tears slid down her cheeks and she wiped them impatiently away. "I confess I prayed for my sister to die," she said quietly. "I *wanted* her to die. She was a sweet simple girl, and now she was nothing. And it was all my fault.

"She was in the hospital for many months. Her face healed, but the scars were terrible. Eventually she came out of the coma. I believe she recognized me, though she couldn't say my name because she could no longer speak.

"Pitiful, selfish woman that I am, I'd never been able to admit to having a plain country bumpkin sister, and now I couldn't just bring her home and say, 'Here she is and she's crippled and scarred and brain damaged.'

"I'll hate myself for the rest of my days for what I did next, but I still couldn't have her live with me. So I bought her a little house, right there near the hospital in Lyon, where she could get the help she still needed. I found an experienced caregiver, a nurse who lived with her and took care of her needs. She had a little garden, a home of her own. And no sister there to say she loved her." Diane stopped. She closed her eyes. "My shame is complete," she said, and the tears fell down her face.

"After Bob divorced me, it became more and more difficult to pay for Alice's care. I was forced to sell my jewelry, to borrow from loan sharks. And of course I gambled, always hoping for the big win that would solve all my problems, always worried that Alice would lose the only real home she'd ever known."

She looked at her silent audience. "Anyhow," she said finally, "that's my story, and that's what Bob wanted me to tell you. And you know what? I'm grateful to him for making me finally admit my guilt. And I'll be forever grateful to him for the château. He's taken me out of the despair I've been living in these past few years and given me a purpose in life. Bob's given me that second chance I know I don't deserve, but Alice does."

# 50

*Bob*

There was silence as Montana took out the next sheet of yellow paper. A flash of lightning lit the room like a searchlight at a Hollywood premiere, and people shifted in their chairs, staring uneasily out of the windows.

"This one's for Davis Farrell," he said.

"*Well, Davis,*" Bob had written,

*"did you ever think it would come to this—me speaking to you from across the great divide where you might stand accused of dispatching me? Did you kill me, Davis? Come now, let's speak the truth. There's nothing more to lose, is there?*

*"You hated me for what I did to you, shutting you out of the financial paradise you'd created, turning you out into the cold, cold world to 'make something of yourself.' You'd had every chance, and you abused it in every way. You cheated, stole, lied, turned on your friends even . . . all because you worshiped that tired old despot—Money.*

*"Money ruled your life, and in a way it ruled mine, though I liked it only for the game I could play making it. It never controlled me the way it did you. I didn't turn you in though, I didn't let you stand trial, go to jail. I still saw something in you that made me set you free to do with your life what you would. By turning you away from Money, I thought I would save you from yourself. I thought I'd given you a second chance at life. How sad, then, if you are the one who took my life from me.*

*"Still, I'm giving you the benefit of the doubt, unless Montana proves me wrong, that is. I've heard about your work. You're doing an admirable job helping the ignorant and the disenfranchised. I commend you, Davis. And it's for that reason I'm leaving you the sum of fifty million dollars to establish a foundation that will enable you to pursue your philanthropic dreams of a better life for others. I think I can say without hesitation that I know, this time around, the money will be well-spent."*

There was a stunned silence, then Davis got to his feet. Hands in his pockets, he looked casually around. "Sure, I thought about killing Bob," he said. "But I'm a white-collar crook, not a murderer. Technically, I didn't 'steal,' I just cleverly shifted monies around to suit my own ends, which were always, of course, to make money for me. I was heading on that long, slippery upward road to corporate stardom, on my way to becoming one of those billionaire heads of companies who line their own pockets using the workers' pension funds and throwing million-dollar parties with money skimmed from shareholders. Bob caught me, and he forced me out of the world I belonged in. Bob Hardwick changed my life—and not for the better. I'd already started to edge my way quietly back into the financial arena before Bob died, but then I had the freedom to pick up where I left off when he showed me the door.

"I sympathize with the disenfranchised. Let's not forget that because of Bob for a few years I became one of them. But it's not who I am, and a philanthropist is not who I aim to be. I don't want Bob's fifty million. And I don't want to run a foundation. Oh no, what I want is to be the next Bob Hardwick, and trust me, my fellow suspects—and by the way, I wonder which one of you *did* murder Bob—I will get there. Forget Gordon Gekko. I'm no murderer, but like him I'm a killer on the Street, and it's my name you'll be seeing on a daily basis in *The Wall Street Journal* and the *Financial Times*. And I'll use every ounce of my devious smarts to make sure I stay there.

"Bob called it wrong on this one, Montana," he added. "He can keep his fifty million. Get someone else to head the foundation.

"And you know what else I have to say to Bob Hardwick? Forget it, Bob, I'm a guy who makes his own second chances. I don't need yours."

He sat down to a stunned silence.

"You have thirty days to rethink your decision," Montana said.

Davis shrugged. "I don't need it. I know what I want and this time nothing is going to stop me."

Montana turned to Filomena. "And now it's your turn," he said.

She bit her lower lip nervously. Then, "I didn't kill Bob," she cried. "I'd never do anything bad like that—"

"Wait," Montana said. "And listen to what Bob wrote to you."

She sat on the edge of her seat, head down, twisting her hands together, a picture of guilt.

*"Filomena, my lovely Filomena. How I wanted you to love me. Really love me. I was reflected in the glow of your beauty, poor ugly older man that I was, seeking something I never had and never would have had if it was not for my extraordinary ability to make great amounts of money.*

*"Of course it was asking too much. What we had was a simple form of exchange. You paid your price, I paid mine. Which doesn't mean to say I didn't love you. Of course I did, in my way. I loved the shortness of your upper lip, the curve of your mouth, that little pout. I loved the way you looked—you might have noticed I couldn't take my eyes off you. But I made a mistake, Filomena. You were a young girl, and I was an older, experienced man. I took advantage of your youth and I've been ashamed ever since. I tried to make it up to you, but enough never really seemed to be 'enough,' and you started to make my life hell.*

*"Thinking about it now, I'm forced to wonder what your life might have been like had you not met me. Would it simply have been some other rich man? Or would you have fought your way out of the 'beauty trap' and made something of yourself?*

*"I wonder, have you been asking yourself these same questions lately, dear little Filomena? Have you asked yourself what's left in life for you? Why not ask instead 'What's life got in store for me?' And you*

*can interpret that two ways. It's either What's yet to come? Or Why not a store?*

*"I've bought you a boutique on the best shopping street here in Capri. Along with it comes a small very pretty house—I've seen photographs—where you can finally make a proper home because, you see, I believe you are two things: a true merchant and an old-fashioned homemaker. I can just see you cooking pasta in your own proper Italian kitchen.*

*"There will be enough money to start up your business and keep you going, but just to make sure, the sum of ten million dollars has been placed in trust for you. The income from this will be paid annually into your account. You are set for life, Filomena, and I wish you luck. And of course you didn't murder me. After all, it might have ruined your dress."*

A ripple of subdued laughter ran around the room as Filomena got to her feet.

"Bob was right," she said, still twisting her hands nervously together. "I *am* a merchant at heart. Clothes and fashion are what I understand, and I know I'll make my boutique a success." She clapped her hands together, realizing it was a dream come true. "I can't believe it, I just can't believe it. Not only does Bob give me a shop, but he buys me a house! No more damp rented rooms in poor palazzos in Venice. I am to have my own home. I can invite my family and they can be proud of me. Bob has given me material things but he's also given me my dignity back. And I'm very grateful for that, and for my second chance."

She looked uncertainly around, then making up her mind, she said quickly, "I would have never admitted this before, but now that Bob has put me in a position of trust, I too must make my confession. I stole things from the boutique where I work, small things, stuff that was returned or was going on sale. I lied and blamed it on shoplifters. We get them, you know, even in a smart store like that. But I promise I'll return every cent they cost. I will not start my business with this on my conscience."

A rumble of thunder drowned out her little speech. It wasn't raining yet, but the black clouds had changed day into night and the garden was still silent; no birds sang, no crickets chirruped.

"Charles Clement, it's your turn," Montana said.

*"Well, Charlie, I believe I have to call a failure on this one. I gave you your chance. I closed down your call-girl business but I didn't have you put in jail as you deserved. However, you have not changed for the better. You are worse."*

Charlie leapt to his feet. "Stop this nonsense," he yelled. "Stop it right now. I demand to have my lawyer present."

"Sit down," Montana said in an icy voice, and Charlie subsided, though he was still muttering.

*"I gave you a chance, Charlie, even after you brought the poor little girl to Sneadley as a 'gift' for me, your usual method of touting for business I heard later. This time, though, you made a mistake. You made a serious misjudgment of my character. By closing you down, I gave you a chance and you betrayed that. It's my belief you simply took your child pornography, your child selling, abroad—"*

Charlie was on his feet again, his face mottled with anger. "Bob Hardwick is lying. He was a pedophile, he had me find girls for him, nine- or ten-year-olds, sometimes even younger. . . . You don't know the true Hardwick, the liar and child pornographer—"

Montana was out from behind the desk. Hands clenched into tight fists, he stood in front of Charlie. "One more word and I'll personally take great pleasure in giving you the beating of your life," he said in a voice filled with quiet menace. "And let me tell you that, as we speak, the École de Nuit—charming name, isn't it, for a bunch of poor kids sold into sexual slavery—is being closed down by the Paris vice squad. You're finished, Charlie. It's over for you."

Charlie pushed back his chair. He turned to run, tripping over Reg and shoving Ginny out of his way. Reg had none of Montana's compunctions; he smashed his fist into Charlie's nose, sending him reeling, blood spurting. Montana grabbed Reg and held him back from plastering Charlie again.

"No bugger talks that way about Bob Hardwick," Reg hissed. "*No* bugger, especially one like you." He aimed a kick at Charlie's knees, grunting with satisfaction as his foot connected.

Limping, and with blood still dripping all over his expensive shirt, Charlie lunged for the doors. Heads turned to look as Montana called after him. "By the way, Charlie, Bob thought it was quite possible you murdered him. 'You never know with a man like that,' is what he said."

Ignoring him, Charlie eyed the guards warily, ready for more trouble. To his surprise they moved aside and even opened the doors for him.

He stepped outside, congratulating himself on being a free man. And walked right into the waiting arms of two very large Italian policemen. He was told they had an arrest warrant issued by the international police; then they handcuffed him, read him his rights, bundled him into the back of a police van, and drove him away.

"How dare he talk like that about Bob?" Ginny said angrily. "I always knew he was scum." Reg rubbed his skinned knuckles, the look on his face expressing what he felt about Charlie, while the others whispered together, shocked.

Montana called their attention back to Bob's will. This time it was Dopplemann's turn to squirm.

*"And now you, Dopplemann. I suppose I should call you Marius, though nobody ever does. Dopplemann you were and Dopplemann you remain, with occasionally the 'Herr' in front, to show due respect.*

*"I was your great admirer, Herr Dopplemann. I myself was merely a man who knew how to make money, while you are a genius. Did that excuse what happened? I think not. Of course I would willingly have given you money had you needed it, but there was no need. Only a reason. A woman. And that 'reason' has been a destroyer of many a man before you.*

*"I had my contacts in the corridors of power, I heard rumors. I tried to dismiss them but in my gut I knew they were true. Yet I did nothing because I had no proof. Then someone came to me with a couple of disturbing stories: about secret meetings in a Georgetown park; about messages passed in out-of-the-way cafés. . . . It didn't take a genius, Dopplemann, to guess you were being recruited to sell out America, the country that had given you honor and access to its secrets. You were*

*about to hand them over to a foreign power. And all because of a woman.*

"Now, I understand the pressure you were under and your feelings for this woman, but as I told you when I confronted you, selling out the country that made you who you are was not the act of a gentleman, as many another spy has found to his cost.

"Fortunately, I stopped you before you acted. I offered you a choice. Leave immediately and never darken Lady Liberty's doors again. Or take the consequences. And we all know from the media coverage of spies caught in the act what that would have meant. Total disgrace and a lifetime in jail. It was only because you had hesitated, not taken the final step and actually committed the crime, that I felt able to offer you a way out. You took it; you left America and disappeared who knew where.

"I saved you, Dopplemann. I gave you a chance, and yet I'm sure that for the rest of your life you'll curse me for taking away what you were. A scientist. A genius. A man dedicated to his work. And a man with a terrible weakness.

"Did you kill me, Herr Dopplemann? I think it's possible. That's up to Montana to say. It would be a pity if you did, though, because I'm about to offer you and your genius a second chance.

"The world needs men like you, men with your vision, with your talents, your incredible far-reaching, ever-searching brain. I've discussed you with people I know, and we feel there's no risk factor in taking you back onboard. You'll find a job waiting for in the private sector. Your life is being handed back to you on a plate, Dopplemann, while mine, sadly, is over. You might want to think about that.

"I'm also leaving you the sum of one million dollars in trust, with

*the income to be paid annually. Along with your salary, this will be*
*sufficient for you to live on. Just keep away from the women. And I'm*
*leaving you the contents of my wine cellar in New York. I think you'll*
*find enough good Bordeaux there to keep you happy for a long, long*
*time. If you did not murder me, then I wish you luck."*

Everyone looked at Dopplemann as he got to his feet. His
head was held high, and for the first time we glimpsed the man
he once was.

"There were times over these past few years when I thought
it would be a good thing to kill Bob Hardwick," Dopplemann
said in his odd hissing voice, "but I did not do it. I admit the
urge for revenge burned in me until I could no longer think. I
couldn't have done the work I used to because my brain
stopped like a broken watch on the day Bob confronted me. I
blamed him for my downfall when I should have blamed the
woman. Bob let me go free and now he's given me a second
chance. I'm humbled by his generosity of spirit. You can be
sure I'll never make the same mistake again."

# 51

## Bob

"Rosalia." Montana's voice was low and gentle as he spoke her name. "This is to you from Roberto."

*"Rosalia, my true love. I've wondered countless times how it would have been if we had stayed together. I've missed you every day of my life, and no doubt I will continue to do so in death. That's the strength of my love for you."*

Rosalia's face softened; she took her daughter's hand and gripped it tightly. There was an innate dignity about her, in the way she held her head, the long, elegant neck that spoke of past beauty, a gentleness of demeanor and even after more than forty years, a lifetime without him, it was clear she still loved her Roberto.

*"I still have the letters I wrote and that you returned, unopened. For the longest time I couldn't figure out where I'd gone wrong. I loved you, you knew that. I was a hard worker—you saw that too. I wanted to give you everything in the world: as many fancy jewels as you could wear, a magnificent home or maybe two or even three, whatever you wanted. And of course, children. Rosalia, my love, I wanted so badly to have children with you that all these years I dreamed about what they might look like. A son like me? A daughter like you? Hey, maybe even twins. . . .*

*"The truth is, though, I wanted something else more. I was ruled by ambition. My mistake was not recognizing how the changes in my life would affect you, not understanding that you were afraid of the kind of life I was carving out for us. I failed to understand that you were unable to cope, that separation was the only answer, that you needed your life to go on the way it always had.*

*"I failed, but unlike the people gathered here at the Villa Belkiss, I was not given a second chance. Your decision was final and eventually I was forced to accept that. You went on with your life and I with mine, never to meet again. Until now.*

*"You must know, as you listen to my words, that I am here with you today. Nothing could keep me away. I wanted to give you everything in life, but now I must give it to you after I am dead."*

Rosalia clung to her daughter's hand. Behind her, Hector leaned forward and put a comforting hand on her shoulder.

Montana read on.

*"I am leaving you, Rosalia Alonzo Ybarra Delgado, the sum of one hundred million dollars."*

A bolt of lightning flashed through the room followed by a violent clap of thunder that rattled the villa's windows. Filomena screamed and everyone jumped and looked nervously around. Montana read on.

*"I also leave the sum of ten million dollars to my daughter, Magdalena Alonzo Ybarra Delgado Ruiz."*

There was an astonished murmur and all eyes fastened on Magdalena.

*"I didn't find out about our daughter for many years and now I'm attempting to make up for what she might consider my neglect. Know this, my Magdalena, I would never have neglected you.*

*"The money is to be held in trust for any grandchildren, both mine and those of Juan Delgado, the man who was lucky enough to marry you, Rosalia, and give you more children. The income will be paid annually and my lawyer, Arnold Levin, and my friend Harry Montana will be the senior trustees. These are men I can trust and I ask you to give them your trust too.*

*"So, my Rosalia—I feel I may call you 'mine' at last—this is finally the end of the road. Unlike the others, you are not under suspicion of murdering me. Your honor is not even in question. There is no room for evil in your lovely soul.*

*"And now I shall say a brief hello to the daughter I never met, and a sad good-bye to you, my love. Know that, even across this great divide, behind this final curtain, I will always love you."*

Montana put the long sheets of legal paper down on the desk, watching as Hector got up and went and knelt in front of Rosalia. He took her hand and Magdalena's, peering into their downcast faces, looking like a man praying.

The room was silent. Outside a wind rustled through the trees. "I don't deserve this gift," Rosalia said quietly. "I cannot accept it."

Hector jumped to his feet. "But Rosalia, Bob was so generous and he loved you so much. And besides, it's not meant only for you, it's for the children and the grandchildren."

She shook her head. "I didn't know I was pregnant when I left Bob," she said. "My whole life was in disarray. I thought the obvious signs of pregnancy were simply because I wasn't eating. I was thin, I was worried. I was afraid. When I finally understood, it was already five months."

"Rosalia," Montana said gently, "there's no need to tell us your story. It's private, personal . . ."

She shook her head. "No, I need to. I've told only three people my secret, but now, because of the inheritance, I have to tell you why I cannot accept.

"I was a waitress in a small workingmen's café. Juan Delgado was my boss and also the cook. The food we served was the simple inexpensive fare of Andalusia: fish, paella, tapas. Juan was older, a nice man in his forties and never married. I'd been working for him for five months and he'd noticed my growing waistline, though I tried to disguise it behind a large apron. At night after the café closed, it was our custom to eat dinner together. Juan would cook whatever I fancied, and we would sit and talk, he with a glass of wine, I with only water because of the child.

"One night, it grew late, but I still wanted to talk. I wanted to tell him about Bob and why I'd left him. I cried and Juan listened and then he said to me, 'And what will you do now about the baby? Will you tell him?'

"I hadn't thought he knew, but when I looked in his eyes I saw only kindness. I said I would never tell Bob because then I would be forced to go and live a life that would destroy me.

"'But what about your child?' he asked. 'It will never get to see its real father.' But I told him that was the way it had to be. I would look after my child myself.

"Juan said he'd fallen in love with me and he wanted to marry me and look after me and the baby. I loved him too, in a gentle, undemanding way; we were friends, compatriots, and now we would be parents.

"To protect my name Juan delayed reporting Magdalena's birth. He registered it as six months later than the actual date. That way, he said, Bob would never suspect he was Magdalena's father. And yet," she added, with a half smile, "somehow later Bob seems to have found out. I thought only Juan knew. I'd told Magdalena the truth when she was old enough to understand and because I couldn't live with the lie. And much later I told Hector, because he's my good friend and I keep no secrets from him.

"I know now, of course, that I was wrong. I should have told Bob about his child. I cheated him of the pleasure of being with his daughter, but I was so afraid of losing my baby, afraid Bob would take her away from me. A man with all that money has the power to do anything. It's for that reason I cannot accept Bob's gift, though of course his daughter must take what her father has so generously given her."

Rosalia sat down. Everyone looked at her, but she bent her head and cried softly. For her it was the end of a love affair.

# 52

*Daisy*

It was my turn. I looked at Montana as he began to read, wondering nervously what secrets Bob might divulge about me.

*"My Daisy, I left you for last because you are the closest to me. You've put up with me for quite a few years now, longer than any other woman, and that's living in close proximity with me, sharing my good moods and my bad, though it has to be said that you can act as ornery as any woman I've ever known, as you'll remember from our first 'date' at my favorite London restaurant. I still bear the scar from that awful cheap brooch you wore, and that's why I want you to go out and buy another one. The real thing this time. Go to Asprey in London, they'll have exactly what you want. Charge it to my account—ah well, actually no, charge it to your own account, lass, because you'll have money in it by then.*

*"Did you really think I would leave Sneadley Hall to anyone but you? Actually, it's Rats's home—you'll just be there to look after him.*

*Ha ha, just joking, of course. No, lass, Sneadley is yours. I know you love it as much as I do, and I like to think of you there on a winter's night, snug in front of the fire with Rats on your knee, or on a summer afternoon, handing out prizes at the village fete with the band playing 'Jerusalem' under the hundred-year-old chestnut tree. It's all yours, Daisy, just remember to lift a pint to me next time you're with Reg and Ginny at the Ram's Head.*

*"As for the Villa Belkiss. Of course I've never seen it, but I pored over those photos many times, until I almost felt I knew it. What I do know is that it's beautiful. It's different, unusual, dramatic, and it has a history. Sounds just like you, my love. So it's yours. I'd like to imagine you there too, under that vine-covered arbor, sipping wine and maybe thinking of me.*

*"After certain other bequests have been taken care of, I'm leaving you, Daisy Keane, my entire fortune. Why? you might ask. Because I can't think of anyone who deserves it more. You've been my loyal companion through thick and thin. You've put up with my moods just as much as I put up with yours. You've seen me through sickness—and health. In fact, I don't know why we're not bloody well married—except I know you didn't love me, at least not in that way. You are my best friend, Daisy, and always will be. I love you, and I always will and I'll look after you—even from across the great divide. So take what I'm offering and make of it what you can.*

*"So, my little lass, this is your second chance at life. These will not be the final words you hear from me. Remember, there's another letter still waiting to be read when you return to Sneadley.*

*"Think of me then, Daisy, because you can bet I'll be thinking of you. And I'll be blessing the day I found you at that awful party, trying to pretend you were a gossip columnist, with that half-starved look in*

*your eyes. Always remember I was the man who saved you from those awful canapés. It's not a bad memory to go out on. Know I love you. Always."*

Everyone was looking at me, waiting for what I was going to say after suddenly inheriting billions. I met Montana's eyes. He smiled and said softly, so only I could hear, "It's what Bob wanted. Don't worry about a thing."

He understood I was already feeling the weight of Bob's inheritance, but more than that, I was missing him. I didn't want the money, I just wanted Bob back.

I got to my feet and looked around at the faces, reading their different reactions: astonishment, anger, delight, envy. But even blindfolded I could have guessed which emotion belonged to which person.

"I loved Bob," I said. "And some of you here loved him as well. I was near the bottom, emotionally and financially, when I met him. He picked me up off the floor and gave me a job. Now he's given me a second chance, he's given me a home, Sneadley Hall, and this lovely villa. I'll do my best to keep them exactly the way he would have wanted. And I'll love and cherish Rats for him, just the way he would have himself."

I sat down abruptly, near to tears and a thin spatter of applause rippled around the room.

But all was not over yet. Now it was Montana's turn.

# 53

*Montana*

Montana stood behind the graceful ebony desk where Vassily Belkiss had penned his memoirs, spilling secrets the way the suspects had spilled theirs. He looked very cool and very much in command of the situation. The doors were closed and the two guards stood, arms folded, ever alert, watching, listening. The room crackled with tension and outside the black clouds pressed so close they almost rested on the house. A sudden spatter of raindrops, large as silver dollars, bounced off the terrace and a zigzag of lightning cleaved the sky, burying itself in the blackness of the sea. Daisy counted off the seconds . . . one, two, three, four, five . . . then the peal of thunder shook the house as though the God of Thunder was using his magical hammer to beat the sky.

Montana said, "And now I want to tell you exactly how Bob Hardwick died." There was another shocked murmur and the suspects sat up straight, watching him.

"Bob was on his way to a mountain resort for a conference. It had been arranged some months before and he was driving there alone because Daisy had the flu. Of course he couldn't know that an explosive device had been affixed to the car's engine and that a cell phone, set on 'tremble' so it couldn't be inadvertently activated by someone dialing Bob's own number, was planted under the driver's seat. The killer didn't even have to be on the scene. All he had to do was dial a certain number and the vehicle would explode."

The silence was almost tangible. Magdalena took her mother's hand again and held it tightly. Diane leaned back in her chair, eyes closed, her face pale. Filomena put a shocked hand over her mouth and tears rolled down her cheeks and dripped off her chin. Dopplemann stared blankly ahead like a man looking into space. Davis, arms folded tight across his chest, eyes half-shut, looked at the floor, and Reg and Ginny glanced worriedly at each other.

Montana said, "Of course, the question is not just *how* Bob died, but *why*. Bob came to me a few days before his death and told me he was worried about crank e-mail messages he was receiving. To me they sounded like the beginning of a blackmail plot, but as far as I knew Bob had led an exemplary life and there was nothing to blackmail him for. Of course no man is perfect and I could have been wrong, but I had a gut feeling about this. There was more to it than met the eye.

"At the same time, Bob gave me a list of the six people he reckoned had grievances against him, bad enough, he said, for any one of them to want to kill him.

"And all it took to kill Bob was one phone call." He turned and looked at Rosalia. "That call was made from Andalusia."

The color drained from Rosalia's face and she suddenly looked years older and a lifetime sadder. After a moment, she got slowly to her feet.

Her voice had lost all its soft charm, all its life, as she said, "I killed Bob Hardwick." She turned to look at Hector. "And the man I called my friend asked me to do it. Hector was in New York that day; he asked me to call him at a certain time, at a certain number. I made that call. He had me kill the man I loved, the father of my child—"

Hector was already on his feet. "She's lying," he shouted over the crackling thunder. "I happened to be in New York on business. Rosalia's always had it in for Hardwick, she told me so herself, told me how she hated him because he'd deserted her, left her pregnant and with no money. She said she would get even with him one day. She killed him and now she's using me to try to escape the consequences."

"*You* sent those e-mails, Hector," Montana said coldly. "*You* found out where Bob parked his car. It was a matter of seconds to affix the device and plant the phone. *You* called Rosalia, told her the time, gave her the number . . ."

Hector made a run for the door but the guards moved to block him. He spun around and headed for the French doors with the guards after him. Everyone was on their feet, and as he ran past Daisy grabbed his jacket. Snagged, he swung around, got her neck in a headlock and held her in front of him. Choking, unable to move, she stood in his stranglehold.

Everyone stopped in their tracks. Bordelaise screamed Daisy's name and the other women stared, hands to their mouths, terrified. The men moved in front of them. Reg's face was mottled with fury as he crouched ready to tackle, but Montana held him back.

"Let her go." His voice fell icily into the new silence.

But Hector edged backward toward the closed French doors. Suddenly, with a great whoosh of wind, they burst open and the storm was in the room. The wind swirled with a banshee wail, lightning zigzagged outside, thunder roared, the windows shook, and the women screamed. Dragging Daisy in front of him, Hector edged out onto the terrace.

Rain stung Daisy's face, sharp as spears. In seconds she was soaked to the skin. Her hair hung in wet strings in front of her eyes and she was unable to see. Fear paralyzed her and she went limp in his grip. She knew she was about to die, Hector would kill her rather than be caught. "Help me, Bob. *Please* help me," she begged silently.

The mini-tornado came out of nowhere, circling and swirling, shafting between them like a sword. Hector was knocked to the ground. Montana grabbed Daisy and shoved her out of harm's way. He lunged for Hector but the Spaniard was already up and running, making for the little blue door that led from the garden onto the cliffs. He wrenched it open and disappeared into the storm.

Montana held up a hand to stop anyone from following him. The door banged back and forth in the wind. "It's too dangerous in this storm," he said as lightning forked down again. "Besides, there's nowhere for him to run. We're on a small island, and the police are waiting for him."

Daisy was sitting on a lounger, weeping. He went and sat next to her. "I'll never forgive myself for this," he said. "I'm so sorry."

She nodded it was all right. Rubbing her bruised throat, she said hoarsely, "You'd better speak to Rosalia. She's the one who's never going to forgive herself."

He took her arm and led her back inside. Everyone was standing around, windblown and wet and looking shocked and angry. Montana apologized to Rosalia and to everyone else. "I'd have preferred to do this another way," he said, "but it was Bob's last wish that it be played out like this. I know you're all wondering why Hector killed Bob when he didn't even know him. It was money, of course.

"I'm sorry to tell you this, Rosalia, but Hector is an expert con man. He has prison records on three continents. He latched on to you at your peaceful hotel, tucked away from the police and from his past, and convinced you he could run the place better than you did. He said he could make life easier for all of you, and I'm sure at first he did just that. He became your trusted friend, a man you knew would do anything for you. Eventually, you turned the management of your business affairs over to him.

"You trusted him," he said. "When he brought you documents to sign, you signed them without question, and Hector became expert at forging your signature. He also borrowed against your property and pocketed the money. When the banks threatened to foreclose, he knew he would have to leave, which is what con men like him always do. Just disappear. Then he remembered you'd told him Bob Hardwick was Magdalena's father. At first he thought of blackmail, hence the threatening e-mails. He was just working up to it when he saw it was a fool's game and it was too easy to get caught. He realized that when Bob died, his only child, Magdalena, would be the legal heir to his fortune. Bob had no other family, there was no one else to contest it.

"It was a plot for murder made in Hector's kind of heaven. And the beauty of it was he could never be accused of it, because you, Rosalia, would be the one who had, so to speak, 'pulled the trigger.' Magdalena would still inherit and once again Hector, as the family's trusted friend, would take over. He couldn't lose."

"I'll never get over that I killed Bob," Rosalia wept. "I always loved him, I'm sure he knew that. That's why he never came to me about Magdalena. He knew she was his and he let me have her. He was a good man, you all know that." She looked around at the frightened group, shivering and soaked.

"Hector won't get away," Montana assured her. "The police are down the road, waiting. Don't worry, they'll get him, or the storm will."

Looking at the lightning and at the wind swirling like a tornado, Daisy bet on the storm. She had no doubt that Bob had come back to save her and no doubt that he would get Hector. Only then would Bob rest in peace.

# PART X

# BACK ON THE *BLUE BOAT.*
# THE LAST NIGHT.

*Experience is the name everyone
gives to their mistakes.*

—OSCAR WILDE,
*LADY WINDERMERE'S FAN*

# 54

*Daisy*

We were a subdued and very wet bunch climbing back up the gangway to our beautiful *Blue Boat*. Montana and I escorted Rosalia. Her step had lost its lightness and she trod like an older woman, as with Magdalena's arm around her, she returned to her suite.

Montana walked me to my door. I leaned against it, hands behind my back, looking seriously at him. There was no backchat between us now, no man-woman games being played.

"I would have killed Hector if he'd harmed you," Montana said quietly.

"No need. Bob did it for you." He raised his brows in a question. "The tornado that came from nowhere," I said. "The island doesn't get winds like that. And didn't you notice it wasn't blowing anywhere else, just on the terrace? In his letter Bob said he would be with me to make sure I came to no harm. I believe he kept that promise."

I could tell Montana thought I was being irrational, frightened by the day's happenings into believing something that was impossible. Still, he humored me.

"Believe what you will, I'm just glad you're all right." He tilted my chin with his finger and planted a soft kiss on my lips. "Do we have a dinner date?"

"Please," I said. He kissed me again, and I watched him stride off down the long blue-carpeted corridor, my heart jumping again for joy.

It was the last night of the cruise and we were supposed to have a gala farewell dinner. Despite all that had happened, and because I knew it was what Bob would have wanted, I contacted the remaining guests and asked them still to dress up. I wanted us to show up looking good and as though we hadn't a care in the world. Which, I supposed, except for Rosalia, now we didn't.

Later, dressed in my sea foam chiffon, with the peridot necklace I'd bought only four days and a lifetime ago in Saint-Tropez covering my bruises, my eyes still faintly red from crying and my hair piled on top and threatening to fall down, wearing Bob's whopping yellow diamond ring and thinking amazed I could easily buy ten of these now and hardly feel the pinch, a bit wobbly in my too-high heels, I walked to the bar to greet Bob's guests. It was my last night as hostess and with all suspicions gone, I knew he'd have wanted everyone to have a good time.

Diane and Filomena were already propping up the bar with Bordelaise between them, keeping the peace I supposed. Diane looked more beautiful than I had ever seen her. Her red hair was pulled back in a knot and she wore a simple black Chanel dress with the signature white gardenia at the shoulder. Filomena was in a wild jungle print and Bordelaise looked the innocent in a white lace outfit I seemed to remember from one of her weddings.

I called hello to them, and this time I saw their faces light up in genuine smiles. It was so different from the way it had been before and I knew it was all thanks to Bob. Ginny, flamboyant in scarlet lace, was playing backgammon with Brandon, who was just straight-ahead handsome in his tuxedo. Texas had discarded her crutches and was talking with Melvyn, who was playing our old favorites. Only Rosalia and Magdalena were missing, but I'd expected that.

Dopplemann was there, though, still in his awful green jacket, but I could tell he felt better about himself and more confident.

Davis stood alone by the window, a glass of Perrier in his hand, observing the scene, part of it and yet not. Somehow I knew that the next time Davis was on a yacht it would be his own—and it would have to be bigger and better than anyone else's.

Reg was telling Texas and Melvyn, who played on, about the Ram's Head, drinking Peroni beer and looking happy again.

It was a relief not to have to look anymore at Charlie Clement, sporting his superior little half smile as he eyed the women. I wondered uneasily where Hector was. Montana said it was impossible for him to escape but I was still worried. And anyhow, as always, Montana was missing.

I joined the women at the bar and asked for my usual cosmo. Taking a sip, I glanced up and saw all three of them looking at me. "What?" I stared down at my cleavage to see if anything had escaped.

"It's just that you look like a different woman tonight," Filomena said.

"Is that good?"

They laughed. "You look years younger," Bordelaise reassured me.

"It's the relief, knowing none of you are murderers," I said, and Bordelaise raised her glass and said she would drink to that.

We clinked our glasses, four women united by Bob Hardwick's life and his death in a cautious new friendship.

"How is your poor throat?" Diane peered at me but my peridot *collier* covered Hector's thumbprints perfectly. "Such an evil man." Diane shuddered. "Poor, poor, Rosalia."

A whoop of delight came from the backgammon table. Ginny had beaten Brandon at his own game. He was stammering his congratulations to her, and she was laughing and yelling her delight, completely uninhibited. That was the great thing about Ginny; it didn't matter who you were or how rich you were, she treated everybody the same. And so did Reg. Just look at him now, offering Texas his arm to escort her into dinner.

We drifted onto the afterdeck, where we would dine under the stars, with the lights of Capri twinkling brightly. And still Montana was not here. I wondered if this was to be the story of my life.

# 55

*Daisy*

I took my seat next to his empty chair, acting as though I didn't care, but I was smoldering behind my smile.

The night was clear after the storm, the stars were out, champagne was being poured, caviar and fois gras served. Still no Montana. I asked Diane what she intended to do with her château in Saint-Tropez.

"I'll make it into the best hotel there, of course," she said, as though there was no question about it.

"And I'll bring my sister to live there. I'll give Alice the best rooms overlooking the sea, where she can watch the boats go by. I'm so sorry for all the bad things I said about Bob, the way I behaved. And I'm sorry I was rude to you, Filomena."

Filomena said, "That's okay. And you know, it's odd but I only ever thought of Bob as a man who made money and didn't particularly care about anything else, except maybe his dog. Now I see he cared about all of us. He understood who I was, and now I'll never have to be another man's mistress."

I looked at Davis, sipping his Perrier, saying nothing. "And what does the future hold for you, Davis?" I asked.

He lifted an indifferent shoulder. "Success, of course. What else matters?"

"And Herr Dopplemann?"

Dopplemann scrambled to his feet. As usual he clutched a glass of fine Bordeaux, a Léoville Las Cases, a particular favorite of Bob's that, feeling guilty of having misjudged him, I'd ordered to be decanted especially for him.

"Some years ago I made a very foolish decision," he said. "Now, thanks to Bob, I am being given a second chance. He had confidence in me and I'll work hard to prove him right." We toasted to that as he sat down again.

By now we had finished the appetizers, and the fish—a delicious John Dory—was eaten and the plates cleared away. Salads decorated with pretty edible flowers were tasted, along with perfect cheeses.

Bordelaise said, "And what about you, Daisy? What do you plan to do with your life now?"

I'd planned nothing beyond finding Bob's killer. In my mixed-up mind the future had somehow involved Montana, but obviously that was just another pipe dream.

"I don't know," I said, blushing under their gaze. "It hasn't sunk in yet. I'll donate a lot of the money to a foundation, I suppose—to help sick children, the fight against famine, oh, and the local Society for the Prevention of Cruelty to Animals. Bob was always a big supporter of that. And of course, Sneadley will be my home, though I expect I'll spend a lot of time at the villa in summer."

I got up, glass in hand, and said, "I want to propose a toast to Sir Robert Waldo Hardwick, Knight of the Queen's Realm, a fair and just man. A good man, even though he could be a bit of a despot at times," I added, making them laugh as we finally celebrated Bob's life, just the way he'd hoped we would.

Montana finally showed up with the Baked Alaska, another of Bob's old-fashioned favorites. The lights were dimmed and on a drum roll the waiter appeared bearing aloft the flaming silver platters, and laughing, everyone applauded.

As he slipped into the seat next to me, I threw Montana a scathing sideways glance that left him in no doubt I was totally pissed off.

"I apologize for being late, I was delayed by business calls," he said to the table. "I have news. And by the way, I've already told Rosalia this. The chief of police informed me they surrounded Hector on the cliffs. He made a run for it, it was dark and wet, he didn't know the terrain. A fissure runs deep into the cliffs there; obviously he didn't see it. They found his body on the rocks below."

There was a stunned silence, then Dopplemann said thank you, and everyone joined in a chorus of thank-yous to Montana, the man who had, by putting together all the pieces of an international puzzle, solved the mystery of Bob's death.

He turned to look at me. "Sorry I'm late." I shrugged my shoulders indifferently and took another sip of champagne.

"What do I care?" I eyed him over the rim of my glass.

He laughed, knowing I was pretending. "Bob warned me you tended to lie a bit," he said. "I guess he was right."

# 56

## Daisy

We were alone on deck. It was past midnight; the sky was a
dark blue, and the stars were out. The water parted smoothly
over our bow, the wake frothed behind us and brilliant stars
flickered like candle glow. We stood side by side, not touching,
as *Blue Boat* steamed toward Naples, where we would disem-
bark. It was over.

Montana broke the long silence. "There's something you
need to understand about me," he said. "It began when I was
just a boy. You remember I told you about the mare I rode to
school every day? She was my closest companion and I loved
her the way only a boy who has nothing else to love can. One
day, without my knowing it, one of the cowboys took her out
on the range. There was barbed wire; she caught her flank, got
badly cut up. The wounds were neglected. By the time they
brought her back to the ranch, the cuts were severely infected
and the limb had swollen to twice its normal size. My father

took one look at her, shrugged his shoulders and went to the barn and got his gun. He shot her right in front of my eyes. She screamed as the bullet hit her. I watched her legs fold under her as if in slow motion, saw her roll over. She looked up at me as though asking why, then her eyes glazed over.

"'Get rid of her,' my father told his boys and in minutes they had lassos around my mare and were dragging her away. At that moment my life changed. Mentally, I was already out of there. It was only a matter of time before I left. And I swore I would never love anything or anyone again."

I touched his arm tenderly. "But you must have cried," I said.

"I didn't allow myself to cry. It wasn't until the night I met Phineas Cloudwalker that I realized it was all right to cry. I finally understood that love takes a toll when bad things happen. And it's because of him that I began to understand that good things can also come from love."

He turned his head and our eyes linked. "How can I care this much? I've known you such a short time," he said.

"I know." My voice was still hoarse from Hector's stranglehold. "And we've seen each other how many days altogether?"

"Very few," he said.

"Not enough," I said.

"It's a beginning, though."

I nodded, yes, it was.

"A new beginning for me," he added.

"And a second chance for me." I smiled as I echoed Bob's words.

"I guess that's what life is all about," Montana said.

"I guess it is."

"Then will you kiss me?" he asked.

"Why not?" I said, breathless now. "At least it's a start."

# PART XI

## ONE YEAR LATER.

*The good ended happily, and the bad unhappily.*
*That is what fiction means.*

—OSCAR WILDE,
*THE IMPORTANCE OF BEING EARNEST*

## 57

*Daisy*

It's a Saturday night and Bordelaise and I are taking Rats to the Ram's Head for a banger and a pint of Tetley's bitter the way Bob and I used to.

Rats snuffles happily along the familiar road, lifting his leg at favorite trees and wagging his stumpy tail at people he knows, and they stop to say hello to him, and to me. I'm part of Sneadley's tapestry of life now, the lady of the manor, as they say. I spend most weekends here, though I'm in London during the week, or sometimes New York, running the charitable foundation I formed in memory of Bob. It keeps me busy and out of mischief, and I'm proud of what I do. Proud to be a part of an international team working for the good of children everywhere.

Bordelaise is visiting from Chicago and everyone here loves her. Tomorrow I'm giving a lunch party. I'll see if I can get her off with one of the local county gents, though nobody else I know around here has been married three times. Still, it would be a novelty and she'll charm their socks off, have them eating out of her hand in a flash—though, come to think of it, even with an Aga, her cooking's not so hot. In fact, the cruise is the best thing that happened to Bordelaise, and I know she's still in touch with Captain Anders. She's already signed up for another cruise, on a big ship this time, leaving next week out of Rome, and then a second one in winter to Australia with half the world in between. Cruises seem to suit her need for constant change, and she swears she'll end up as the ship's mascot, an old lady adopted by the crew, with her own permanent cabin, folding table napkins to help out and keep busy.

Somehow I don't see it that way. Bordelaise will be flighty and free until the next charmer comes along, and no doubt I'll be matron of honor one more time.

Next week I'm off to Saint-Tropez for the opening of Diane's hotel. Of course, I've already seen it and she done a marvelous job. How could she not—a woman with her taste? *And* her money, I can hear Bob saying with a laugh.

Her sister, Alice, is sweet, like a child really, and Diane says she can tell she feels at home at the Château de Valentinois. She's happy and playful, and Diane got her a little dog, a white bichon frise named Billy. She grooms it every day and feeds it herself, and it sits on her lap in her electric wheelchair, going for rides along the paths in the pretty gardens.

It's odd, but Diane doesn't seem to care much anymore about the way she looks; she's comfortable in pants and a shirt, very much the chatelaine, very much the boss. I can guarantee she drove her team of workmen crazy, but she got the job done in record time.

As for Filomena, of course I see her because I'm often at the Villa Belkiss. She's in her element, buying for her boutique with its tempting window displaying the one perfect bag fringed with beads, or the sexiest little persimmon top, or the most gorgeous summer gown. She's proven to be a great saleswoman, selling her customers from top to toe when all they really came in for was to ask the price of the bag in the window. And her little house, tucked up an arched flight of steps with an eagle's-eye view of the town and the sea, is a cool pleasure in blue and white, a bit like *Blue Boat,* now I come to think of it. There's a man in her life too, the owner of one of the island's nicest restaurants. Life is looking good for Filomena.

I hear about Davis Farrell, of course, though I never see him. True to his promise, he's mentioned almost daily in the financial papers. He's already living up to his previous reputation as a skilled and devious manipulator, and his success is guaranteed. Bob offered him back his soul and he turned it down. So be it.

I haven't seen Dopplemann either, but he reports in with an e-mail every now and then. He's working for a Swiss company and from what he says he's in his element. I wish him well.

And now Rosalia. A few months after the cruise, Magdalena wrote saying she would like to see me, so I went to the Finca de los Pastores. I found Rosalia sad and remote. She no longer took an interest in her hotel; she didn't cook, or even speak with her guests.

I sat with her in the courtyard of her pretty home, where a white peacock spread its tail for us, like a cloud shimmering in the sunlight. Magdalena had persuaded Rosalia to keep Bob's legacy, and now she asked me what she should do with it. She said it didn't feel right using it for her own needs, though it had enabled them to buy back their property from the banks, who because of Hector's fraud had been on the verge of foreclosing. I urged her to continue with the plans to build an annex and the new hotel in the foothills of the Sierras she'd always dreamed about.

"You can do it," I said, knowing it was true. "You've done it before, under much tougher circumstances. Now you have no young mouths to feed. Forget Hector, forget the bad things and move on. It's time to *live*."

My persistence must have paid off because the night before I was to leave, Rosalia took over her kitchens again and cooked me a dinner I will never forget. And Magdalena writes me that she's back in charge and going ahead with the plans for the new hotel.

I can hardly bear to mention the evil man's name, but anyhow, Charlie Clement is doing plenty of time in a French jail. Exactly where he belongs.

Reg Blunt tells a good story to anyone who comes into the pub and can bear to listen (they've all heard it a million times by now) about *Blue Boat* and the people he met and what a wonderful time he had. He does not go into detail about the other happenings; he's a discreet man, which is one of the reasons Bob liked him. He also doesn't talk about the hundred thousand pounds Bob left him, and he keeps the Ferrari he also left him stashed in his garage and polishes it every day. I don't know if he'll ever take it out for a spin; he thinks it's too good to get "mucky."

And Ginny is . . . well, she's just Ginny. The fifty thousand Bob left her is safely invested, and I see her driving Bob's Mercedes convertible through the village on her way to Harrogate to shop, always smiling, always flirting, always busy with her family. No special man yet, but she's hoping.

Mrs. W still works for me as housekeeper, along with Brenda, and Stanley, who all benefited under the will. Bob forgot no one—he even left money for repairs to the church.

Texas and Brandon got paid well for their stints as red herrings, and the small financial security has given Texas a new confidence. Brandon has music biz "connections," and now she's playing the good clubs and also has a small part in an upcoming movie. She's hoping for a winner this time.

As for Brandon, he's found a new life on cruise liners. "Have backgammon board, will travel" is his motto. I believe he makes a fair living that way. Onboard ship he lives like a king, and of course, women dote on him. It's a life that suits him. At least for now.

Bordelaise and I finally arrive at the pub. Ginny waves at us from behind the bar, and Rats runs to her, ready for his treat. The old boys nod a greeting over their pints as we go by, then Reg calls me over. He has an odd look on his face.

"I could swear I saw old Bob just now," he says. "Right here, sitting on the old settle over a pint like he always did. Out of the corner of my eye I saw him; then I turned my head and he was gone."

"I'll bet you did," I say, smiling. "I'll bet he's come home after all."

I've never been lucky enough to see Bob, though I still feel his loving presence the way I used to in that soft breeze. I like it, it makes me feel good, but then Bob always did that. And no matter what anyone else thinks, I'll believe to the end of my days that he saved me from Hector.

Do you remember there was one last letter, not to be opened until the time was right? When I first returned to Sneadley, I sat alone in the lovely golden drawing room with the evening sun slanting in and Rats on my knee, and I opened it.

*"Daisy, my love,"* Bob wrote.

*"You have to give me my due, I set you up royally for what I'll bet you thought was a wild-goose chase. Didn't turn out quite like that, though, did it? Of course I don't know who my killer was, otherwise Montana would have taken care of him before the fact and not, unfortunately as it turned out, after. In my heart of hearts, though, I'm still hoping it wasn't one of my second-chancers. I thought they all had something better to offer the world if they could overcome their weaknesses and straighten up. I failed with Charlie Clement, but he was always a long shot.*

*"Anyway, love, now you know I have a daughter. I didn't tell you or Montana, because I wanted to respect Rosalia's privacy. I finally found out about her, years later, when Rosalia was already married. I knew she didn't want me to interfere, so I kept out of it, though Lord knows it was hard. I also knew she wouldn't take a penny from me when I was*

alive; that wasn't her way. I've had to leave it until now, when I'm dead, to do the 'right thing' for them. I hope she accepted this in the spirit of love in which it was given.

"Meanwhile, lass, I'll bet you put on a good show at the Villa Belkiss. I'll bet it turned out exactly the way I planned, weather permitting, of course, though I might have a hand in that too . . . you never know.

"So, now you're a rich woman. How does it feel? Does money make you happy? Let me tell you from experience what money does. It buys freedom. Freedom from want and freedom from worry. It does not, as they always so rightly say, buy happiness. I know you'll do good things with it, just as I know you'll look after Sneadley Hall—our home together, lass, for quite a few years. I know you think of it as home, and that you care. And the Villa Belkiss seems the perfect place for you to find peace and sunshine, and who knows, maybe even love.

"Speaking of love. Remember I was always trying to fix you up with guys? All of whom you rejected—too tall, you said, too short, too boring, thinks he's too clever, don't like mustaches. You had every excuse under the sun, and all because you were afraid to fall in love again. Remember I told you I thought I'd found exactly the man for you? Not only that, I knew he'd love Rats too, and that's important. Give Montana a chance, Daisy. And yourself too, this time around.

"Remember I also said in my first letter I'd be there to take care of you if danger presented itself. You'll probably know by now I spoke the truth.

"I'll miss you, Daisy Keane. Take care of yourself. And of Rats. And of my man, Montana.

"And remember, Daisy. Live in the present. There's no guarantee about tomorrow.

Your loving B.H."

As always, Bob, my ogre at the top of the beanstalk, my intelligent Shrek, my all-knowing, all-seeing best friend, had the last word.

And what about Montana? Because of Bob, I finally met the man of my dreams, and he's so different from anything I ever expected he's turned my world upside down. He's a man wounded by lack of love, and I'm a woman scarred by wrong love. How could we possibly make a go of it?

Are we in love? Yes, oh yes. Does he say he loves me? Finally, yes. Do I love him? Of course. But Montana is a man dedicated to his work, and that work takes him around the world, often without much notice.

They say you can never change a man, and I don't intend to try. Rosalia left Bob because she knew she would never be able to change him and I'm not going to make that mistake. Montana is the man he is. His life is what it is. I'll take what I can get and what's more I love it.

Our life is a perpetual romance. We have our long weekends at Sneadley and our summer weeks at the Villa Belkiss. We meet at small hotels and pensions in Istanbul or Marrakesh, in Kyoto or Rome . . . anywhere in the world. We drink wine, smooch in quiet corners of intimate restaurants, stroll hand in hand down cobbled alleys in small Mexican villages, wander sandy paths in out-of-the-way seaside resorts, and make love anywhere and everywhere. Life is different every day with Montana, and that's what I love about it.

Does this scenario make for happiness? For us it does. At least for now. And to tell the truth, since all this happened, I've taken Bob's advice and become a live-for-the-day woman.

Take it and be happy is my motto. And if you ask me now, Well, are you happy? Well, yes I am. And with luck—and Bob Hardwick—on my side, I believe it will last forever. And maybe this time, *I* will have the last word.

Elizabeth Adler

# The House in Amalfi

**Once Lamour Harrington was a carefree little girl, following her charming, hard-up, writer father around Italy: first Rome, then the lovely Amalfi coast. Lamour will never forget the tiny cottage where they spent the happiest years of her life.**

Now, nursing a broken heart, she decides to leave Chicago and her career as a landscape architect to rediscover the Italy of her memories.

In Amalfi, the Castello Pirata with its Japanese garden still stands; their cottage still waits for her. It even seems as though love has come back into Lamour's life as the heir to the castello – glamourous Nico Pirata – sweeps her off her feet. But why does his father Lorenzo hate a woman he only ever knew as an innocent child? As Lorenzo plots to make Lamour leave Amalfi forever, long-hidden secrets come to dangerous life again.

**HODDER**

Elizabeth Adler

# Invitation to Provence

**Nothing ever changes much in the village of Marten-de-Provence . . .**

until Rafaella Marten decides she has lived alone in the Château des Roses Sauvages for too long, and that the time has come at last to bring youth and energy, love and laughter back to the old house.

Franny Marten, hard-working California veterinary surgeon, accepts the invitation from a relative she has never heard of at a moment when her life is at rock bottom.

Jake Bronson can't resist – he is still a tiny bit in love with the charming woman who was once his father's glamorous lover.

And two more unexpected guests arrive: Rafaella's long lost son, and a terrified little girl from Shanghai with the Marten blue eyes.

Soon the sleepy French village is alive with more romance and danger than Rafaella ever dreamed of.

**HODDER**

Elizabeth Adler

# The Hotel Riviera

**Of all the hotels he could have walked in to, he had to walk into hers.**

Lola Laforêt has no time for love. Her disreputable husband has disappeared, the police consider her a prime suspect and her beautiful home and business seem to belong to an ex-arms dealer.

Lola doesn't go looking for danger, it just seems to walk through the door. And when it walks through the door in the form of the delectable Jack Farrar she knows she's in real trouble.

**HODDER**